"You... we're..."

Ellis said. "I want you too much to spend another night under the same roof with you without touching you. Tasting you. Knowing all of you."

Sydney felt the heat of his gaze burn into her soul, and she knew he was telling the truth.

"I'll ask you one last time, Syd. Do you want me to come back to stay, at least until I can find the help my son needs?"

She knew what he was saying. They would become lovers, but eventually he would have to leave again. He'd made a promise, and that promise was to his son.

She stepped closer to him and gave him temporary custody of her heart. "Come back, Ellis. I want you too much to fight it any longer."

Dear Reader,

Summer's in full sizzle, and so are the romances in this month's Intimate Moments selections, starting with *Badge of Honor,* the latest in Justine Davis's TRINITY STREET WEST miniseries. For everyone who's been waiting for Chief Miguel de los Reyes to finally fall in love, I have good news. The wait is over! Hurry out to buy this one—but don't drive so fast you get stopped for speeding. Unless, of course, you're pulled over by an officer like Miguel!

Suzanne Brockmann is continuing her TALL, DARK AND DANGEROUS miniseries—featuring irresistible navy SEALs as heroes—with *Everyday, Average Jones.* Of course, there's nothing everyday about this guy. I only wish there were, because then I might meet a man like him myself. Margaret Watson takes us to CAMERON, UTAH, for a new miniseries, beginning with *Rodeo Man.* The title alone should draw you to this one. And we round out the month with new books by Marcia Evanick, who offers the very moving *A Father's Promise,* and two books bearing some of our new thematic flashes. Ingrid Weaver's *Engaging Sam* is a MEN IN BLUE title, and brand-new author Shelley Cooper's *Major Dad* is a CONVENIENTLY WED book.

Enjoy all six—then come back next month, because we've got some of the best romance around *every* month, right here in Silhouette Intimate Moments.

Yours,

Leslie J. Wainger
Executive Senior Editor

Please address questions and book requests to:
Silhouette Reader Service
U.S.: 3010 Walden Ave., P.O. Box 1325, Buffalo, NY 14269
Canadian: P.O. Box 609, Fort Erie, Ont. L2A 5X3

A FATHER'S PROMISE

MARCIA EVANICK

Published by Silhouette Books

America's Publisher of Contemporary Romance

If you purchased this book without a cover you should be aware that this book is stolen property. It was reported as "unsold and destroyed" to the publisher, and neither the author nor the publisher has received any payment for this "stripped book."

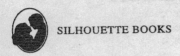 SILHOUETTE BOOKS

ISBN 0-373-07874-9

A FATHER'S PROMISE

Copyright © 1998 by Marcia Evanick

All rights reserved. Except for use in any review, the reproduction or utilization of this work in whole or in part in any form by any electronic, mechanical or other means, now known or hereafter invented, including xerography, photocopying and recording, or in any information storage or retrieval system, is forbidden without the written permission of the editorial office, Silhouette Books, 300 East 42nd Street, New York, NY 10017 U.S.A.

All characters in this book have no existence outside the imagination of the author and have no relation whatsoever to anyone bearing the same name or names. They are not even distantly inspired by any individual known or unknown to the author, and all incidents are pure invention.

This edition published by arrangement with Harlequin Books S.A.

® and TM are trademarks of Harlequin Books S.A., used under license. Trademarks indicated with ® are registered in the United States Patent and Trademark Office, the Canadian Trade Marks Office and in other countries.

Printed in U.S.A.

Books by Marcia Evanick

Silhouette Intimate Moments

By the Light of the Moon #676
His Chosen Bride #717
A Father's Promise #874

MARCIA EVANICK

is an award-winning author of numerous romances. She lives in rural Pennsylvania with her husband and five children. Her hobbies include attending all of her children's sporting events, reading and avoiding housework. Knowing her aversion to the kitchen, she married a man who can cook as well as seemingly enjoy anything she sets before him at the dinner table.

Her writing takes second place in her life, directly behind her family. She believes in happy endings, children's laughter, the magic of Christmas and romance. Marcia believes that every book is another adventure waiting to be written and read. As long as the adventures beckon, Marcia will have no choice but to follow where they lead. She hopes that you will join her for the journey.

This book is dedicated to the volunteers of the
Leukemia Society of America and to anyone who is
listed on a marrow donor registry.

Bless you all.

Prologue

Ellis Carlisle stared out the window at the sprawling snow-covered city and the mass of bundled-up humanity fighting their way through it all. Philadelphia was one depressing mess when it snowed. The white fluffy flakes quickly turned soot gray and blanketed the city with its dismal chilly coat. Mother Nature had decided to welcome in the first week of the new year by dumping ten inches across the East Coast. Six months ago he would have thumbed his nose at the weather and tell it to do its worse. Today he hadn't even known about the storm until he'd looked out the window. Who had time for something as mundane as the weather when his son was fighting for his life?

He blinked back the tears that filled his eyes as soon as his thoughts touched on Trevor. He should be pleased by the news the doctors had just given him. His child had been given a chance. The deadly disease invading his five-year-old son's body had stopped its advance and, for all apparent purposes, disappeared totally. The doctors had warned him, and warned him well, that in all likelihood it would relapse. The fight hadn't been won, only a temporary cease-fire had been called. It was time to regroup and plan for the next attack.

"Hey, Dad?"

Trevor's sweet high voice tore at his heart. How was he to go on living if Trevor lost his courageous battle? He blinked away the tears and forced his mouth to smile as he turned and faced his son. "What, Trev?" He walked over to the hospital bed and sat on the edge of the mattress. His fingers shook as he brushed back a short unruly lock of his son's brown hair.

Trevor's teeth worried his lower lip as he nervously played with the mane of the huge stuffed lion Ellis had just purchased from the gift shop four floors below. "This re...re...re..."

"Remission?"

"Yeah, that's it. It's good, right?"

He smiled and pulled his son onto his lap. For the past several months he had been praying for Trevor to go into remission. Now that it was finally here, he had more important things to pray for, such as a bone marrow donor. "Yes, remission is good. Very good." Remission was one word he wouldn't mind his son learning. No child should ever have to learn to say the word *leukemia* as Trevor had done six months ago. He pulled his son closer and tightly wrapped his arms around the boy's little frame. He now had a new battle to fight and this one would determine the outcome of the war. Trevor needed a bone marrow transplant, and he needed it fast.

"I'm going to be okay now, right?"

Ellis looked into his son's worried brown eyes and felt his heart start to splinter into a million pieces. Pieces that would never be put back together if something should happen to Trevor. The doctors had warned him to stick to the truth as much as possible when Trevor asked questions. How could he meet his son's anxious gaze and tell him no, that everything isn't all right now? That he still might die. Ellis couldn't.

Trevor knew he had been sick, very seriously sick. But never once did the word *die* tumble from his young lips. Ellis was thankful for some small blessings. Trevor's strength through everything had given Ellis the courage to test his own depth of strength. If it hadn't been for Trevor's courage he would have lost all faith and fallen apart months ago. And if a five-year-old boy could meet this disease head-on, then surely a grown man, such as himself, could stand tall beside him and help him make the trek ahead. Some mountains were just too steep for Trevor's short little legs to climb on his own.

Ellis swallowed the lump of tears blocking his throat and rumpled Trevor's hair. His son had been such a good brave boy throughout this whole ordeal. Trevor didn't deserve this disease—no kid did.

Trevor deserved a normal childhood and a long, happy life and Ellis was going to do everything within his power to make sure his son got what he deserved. "I won't lie to you, Trev, it's going to be a long hard road ahead of us, but you're going to be fine." He brushed a kiss across Trevor's forehead and feverishly prayed he was telling his son the truth. "I promise you, Trev, you're going to be just fine."

Chapter 1

Sydney St. Claire wasn't having a good day. Hell, she couldn't remember the last time she'd actually had a good day. It had to have been over six months ago. After all, it had been six months, yesterday, that the accident had occurred. Six months since some drunk ran a stop sign, killing her mother outright and leaving her father blind. Six months since her world started crumbling beneath her feet. She still hadn't managed to get on firm footing.

Her father was worrying her sick. She expected him to grieve for the loss of his wife, Julia. She expected him to rage against his blindness and the loss of his career as the town's police chief. What she hadn't expected and wasn't prepared to handle was this deep, solid wall of depression that he refused to allow her to penetrate. Not being allowed in to help him heal was ripping at her soul. Standing helplessly by while he sank deeper and deeper was breaking her heart.

Sydney glanced at the barely touched tray she was holding. Her father once again had hardly eaten a thing. She opened the kitchen door and looked back at her father sitting so alone, so silent beneath the massive oak in their backyard. Tiny green buds were just beginning to sprout along the winter-barren branches. Spring, the busiest time for her, was arriving and it really didn't care if she was ready or not. How could she possibly be ready when every ounce of energy she possessed was spent worrying about her father?

Twenty years ago, her mother had started Ever Green Nursery with nothing more than a couple of hundred dollars, a barren cornfield and a pocketful of dreams. Immediately upon graduating from college Sydney had become partners with her mother in the nursery business. Today Ever Green Nursery was the county's finest nursery and employed a dozen full-time people and a handful of part-timers during their peak season. Peak season was approaching and for the first time she was alone at the helm. After the accident the employees had pulled together and kept things going. Now they were looking for direction from her, and all she could think about was her father.

Thomas St. Claire was the most important man in her life, and had been since she had first laid eyes on him when she was ten years old, when he and Julia St. Claire became the parents she never had. Thomas had been there when she needed him so desperately eighteen years ago. She still needed him today. He was one of the few remaining family members she had left in the world, and he was wasting away before her very eyes. Thomas had dropped a good forty pounds since the accident and no amount of cooking or begging on her part had perked up his appetite.

With a heavy sigh she entered the house and started to clean up the lunch fixings while keeping an eye on her father through the window above the sink. The afghan she had tucked across his lap and legs had been tossed aside as soon as she had closed the door. She knew he would shrug off her careful attention to him, but she kept on trying. Spring might be here, but the air still had a cold bite. It had taken her weeks to convince him to sit outside for a little while each day and get some fresh air. Since the accident he never left the house, except for the occasional doctor's appointment.

She'd dried and put away the last glass when the doorbell rang, pulling her away from the kitchen and her troubled vigilance over her father. As she walked toward the door she prayed it wasn't one of her father's friends stopping by for a visit. Thomas St. Claire refused all visitors and it would break her heart to send away another family friend. Since the accident her father had developed a very strong trait known as stubbornness.

Sydney opened the door and stared at the man standing there. The welcoming smile she had put on her lips slipped a notch as a slow heat started to build in her stomach. Her smile went from friendly to curious. The caller was definitely a stranger because she would have remembered him had she met him before. The small town of Coalsburg, Pennsylvania, was known for its two still-operational coal mines and for the pies at Betty's Diner down on the interstate, not for its model-gorgeous men. And the blond-haired, gray-eyed hunk definitely fell into the model category.

She had to swallow twice before she could manage a

simple, "Hello, may I help you?" Whatever he was selling, she was buying. She just hoped it wasn't a vacuum cleaner because she just went out and bought a new one last month. What in the world she was going to do with two vacuum cleaners was beyond her.

The stranger didn't return her smile. "I would like to speak to Thomas St. Claire."

"I'm sorry, but my father isn't accepting any visitors at this time." She felt her smile slip from curious to concerned and the heat that had been bubbling in her stomach started to cool. The stranger on her doorstep wasn't some sweet-talking salesman. Door-to-door salesmen didn't dress in expensive suede jackets or wear Italian leather shoes. She glanced at the car sitting in the driveway and frowned. Nor did they drive a brand-new Mercedes. She returned her attention to the stranger and met his gaze head-on. "Maybe I can help you?"

"I'm sorry, but what I need to discuss with your father is personal, Sydney."

"You know my name." She went straight past being concerned and directly into the worried stage. She didn't like strangers knowing her name.

"Yes, Sydney, I know your name. I also know that Thomas and his wife adopted you when you were ten and that Mrs. St. Claire passed away six months ago." He made no move to shake hands, offer a normal greeting or express any sympathy on her mother's passing. "I'm Ellis Carlisle and I need to speak to your father on personal business."

She shook her head. "I'm sorry Mr. Carlisle, but the answer is still no." She tightened her grip on the doorjamb as a wave of fear skidded down her back. "Since you are so informed about our family history, I'm sure you know my father was also injured in the accident that took my mother. He still isn't ready for visitors."

"I was under the impression that the only injury your father sustained was to his eyes."

Now Mr. Carlisle looked concerned. Not so much by her father's injuries, but by the fact he might not have gotten all his information correct. The cold lump of dread forming in her stomach quickly turned to heat once again. This time the heat was solely due to her temper. Her father had once teased her about having Irish blood coursing through her veins, not only because of the red highlights tinting her brown hair, but because of her hotheaded nature. Mr. Carlisle had managed to tap into that temper quite easily.

She felt the flush of her anger sweep up her cheeks as she confronted this ignorant and rude stranger. "If you want to consider burying your loving wife of thirty years, losing your job as well as your career and being blinded in the same instant as 'only an eye injury,' then yes my father sustained only injuries to his eyes." She knew her voice rose with each word but she didn't care. Who did this Carlisle guy think he was to demand to see her father and then belittle his injuries?

"I truly didn't mean that to sound the way it did, Sydney. You have every right to take offense, but I still need to speak with your father. It's of the utmost importance and it really can't wait until he is feeling up to visitors."

She had heard better apologies in her life, but at least he appeared sincere.

She stared at his dark blond hair, expensively cut and styled, and his perfectly straight white teeth. His jaw was clean shaven and strong. His penetrating gray eyes contained the intriguing mix of intelligence, fatigue and a touch of sorrow. His nose had a slight bump at the bridge—more than likely it had been broken—and in other circumstances, she might have found this characteristic endearing. If she had to guess, she would say he was around thirty-five years old, and judging by the dark smudges beneath his eyes, he hadn't been sleeping very well. Great, that made two of them.

For a moment she wondered if Ellis Carlisle knew her father because of business. He looked as if he could be a cop and that would explain how he knew so much about her family. The only thing preventing her from believing in that connection was Carlisle said that the reason he needed to speak with her father was personal, not professional. "I'm still sorry, but unless you tell me what's so important I'm afraid you cannot see my father."

"I really don't think this concerns you, Sydney. My business is between your father and me."

That tears it! She had been worrying herself sick, living on five hours of sleep a night and juggling so many balls in the air that she was beginning to feel like a circus performer. Who did this joker think he was, demanding to see her father and trying to knock one of her balls out of the air? Her father must have been right all those years ago when he'd teased her about having an Irish temper because right now she was seeing red. Mind-numbing, heart-stopping red. "Who in the hell do you think you are?"

Ellis Carlisle took a deep breath, met her glare straight on and softly whispered, "I'm his son."

Sydney's heart stopped beating as she visualized every one of the balls she had been mentally juggling come crashing to the ground. There was no way she could have heard him correctly. The lack of sleep and constant worrying had taken their toll. She was now imagining things. "Excuse me, but could you repeat that?"

"I said Thomas St. Claire is my father." Ellis squared his shoulders as if he was daring her, or the world, to disagree with him. "I'm your father's son."

"What you are is a liar." There was no way on this green earth that Ellis Carlisle was her father's son. She would have known.

Ellis reached into the inside pocket of his jacket and pulled out a sheet of paper and handed it to her. "I'm not here to cause any problems, Sydney. I just need to speak to your father."

She took the paper and slowly unfolded it. It was Ellis's birth certificate. His mother was Catherine Carlisle and she had been nineteen years old when she had given birth. His father was listed as Thomas St. Claire, age twenty-one. She quickly calculated the year Ellis was born and frowned when she realized that her father would have been twenty-one at that time.

This still didn't cut it. Ellis could have a truckload of birth certificates listing Thomas St. Claire as his father and she still wouldn't have believed him. The only child Thomas St. Claire had was herself, and she had come to him walking, talking, with a chip on her shoulder the size of Texas and already in the fifth grade.

She neatly refolded the certificate and handed it back to him. With a smooth calm voice she politely told him, "You must have the wrong Thomas St. Claire. My father couldn't possibly be your father." She closed the door right in his surprised face and leaned against it.

Deep inside she felt the crumbling of the solid wall she had built to hold back all her worries. The worries were like those the curious Pandora had released when she opened the box. Wicked shadowy figures swooped and swirled their way around the inside of her head. If Thomas was someone else's real father, where did that leave her?

All of a sudden she was ten years old again and running away from the foster home Youth Services had just placed her in. The older foster children didn't want her there. The woman of the house only wanted her to scrub floors and wash dishes. It was the man of the house that had frightened her into running. There was something about the way he used to watch her all the time that sent chills down her spine. She might have only been ten years old, but she knew enough to run. Run until she found someone who really wanted her.

She had run until she found Thomas and his wife.

She held her breath as she waited to see what Ellis Carlisle would do now. Was it too much to hope for that he would get back into his fancy Mercedes and quietly drive back out of town?

Sydney released her breath as Ellis amazingly did exactly that. At least she was hoping he was heading out of town. She pulled back the lace curtain in the living room a fraction of an inch and watched as he backed out of the driveway and headed in the direction of the interstate.

She should be cheering her victory. So why was she more worried now than she had been before? Something was telling her that Ellis Carlisle didn't seem like the type of man to quietly go away when things didn't turn out the way he had planned. That same something was telling her that she was going to be hearing from Ellis again. Real soon.

Ellis's grip on the phone tightened as he glanced out the window to the vertical sign at the edge of the parking lot. The *T* in the lighted red Motel sign was flickering away, and dusk was settling in. "Yes, Trev, I miss you, too."

This was going to be the first night away from his son since the initial diagnosis of leukemia. Every night, every day, every hour with Trevor was a small blessing and he didn't want to waste one precious minute of it. He hated to be away from Trevor, but he was out of options. He had reached the end of the line. His last desperate hope went by the name of Thomas St. Claire.

"Yes, I love you, too." The sound of his son's voice brought tears to his eyes. "I want you to listen to Mrs. McCall and do everything she says. I'll call you in the morning."

He smiled as Trevor promised to listen to the housekeeper who cared for him, and then asked him if he'd seen any jungle animals. "Not today, Trev, but I promise I'll look tomorrow." His son's room was floor-to-ceiling stuffed animals. Trevor's latest obsession was collecting jungle animals and he had willingly obliged his son. "Good night, Trev. I love you."

His son's loving response stayed with him long after he replaced the receiver into the cradle. He would have given anything to be in Jenkintown, Pennsylvania, with Trevor than in this cheap room at the Starry Night Motel.

Coalsburg, Pennsylvania, didn't have an abundance of overnight accommodations to choose from. It was either the Starry Night Motel with its clean sheets and threadbare carpet or the ever-popular Hide-Away Motel that actually charged by the hour and listed X-rated videos by title on a blinking billboard five feet off the interstate. The choice was obvious since his business in Coalsburg was going to take a bit longer than he had hoped.

Four months ago he had started his search for a bone marrow donor that matched Trevor as soon as he learned his own marrow was incompatible with his son's. Trevor's best hope of a cure was to have the transplant done while he was in remission. No one would hazard a guess as to how long Trevor would be in the remission stage. His race to find a donor was pitted against the clock. Trevor's clock.

So far every relative of Trevor's, near and far, on his mother's side, had been tested. There hadn't been a single match among the greedy, money-hungry lot. His ex-wife, Ginny, had volunteered to be the first one tested. The remaining members of her family all came with a price tag. If there had been a match, he had been committed to dig deep into his wallet before the actual transplant took place.

Both registries for unrelated marrow donors in the United States hadn't turned up a match.

His last hope was Trevor's biological grandfather, Thomas St. Claire, the man who'd fathered him and then abandoned his mother, Catherine, when she was eighteen and pregnant. St. Claire hadn't been worthy of a moment's thought the entire time Ellis had been growing up. Now he would beg, plead or pay dearly for Thomas to take a simple blood test. If he could just talk to the man.

The detective he had hired to track St. Claire had been thorough. Thomas St. Claire had married a couple of years after Catherine left Coalsburg carrying his child. St. Claire and his wife adopted a little ten-year-old girl several years later and never had any children of their own. Six months ago St. Claire's wife had been killed in the same car accident that had left Thomas blind. Thankfully, St. Claire was still in good enough physical shape to be Trevor's donor, if there was a match.

The detective forgot to mention that the little girl they had adopted had grown into one beautiful, if not stubborn and overly protective, woman. Sydney St. Claire was proving to be one gorgeous obstacle.

When Sydney had opened the door earlier he had been thrown off balance, and never did manage to regain his footing while in her presence. In a totally uncharacteristic move, he had been clumsy and rude in his approach to see Thomas St. Claire. He needed Thomas's help, and antagonizing Sydney wasn't going to better the situation.

Fact being, he had in all likelihood worsened his chances of getting Thomas's cooperation. St. Claire probably was relying heavily on Sydney to help him pull his life back together. He had loved Sydney enough to legally adopt her when she was ten. To all the world, Sydney was his daughter.

Ellis glanced at his open briefcase on the bed, the pile of paperwork that needed his attention, and the laptop computer sitting on the room's small table and already displaying a list of figures he had been working on before calling Trevor. Over the past several months he had become quite adept at running his shipping business, One If By Land, out of a briefcase.

Next to the computer was an open bottle of scotch and a quarter-filled cheap disposable cup he had found wrapped in plastic sitting on the bathroom counter. He reached for the cup and turned away from the monitor.

The first swallow of scotch warmed his throat and heated the chill that had been growing in his stomach. Sydney was his father's daughter and the reality of that was finally sinking in. When he had read the detective's report mentioning Sydney's adoption he had actually been disappointed, because there was no blood link between her and Thomas. She was one less person who could have been a possible match for Trevor.

Now, after meeting her, and being in the same town that both his mother and father had grown up in, the town that he had been conceived in, it finally was starting to sink in that Thomas St. Claire had never wanted him. He hadn't been good enough for his father to love or want.

When he had been growing up he had always figured that Thomas St. Claire was some lonely, miserable man who hated children. Ellis had figured that he was better off with just his mom. Now he knew that wasn't true. Thomas had raised some stranger's child to be his own. He had taken a little girl that no one else wanted, and made her his own.

One thought burned through his mind as he finished off the scotch in the cup and stared at the flickering two-foot-high *T* outside the window. Why had Thomas chosen to raise a little girl as his own and not his own flesh-and-blood son? What was so terribly wrong with him that his own father hadn't wanted him?

Chapter 2

Sydney was watering the plants in front of the living-room window when she saw the deep green Mercedes pull up the long driveway and park behind her four-wheel-drive Blazer. Ellis Carlisle was back, just as she knew he would be. This morning she was prepared for him and his wild accusations. She'd had all night to think about what she was going to do when he returned. She just hadn't been expecting him so early this morning. It was barely after nine.

Her father had come down for breakfast, which he'd hardly touched. Then he had retreated to the den and closed the door, once again effectively shutting her out of his life and his pain. For the last forty minutes not a sound had emerged from behind the den's door. Her father preferred the silence of the house to the sounds of the radio or television or even her voice.

She placed the white plastic watering can on the floor

and opened the door before Ellis could ring the bell. She didn't want to disturb her father, at least not yet. The man standing on her doorstep looked slightly different from the man who had stood there yesterday. This Ellis appeared more casual, more approachable. He was still wearing the same suede jacket as yesterday, but this morning he wore faded blue jeans, loafers and a light gray sweater that nearly matched his eyes. The smudges of fatigue beneath his eyes were more pronounced.

Sydney opened the door farther and softly said, "Won't you come in."

A look of surprise flashed across Ellis's face before he schooled his expression back to a bland mask. "Thank you, Sydney."

She glanced nervously at the closed den door off the hallway, before leading Ellis to the kitchen at the back of the house. The huge sunny kitchen with its glass-front cabinets, cheery yellow wallpaper and herbs growing in an array of mismatched pots on the windowsill was her favorite room in the house. Her mother had decorated and loved the room and her memory was stamped into every square inch of it.

She motioned toward one of the wooden chairs sitting around the table. "Would you care for a cup of coffee? I just put on a fresh pot." She had made the pot moments before, hoping the aroma of freshly brewing coffee would draw her father out of the den. Thomas St. Claire had a nose that could match any bloodhound's when it came to coffee.

Ellis seemed to consider the polite invitation for a moment before answering. "Thanks. I take it black, no sugar." He took off his jacket and draped it over the back of a chair before sitting down.

She felt his eyes on her as she poured them both a cup and carried them over to the table. His intense gaze locked with hers as she handed him a cup. "I knew you would come back."

"Why did you change your mind and decide to talk to me?"

"For a couple reasons, but the main one has to do with the truth. Thomas St. Claire isn't, and couldn't be, your father." She pulled her gaze away from his and sat down. Ellis's gaze was too probing. It was as if he was trying to read her soul.

"Couldn't be?" Ellis took a sip of his coffee and watched her over the rim of the cup. "Why *couldn't* Thomas be my father?"

She had given that question a lot of thought throughout the night and well into the morning hours. If Ellis Carlisle was under the impression that Thomas was his father, then he deserved the truth. "Thomas physically couldn't have any children of his own." Sydney remembered the day she had learned this about her father. It was an afternoon, a year or so after she had joined her mother in the nursery business, during one of those rare talks she and her mother had had that not only strengthened the bond between them, but forged a couple of new ones. They were out inspecting a field of trees, to see how they had survived the winter, when her mother had brought up the subject.

Thomas had been devastated when early on in their marriage it was discovered that he couldn't father a child. Thomas had once teased Julia about wanting to father a baseball team of his own, or at least the infield. Julia, who also loved children, had been wholeheartedly in agreement with her husband. When the doctors had delivered the news, Julia had accepted it with the help of her faith. Thomas hadn't been accustomed to relying on his faith and felt as if God were punishing him. Julia had then gone on to tell her how everything had changed the day Thomas had found Sydney traveling the railroad tracks east of town, dragging a huge nylon duffel bag behind her. Thomas had taken one look at the frightened little girl and figured out God's plan.

Her mother had then gone on to tell her that she loved her as much as she would have loved a child she had carried in her own womb, but as the old saying went, she was "Daddy's little girl." Years later she was still "Daddy's little girl," and now Daddy needed her terribly. Only he hadn't realized it yet.

"Are you telling me Thomas St. Claire couldn't have any children of his own, and that's why you were adopted?"

She refused to allow the pain his careless words had caused to show. If Thomas and Julia had had a house filled with their own children, they probably wouldn't have wanted or had room for her. "Yes, that's what I'm telling you."

"Maybe he was the one who made sure he couldn't have any more children after he accidentally got Catherine Carlisle pregnant."

Sydney felt her stomach clench in outrage. She very carefully placed her cup on the table in front of her and narrowed her eyes at the man sitting across from her. In a voice soft as a whisper she said, "Don't you ever say or insinuate such a thing again. Not being able to father any children nearly devastated Thomas St. Claire."

His gray eyes probed once more, but Ellis didn't apologize. "I see you believe that very much."

"Yes, I do." She toyed with the handle on her cup for a moment. She had promised herself last night that she would sit down and listen to what Ellis Carlisle had to say. She took a deep breath and asked, "What makes you so positive that my father is the Thomas St. Claire you are looking for? It's not that unusual a name." Surely there had to be a dozen or so other Thomas St. Claires throughout the country. Ellis's birth certificate hadn't stated where his parents were from.

"My mother and her family moved to Coalsburg when she was twelve years old. Besides a few class trips and a couple of family vacations, she never left Coalsburg until she was eighteen and already pregnant. Unless there's another fifty-three-year-old Thomas St. Claire in this area that the detective I hired couldn't locate, I would have to say your father is my father."

It sounded strange: *Your father is my father.* If she believed Ellis's story, it would mean in some weird, twisted way they were brother and sister—at least legally, if not biologically. Impossible! Her father couldn't be his father. She couldn't think of another Thomas St. Claire anywhere around the area. Her father had a brother, Samuel, and he had a couple of sons, but none were named Thomas. "Maybe there was another Thomas St. Claire living around here thirty-two years ago?"

"There's no record of one, Sydney." Ellis patiently drank his coffee.

"Did you ever think that your mother gave the hospital the name of the wrong man?" His confidence was getting on her nerves.

"Are you saying that my mother might not have

known who fathered the child she was carrying, so she pulled Thomas's name out of a hat?"

There were a handful of explanations as to why Catherine Carlisle might not have known exactly who had fathered her child. None of them painted a pretty picture. "Maybe she purposely named Thomas instead of your real father."

Ellis's smile appeared condescending. "Why would she do that?"

"I don't know." She brushed back a curl that had fallen too close to her eye. "Maybe she wanted to protect him."

Ellis snorted in disbelief. "Protect him from what?"

"There could be other reasons why she named my father." For the life of her, she couldn't think of a single one in this instant. Later they might come, but not right now.

"She wasn't protecting the man who fathered me, Sydney. As far as I know, she never made contact or asked for anything from either Thomas or this other man you keep insisting on. She raised me alone and taught me that my father didn't want anything to do with her or me. I've never given Thomas St. Claire a second thought until now."

"Why now?" That was the confusing part. Why would Ellis all of a sudden, after thirty-two years, look up his father now?

Ellis stood up and walked over to the kitchen sink and stared out the window. She knew that view by heart. A brick patio with an white iron table and chairs. The green-and-white-striped umbrella hadn't been put up yet, but the scene still looked inviting. Many an evening meal had been eaten at that table.

If he turned his head to the right he would see the massive oak where her father sat on sunny, yet still chilly, afternoons. Farther in the distance he would see a couple of the nursery's greenhouses and areas of tiny saplings and larger trees ready to be sold. The nursery's main building and parking lot were a good quarter mile down the road and away from the house. Her mother wanted to be close to her business, yet still have some privacy for her family. It was a view that had been carved into her heart over the years. She wondered what he thought of it, or if he was even seeing it.

"I have a five-year-old son." Ellis jammed his hands deep into the pockets of his jeans but didn't turn around to face her. "His name is Trevor."

So Mr. Good Looking With An Attitude was married and had a little boy. No surprise there. Her best friend and employee, Cindy, always claimed all the handsome men were already taken.

"At the end of last summer Trevor was diagnosed with leukemia."

Her heart skipped two beats and her stomach felt as if someone had just slammed her with a bowling ball. "Lord, I'm sorry, Ellis. You and your wife must be worried sick." Her heart immediately went out to him, his wife and his little boy. He was thinking about his little boy, Trevor, as he gazed out that window. His very sick little boy.

"I'm no longer married. Trevor's mother left when he was six weeks old." He shrugged as if it had happened a long time ago and was now just water under the bridge. "In January, Trevor was diagnosed as being in remission."

"Remission? That's good, right?"

"Yes, it's good. Right now Trev doesn't look or act sick, but it doesn't mean that it's true. His best hope for a total cure is a bone marrow transplant and it should be done while he is healthy and in remission." Ellis lowered his head and stared into the white porcelain sink. "My HLA typing doesn't match his. I can't be the donor."

"I gather that this HLA typing is what they try to match to find a donor?" She had heard about the matching process, but she'd never met or known anyone who actually had leukemia and had gone through a bone marrow transplant. By the tone of Ellis's voice she could tell he felt like a failure to his son for not being a match. "What about Trevor's mom or other relatives? Can't they be tested?" She would have to take back a couple of her thoughts about Ellis. He wasn't arrogant or rude. He was scared to death for his little boy, and she couldn't blame him.

"Ginny and every one of her blood relatives have already been tested and there was no match. Both marrow donor registries have also turned up nothing." Ellis finally turned around and faced her. His eyes told of the enormous amount of stress he had been under lately and the pain tearing at his heart. "My only living relative is my father, Thomas St. Claire." Ellis took a deep breath and met her gaze. "He's my last hope, Sydney. He's my son's last chance."

Now she knew what was so important that Ellis needed to talk to her father about. She wished she didn't. Ellis was setting himself up for another letdown. "Ellis, he can't be your father."

"What if he is?"

What if he is? That's a damn good question. Where

would that leave her if Ellis really was her father's son? She had selfishly hoarded her father's love for the past eighteen years. She wasn't ready to share, but for the sake of a little five-year-old boy named Trevor with a potentially fatal disease, she had to push aside her own fears. "I think we need to talk to my father and ask him why Catherine Carlisle would name him as father to her child."

Ellis gave her a look that clearly stated the obvious answer to her question. Instead of voicing his opinion yet again, he said softly, "Thank you."

"You do understand that my father really isn't up to visitors. He hasn't been in the mood for company since the accident and he might not be very sociable." Classing her father as unsociable was putting it mildly, but she had to at least warn Ellis about what to expect.

"I don't need him to be sociable. I just need him to take a simple blood test."

She could see the hope in his eyes, but she didn't have the heart to remind him that she was almost certain Thomas wasn't his father. Her parents had taught her to try walking in someone else's shoes before criticizing. She couldn't imagine what she would do if she had a critically ill child. There was no telling how far she would go to try to save his life. Allowing Ellis to talk to her father was only one little step. Maybe Thomas could shed some light on why he was listed as the father on Ellis's birth certificate.

Sydney stood up, walked over to a cabinet and reached for a tray that was on the top shelf. "I'll fix him some coffee to take into the den with us. If my father has a weak spot, it's for a good cup of coffee." She busied herself pouring another cup of coffee and fixing it the way her father liked it, no sugar but heavy on the cream. She placed it on a tray with her and Ellis's cups.

Ellis reached for the tray before she could lift it. "I'll carry that, Sydney. Why don't you just lead the way."

She frowned at the three lone cups on the wooden and ceramic-tile tray. "Wait a moment." She hurried to the refrigerator and pulled out a bowl overflowing with green and red seedless grapes. "My father didn't eat a lot of his breakfast. He might be hungry." She pulled two bowls out of a cabinet, filled them with the sweet chilled fruit and placed them on the tray. "There, that's better." Without saying another word, she walked out of the kitchen.

Ellis carefully balanced the tray so the coffee wouldn't slosh over the rim of the cups, and followed Sydney from the room. His gaze once again immediately went to her jean-clad bottom and he admired the view. A man had to be dead and pushing up daisies not to have noticed such a tempting sight. Sydney St. Claire's back view was as enticing as her front. And her front was spectacular.

He was still amazed at how strangely the mind works. One part of his mind childishly resented Sydney because she had been adopted by Thomas. His own father had taken in some stranger's child when he wouldn't even acknowledge his own flesh and blood. He knew the resentment should be, and most of it was, directed at Thomas and not Sydney, who had only been ten when she'd come to live with Thomas. But still, in some deep dark corner of his mind the question was still being shouted, *Why Sydney and not him? What was wrong with him?*

The other part of his mind was remembering how long

it had been since he had been with a woman. He glanced again at her rounded backside as she opened the door and stepped into the den. It had been too damn long and he silently cursed the direction his mind had taken. He had more important things to think about than the way Sydney's short-sleeved green sweater clung to her nicely curved breasts or how denim lovingly adhered to her every curve. Sydney St. Claire was one distraction he could do without.

He took a deep breath and stared at the doorway in front of him. His father was less than ten feet away. He was about to come face-to-face with the man who had abandoned him and his mother thirty-two years ago. He was about to meet the man who had never wanted him.

The heat of desire that had been building low in his gut turned to a solid block of raw, jagged ice. The thought of Trevor bravely battling a deadly disease gave Ellis the strength to follow Sydney into the room and meet Thomas St. Claire.

"Dad, you have some company," Sydney said.

Ellis stared at the man sitting in the dark brown leather recliner. Thomas St. Claire looked older than his fifty-three years. His hair was dark gray and on its way to becoming white. A pair of dark sunglasses covered his eyes. His face was pale and slack. From the way his clothes bagged, he could tell the man had lost a lot of weight recently. Thomas had the faded appearance of once being a big robust kind of man. Now he sat slouched in his chair silently, obviously fighting his inner demons.

"Tell whoever it is that I'm not up to company." Thomas turned his face away as if his words settled the matter.

Ellis hated to disillusion the man. He wasn't about to be pushed away just because Thomas was still depressed. With as much noise as possible he placed the tray down in the middle of the empty coffee table positioned in front of a brown plaid couch. A big-screen television and what appeared to be at least a hundred framed pictures of Sydney taken over the years dominated the far wall. He looked away from the reminder of who was Thomas's child and back to the man. Thomas's head was tilted slightly toward the left and he looked to be staring right at him. Only he wasn't. The detective's report had been brief but accurate. Thomas St. Claire would never see again.

"I'm sorry you're still not up to company Mr. St. Claire, but this is important."

Sydney glanced between the two men and he watched as she tried to instill some normalcy into the situation. "Dad, this is Ellis Carlisle." Her green-eyed gaze landed on him in a brief warning and he saw her possessive look. "Ellis, this is *my father,* Thomas St. Claire."

He had picked up the emphasis on the *my father* part, but chose to ignore it. He wasn't here to take her father away. He was here to save his son. "You don't know me, Mr. St. Claire, but I believe you knew my mother, Catherine Carlisle." Ellis sat on the couch and tried to read Thomas's expression. He couldn't gauge any reaction at the mention of his mother's name, but it was hard to tell since he couldn't see Thomas's eyes.

"Catherine Carlisle? I don't believe I..."

"Go back thirty-three years." He didn't want to hear that Thomas couldn't even remember his mother's name.

Sydney placed her father's coffee on the small table

next to his chair and lightly took one of his hands and rested it near the cup. "You were only twenty, twenty-one at the time, Dad."

Thomas tilted his head farther, as if he was thinking hard. "You mean Cathy?"

He had never heard anyone refer to his mother as Cathy. She had always been Catherine. But "Cathy" made sense. "I guess she could have gone by Cathy back then. She was two years younger than you."

"Right. She lived next door to us back then." Thomas's head turned in his direction. "How is your mother?"

"She died twelve years ago."

"I'm sorry to hear that." Thomas sounded both sorry and a touch confused. "What is it that you need from me? Since you obviously convinced my daughter that your business is of the utmost importance, I can only assume that it is. Sydney isn't easily swayed."

Ellis really didn't know how to start this conversation now that he was here. The important part wasn't that Thomas was his father. The major element was that Thomas might, and it was a very slim might, match Trevor's HLAs. The ideal donor is a tissue-matched family member, usually a sibling. But since Trevor didn't have any siblings, Ellis was reaching far out on the limb of possibilities and making sure every blood relative was tested, including his own biological father.

He glanced at Sydney, who was staring back at him waiting to hear what he was going to say. He knew the concern in her eyes was for her father, and perhaps a touch of it was for his son. The sympathy Sydney had expressed for Trevor had been genuine. But Trevor didn't need sympathy, he needed a match.

"Mr. St. Claire, what I need from you is a blood sample."

Thomas's head jerked slightly at such an outrageous request. "Pardon? I know my eyes went, but I didn't think my ears were bad, too."

"Your ears are fine. What I need from you is a blood sample," Ellis repeated. He clasped his hands together to stop their trembling and silently prayed for strength. Every time he had to tell someone about Trevor's illness it tore at his soul. It brought back those first unbelievable days when his son had been diagnosed. It also made him face the possibility of Trevor's death should a donor not be found in time.

"What possible reason could you have for needing a sample of my blood?"

"I have a five-year-old son named Trevor, Mr. St. Claire. Last summer Trevor was diagnosed with leukemia." He took a couple of short shallow breaths because the pain that was inside him wouldn't allow for anything deeper.

"Being a father, myself, I can only imagine what you are going through." Thomas reached for his cup of coffee and carefully raised it to his mouth. He took a few sips and slowly lowered the cup to his lap. "But I still don't see the connection between your son's illness and your desire for a sample of my blood."

As far as Ellis was concerned, Thomas St. Claire didn't know the first thing about being a father. The first rule of fatherhood is to be responsible. Thomas had failed on that one royally. Ellis forced away his negative feelings toward Thomas and concentrated on the issue at hand. The issue was his son's health. "Trevor has been in remission for nearly four months now. He hasn't been healthier or in higher spirits in a long, long time. Now is the best time to do a bone marrow transplant. I need your blood to see if your marrow will match my son's."

Thomas shook his head. "I still don't understand. Why would you want my old blood?"

"Thirty percent of all bone marrow transplants are done from finding a match within the family. The other seventy percent are from unrelated donors. There are no unrelated donors who match Trevor so I'm tracking down every one of his blood relatives."

"Now I'm really confused. I wasn't related to Cathy. We were just neighbors."

"I agree, you weren't related to Cathy Carlisle. You're related to me. You're my father." He watched as Thomas's hands jerked and spilled some coffee on his jeans. "That means you are Trevor's biological grandfather and that means there's a slight chance that you—"

"Hold up there, Ellis!" Thomas's voice exploded in the room as he hastily set the cup back onto the table next to him. "Go back to the part about me being your father. Where in the hell did you get such an idea?"

"From my mother, Catherine Carlisle." Thomas shouldn't have appeared so shocked. Thomas had known Catherine was carrying his child when she left town. "She told me that you refused to marry her or accept the responsibility of the child you helped create."

"She named me? She told you Thomas St. Claire was your father?"

"No, she never mentioned you by name." He didn't like playing this game with a blind man. He wished he could see Thomas's eyes from behind those dark glasses.

He was a firm believer in the eyes being the window to a person's soul. "I got your name from my birth certificate."

"Sydney, do you believe him?" asked Thomas to his silent daughter.

"I believe he believes you are his father. I've also seen his birth certificate and your name is listed under 'father.' I told him he could speak to you and see if you could shed any more light on this situation." Sydney sat on the opposite end of the couch and fidgeted with the handle on her cup.

"I see." Thomas seemed to study his daughter for a long time before turning back to Ellis. "I'm sorry, Ellis, but I am not your father. I don't know why Cathy named me as the father of her child, but I can assure you that your mother and I couldn't have conceived a child together. We were never romantically involved. We were friends and neighbors, that's all."

"No offense, but I really don't care if you're my father or not. I've managed to get by in life extremely well without one," he said. "But I do care if you're Trevor's grandfather or not. I don't want anything from you besides a vial or two of blood. We'll discuss the transplant later, once we know if there is a match." If he'd learned one thing in business it was that every man had his price. If there was a match, he was confident he would find and meet Thomas's price.

"You have it all neatly planned out, don't you?"

"No, Mr. St. Claire. The only thing I've planned out in the past nine months is the best way to make Trevor well again. How I achieve that is inconsequential. Only that I achieve it matters."

"It doesn't matter to you that your mother named the wrong man as the father of her child?"

"I don't think she did." He studied the man his mother had claimed fathered him. He couldn't see any notable resemblance. Catherine Carlisle had had dark brown hair, brown eyes, and had been only five foot three. It didn't take a genius to know that his dark blond hair, gray eyes and six-foot-plus frame had to have come from his father's side. Thomas St. Claire might have had brown hair at one time, it was hard to tell now that it was all gray. The color of Thomas's eyes were hidden behind the dark lenses he wore. As for his height, he would take an educated guess that Thomas stood about six feet. Thomas could be his father.

"Your daughter also mentioned the same possibility, Mr. St. Claire. I honestly have given it some thought, but I can't come up with one reasonable explanation as to why my mother would have done that." He thought of something he hadn't thought of before. "You knew my mother when she was eighteen. Can you think of one reason why she named you as my father instead of my real father?" Ellis took a sip of his coffee and smiled. "Supposing you aren't my *real* father."

"There's no supposing on my end, Ellis. I'm not your father. I couldn't be your father and I will take any test you want to prove it. I would have never left Cathy, or any other woman, alone and pregnant with my child."

Ellis didn't want to argue with Thomas. The man represented Trevor's last hope. Arguing wasn't going to solve anything. Getting Thomas to take a blood test might, though.

"If I remember correctly, Cathy left home right after

she graduated from high school." Thomas rubbed his chin.

"That's correct. She was already four months pregnant with me. She delivered me in Philadelphia when she was only nineteen."

"She must have been terrified and so alone." Thomas's thumb slowly stroked his jawline as he obviously remembered back and Ellis could see where an electric shaver had missed a couple of spots.

"I imagine she was." Ellis didn't want to think about his mother being scared and alone in a strange big city. He didn't want to think about being the cause that forced her to leave the safety of her parents' home.

"Her father was the minister of the local Methodist church and her mother was the organist. She was very active in the church." Thomas's thumb stopped its stroking as he tilted his head in Ellis's direction. "They left town about three years after Cathy took off. They seemed very upset with her leaving. I think, if I'm remembering correctly, they moved to Texas."

"They did."

"You know them then? Cathy got in contact with them?" Thomas seemed pleased that the family had been reunited.

"No, I never met them. I never even knew I had grandparents until after my mother died. I tried tracking them down then, but I was too late. They both had been killed in a plane crash in the Andes Mountains when I was about twelve. They had been on a missionary trip at the time."

"So there had been no reunion?"

"Not that I'm aware of." Reunion, hell! He had spent the first twenty-five years of his life not knowing what a complex, twisted unit a family really was. He discovered that fact after he had married Ginny and was baptized into a family by the way of hell's fire. Owning his own freight business had left him wide open for a multiple of favors. First her brother needed a job. No problem there until he started coming in drunk. Then there was this unemployed cousin, and then that cousin. Soon it went from jobs that never worked out to loans that were never repaid, to downright handouts. As far as he was concerned, the entire institution known as "family" should be abolished.

"That's a shame. A real shame." Thomas sadly shook his head. "Family is sacred. One's family should never be fractured beyond repair."

"Then you understand my need for your blood sample." There was no way he could control the tremble in his voice as he said, "Trevor is my whole family." He felt the burning of tears behind his eyes but refused to allow them to show. Tears were a sign of weakness. Right now, Trevor needed his strength.

"I'll give you as many blood samples as you want to try to match your son's, on one condition."

"Name it." At this point he was willing to pay any price Thomas named. He was out of options.

"I want you to be fully aware that I am not your father and that the chance of a match is nil. You'll have better luck hitting the lottery than having my blood match your son's." Thomas's voice broke and he had to take a moment to compose himself. "I wish I could tell you differently, Ellis. I wish I were your father so that I could offer you a small section of hope, but I can't."

Ellis ignored the stab of pain that pierced his heart. Thomas sounded sincere and he couldn't afford for him to be telling the truth. "But you'll still give the blood sample?"

"Yes, Ellis, as soon as you want it. I might not be able to see you, but I can hear the love you have for your son in your voice. That alone would compel me to do it."

He felt as if the twenty-pound weight that had been resting over his heart had been lifted. Thomas St. Claire had agreed to the blood test. The first hurdle had been cleared and he was at a loss for words. All of Ginny's relatives had wanted to know what was in it for them should there be a match. He gave the man who he believed fathered him a simple, "Thank you."

"Your mother and I shared quite a few good times together," Thomas said, "but not what you are thinking. We were friends. I never did understand why she hadn't said a word to anyone about leaving. One day, during church services, she had packed one suitcase and was gone. No one, that I know of, ever heard from her again. In a way, I was angry with her for doing that, Ellis. No calls, no letters, nothing but silence. We never knew. But she was my friend and Trevor is her grandson. I'll do whatever I can to help."

"Mr. Carlisle, would it be all right if I give a sample, too?" Sydney asked.

He turned and looked at the woman who had been quiet throughout most of the conversation. "You want to be tested too?"

"Yes. You said seventy percent of the transplants are done using an unrelated donor. I'm unrelated but I have a feeling that my chances of a match are the same as my father's."

"Will you allow the national registry to keep your

results on file?" Over the past nine months he had met more kids with leukemia than he had ever wanted to meet. All of them were praying for miracles. Sydney just might be someone's miracle.

"Yes."

He felt a smile tug at the corner of his mouth. She looked ready to save the world. If only life were so simple. "Thank you, Sydney."

He turned back to his father. "Thank you, Mr. St. Claire. I'll make the arrangements and get back to you both as to where and when." He stood up. His mission for the day was complete; Thomas was getting the blood test.

"Where you are staying?" asked Thomas. "I'm presuming you don't live around here."

"I live in Jenkintown. It's outside of Philadelphia. I'm registered at the Starry Night Motel out on the interstate." He started toward the door. It was time he left, before Thomas could change his mind.

"Know the place well," Thomas muttered. "I have a favor to ask of you."

Ellis felt his whole body stiffen at Thomas's words. Here it comes. The question he had been waiting for: *What do I get out of it if my blood matches?* He stopped in the middle of the room and stared at the man. "What's that?" He knew whatever the favor was, he was going to grant it. He wasn't in the position to refuse Thomas St. Claire a thing.

"Stay here with us until you get back the results. We have plenty of room and I can guarantee you that the accommodations are a lot better than the Starry Night Motel."

He heard Sydney's sudden intake of breath, but didn't

look at her face. She had to be as shocked as he was by Thomas's suggestion. "Why would you want me, a complete stranger, to stay here?"

"You aren't a stranger. You're Cathy's boy." Thomas's fingers drummed on the arm of the recliner. "I would like to hear more about your mother's life. I'm curious if she ever fulfilled any of those dreams she was always telling me about."

His mother never had any dreams that he knew about. She had worked, supported him, taken care of him and worried about him. That about summed up Catherine Carlisle's life. He wanted to turn down Thomas's offer, but knew he couldn't. The man might feel insulted and be annoyed enough not to go through with the blood test. But the main reason he couldn't refuse Thomas's invitation was that it was too good a chance to pass up.

Living with Thomas for the next few days would have its advantages. Golden advantages. If his prayers were answered, and Thomas did match Trevor's HLAs, he would have had ample opportunity to discover what Thomas St. Claire's price would be. He would know exactly what to offer Thomas to guarantee the transplant.

If his prayers weren't answered and there wasn't a match, the only thing he'd lose would be the privilege of not having to pay Starry Night's motel bill.

"Thank you, Mr. St. Claire, I accept your very nice offer. The atmosphere at the Starry Night Motel is a tad unsettling, if you know what I mean." About three in the morning he had been awakened, from what little sleep he had managed, by the noise in the room next to his. It seemed a pair of lovers had checked in and were quite vocal when it came to participating in what had to be their favorite sport. If it wasn't their favorite, it had to be their most exhausting sport.

"Good, and my name is either Thomas or Tom. No more of this Mr. St. Claire business. We'll be expecting you before dinner."

Thomas turned toward Sydney. "You don't mind having company for the next few days, do you, Syd?"

"Of course not, Dad." Sydney shot Ellis a look he couldn't have deciphered if the fate of his business had rested on it. "Mr. Carlisle is more than welcome."

Chapter 3

Sydney paced back and forth in front of the tables containing petunias, or at least in a couple more weeks they would be overflowing with gorgeous blossoming flowers. Now the tables were packed with hundreds of black plastic trays filled with rich dark soil and a three-inch-long green sprig. She turned to her friend Cindy and exclaimed for the sixth time, and in just as many minutes, "I can't believe he did that!"

Cindy continued to examine the trays. "It's his house, Sydney. Your father can invite anyone he wants over." Cindy frowned at a black tray holding four wilted plants and plucked it from the table. "I thought you would be happy that he was finally talking to someone, even if that someone was a stranger." Cindy placed the small tray on the cart behind her that held other sick plants.

Sydney glanced at the wide tables before her and couldn't muster the energy to examine the plants. She had finally managed a couple hours away from the house, and what does she do? She talks Cindy's ears off about her father and the problems at home. "This morning he talked so much he was positively gabby. I'm happy he's talking. Hell, he could talk to Ellis Carlisle all day, every day and it wouldn't bother me. But to invite the guy to stay a few days is something else totally."

In an exasperated gesture, she threw her hands up into the air. "Ellis Carlisle could be an ax murderer for all we know." She kicked at the stones beneath the tables in frustration. A few rocks skidded across the concrete pathway they were standing on. It didn't lower her frustration level. All she got out of the stupid senseless gesture was a sore toe.

"I'd take a chance on him if he looks anything the way you described him. Men like that don't stroll through Coalsburg every day of the week, and believe me, Syd, I've been looking."

Sydney shook her head at her best friend. The whole town knew Cindy had been looking since she turned thirteen. "Yeah, and it's also not every day that men like that claim to be my father's son."

"That means technically he's your brother, right?"

"No, it means technically he's a deeply confused individual." She had seen the flare of interest that had sparked in Cindy's baby blue eyes when she had described Ellis. She needed to set her friend straight on a few matters. "He's not Thomas's son, and the miracle he's praying for isn't going to happen." She brushed back a curl that had fallen too close to her eye and silently prayed that wasn't true. Ellis was here because his son needed a bone marrow match and she really wanted to see that match made. "At least it won't be happening with my father's blood."

"So why did you volunteer to be tested too?" Cindy's look told her she had seen right through her blustering. "He got to you, didn't he?"

"Hearing about his little boy would have made a boulder crumble into gravel." She turned and studied the row of tables on the other side of the walkway. Only someone who actually had a rock for a heart wouldn't have been touched by Ellis's story.

She squinted upward and through the glass roof of the greenhouse. The afternoon sun was stronger than she had expected and the greenhouse was quite warm. The sweatshirt she had pulled on before leaving the house earlier was becoming increasingly uncomfortable. She glanced back down at the tables in front of her. She might not appreciate this much warmth, but the marigolds that were pushing their way toward the life-giving sunlight were thriving.

Spring used to be her favorite season. It was the time of year when life renewed itself and the nursery was at its finest. Now she didn't think she would ever have a favorite season again. Everything around the nursery reminded her of her mother and the fact that they would never share its wonders again.

She pulled her thoughts away from the pain of losing her mother and asked her friend, "Don't you think I have a right to be worried?"

Cindy gave her a cautious look. "Are you asking me as your employee or your friend?"

She knew she wasn't going to like what Cindy had to say when she asked that particular question. "As my friend."

"As your friend, I think you worry too much about everything." Cindy plucked another tray containing shriveled plants off the table. "You're beginning to look like hell, Syd."

"Jeez, I would hate to think what you might have said if you were my enemy." She wasn't blind. She saw her reflection in the mirror every morning. Too many worries and too little sleep had left their mark. "I've got a father who's blind and needs constant supervision. I'm trying to run a business from a quarter mile away, and it can't be done. My employees have nicknamed me their 'ghost employer' and I just received notice that the IRS wants to audit the nursery's tax records."

In an infuriated gesture she kicked at the stones again and reinjured her already aching toe. "And if all of that isn't enough, I get some poor guy with a worse-luck story claiming to be my father's son and making himself at home in the spare bedroom."

"You could send him over to my place. I don't have a spare bedroom, but I'm sure I could think of something."

She chuckled at Cindy. Leave it to Cindy to be thinking of "something" when her friend's whole life was whirling out of control. "And what do I do about all my other worries? I've never been really good at playing Scarlett O'Hara and worrying about them tomorrow."

"Well, dismiss the IRS audit. Leave all that up to your accountants. You don't have anything to worry about on that front." Cindy shuffled a couple of trays to fill in the gaps where she had pulled a few bad trays. "You wouldn't know how to do a dishonest thing if Al Capone himself gave you instructions."

"Al Capone's dead."

"Yeah, right." Cindy glanced over her shoulder and asked, "So who are the bad guys nowadays?"

"Politicians."

Cindy chuckled. "Well, you couldn't be dishonest even if a politician showed you how." Cindy looked a tad guilty before turning back toward the tables in front of her. "You heard about the 'ghost employer' bit?"

"Don't worry about it, Cindy. I can't blame them for labeling me that. I'm hardly ever here." The guilt over that had been ripping at her until she figured she'd rather be guilty for letting the nursery slide than suffer from the guilt over not taking proper care of her father. Now she suffered from both and was learning to live with it. "My father can't be left alone and he's very fussy about who stays with him when I need to go out."

"Is your aunt Mary with him now?"

"Yes. He seems to tolerate his sister's company the best."

"Could be because every time she visits she spends the entire time in the kitchen whipping up more food than the two of you would eat in a week." Cindy grinned. "Which reminds me, if she bakes another one of her famous cherry pies, please remember who your friends are."

"She arrived loaded down with two shopping bags, so it's anyone's guess what she'll be cooking. But she did mention we're having roasted chicken for dinner." Mary might spend hours in the kitchen, but her father wasn't giving her own end results their due respect. He barely touched anything his sister cooked, either.

"Did you tell her there would be three for dinner and that someone was claiming to be her nephew?"

"I did tell her about Ellis staying with us for a few

days, but nothing about his claim or why he's here. I just said he was the son of an old friend of Dad's." Mary had seemed quite interested in all the details, but she hadn't obliged her aunt. If Dad wanted to tell her, that was his business. She had told Cindy because she was a trusted friend who could keep her mouth shut, and she really needed someone's shoulder to cry on for a while.

"I left Mary planning a seven-course meal and muttering about putting clean sheets on the spare bedroom's bed." She glanced at her watch and sighed. "Which reminds me, I've got to get a move on if I'm going to make it home in time to enjoy her cooking. Ian needs me in greenhouse three and Shirley wants my opinions on some of the craft items we'll be carrying this spring." She gave Cindy a small smile in gratitude for listening to all her woes. "Can you finish up here by yourself?"

Cindy was nice enough not to remind her that she hadn't been doing any of the work. "I'll be fine."

She turned and started down the walkway toward the door when Cindy's voice stopped her. "Hey, Syd, about your father..."

"What about him?"

"Stop worrying so much about him. As your friend, I'm telling you, you're babying him too much. He has to adjust someday."

"Adjust? He just lost his wife, his career and his sight!" She frowned at Cindy. She had never known Cindy to be so cruel.

"It happened six months ago, Syd. He can't adjust to it if you're hovering over him and doing everything for him. He needs to get on with his life just like you need to get on with yours."

She stared at Cindy for a long moment before turning

back around and walking out of the greenhouse without saying a word. One part of her was silently screaming that she didn't hover over her father and had never hovered a day in her life. Cindy was totally wrong. The other part heard the sincerity in Cindy's voice and wondered if indeed she was hindering her father's progress by loving him too much. It was a tough call to know when too much love was really too much love.

Sydney made her way home through the gloomy, dusk-shrouded fields. She didn't worry about getting lost or falling into a gopher hole. She had been walking these fields since she was ten and knew every inch of them. Things in Coalsburg never changed, be it the rows in between the acres of trees being grown at the nursery, or the stores that lined Main Street.

In the distance she could see the glowing back-porch light and knew her aunt was still holding things together at home. Mary always turned on the light as soon as dusk shadowed the skies.

Usually when her aunt came over she hurried up whatever business needed to be done at the nursery, left more instructions and headed home. She didn't like imposing on Thomas's sister, even though Mary swore it wasn't an imposition and she could stay as long as Sydney needed her. With all her own children grown and out on their own, Mary had an abundance of motherly instincts that needed to be expressed. Her now-disabled brother, Thomas, was the obvious outlet for all her mothering.

Tonight Sydney had hustled all the employees out the door by five and closed up by herself. It was something she hadn't done in six months. Usually Cindy or Shirley closed for her, but the nickname, ghost employer, had been preying heavily on her mind all afternoon. She needed to regain control of her business. There was a second reason she hadn't been in a hurry to head home. That reason had a name, and it was Ellis Carlisle.

Ellis would be at the house when she got there and she still didn't know how to handle the situation. Then again there wasn't much to handle. Her father had invited Ellis to stay, Ellis had accepted and that was the end of that. Only after the fact did her father ask her if she minded. By then it was a little too late if she did.

Sydney shifted the bundle of paperwork she was carrying as she drew nearer to the house. The nursery might be closed for the night, but there were still hours of work that needed to be done. Paperwork was the bane of her existence. Company or not, it still had to be done.

Her work boots were caked with mud from her walk, and chunks of the stuff came off as she made her way over the brick patio to the small bench beneath the burning light. She carefully set down the folders of paperwork, all neatly fastened with rubber bands, and plopped herself down next to them. Over the years her mother and she had sat on this very bench after walking the field home, and had discussed business or future-expansion dreams. The hunter green bench with its chipped paint brought back lots of memories. All of them sweet.

She bent down and untied her muddy boots. She and her mother used to joke about how pig farmers smelled better than them some of the time, especially when the two of them worked with certain mulches, like mushroom mulch. Today it had felt so wonderful to be outside in the sunshine and fresh air that she had helped Ian turn over a garden or two while adding a nice generous helping of mushroom mulch to enrich the soil. Everyone knew what mushrooms grew best in and tonight she smelled exactly like it.

With a weary sigh she toed off her boots, leaned back against the white clapboard siding of the house and closed her eyes. The question that had been eating at her gut all afternoon returned to take a bite out of her heart. Why had her father invited Ellis to stay in their house? Thomas had never invited anyone to spend the night before. He and Julia had been proud of their home, but they hadn't entertained a whole lot. The only people she could remember spending the night in the spare room had been some college friends of hers, during school breaks, and her mother's sister, Rose, who visited every other year and lived in Minnesota. Beyond that, the room stood unused unless she or her mom needed to use the sewing machine that was in there.

So what had compelled her father to offer the invitation to a virtual stranger? His past friendship with Catherine Carlisle might have something to do with it, but how close had it been? And had their friendship been strong enough to span thirty-two years and another generation? Could there be a chance, no matter how minute or how much her father denied it, that Ellis really was his son? Was that why her father had not wanted Ellis to leave earlier?

She heard the kitchen door open, but she didn't bother to open her eyes. It would be her aunt checking on her. Mary had probably seen her crossing the field from the window above the sink. "I'll be in in a minute, Mary." The aroma of roasted chicken drifted out the door and made her mouth water. "Something sure smells good."

"That's what I told your aunt earlier." Ellis Carlisle's

deep rich voice caressed the evening darkness like a lover's hand.

Her eyes flew open as she jerked away from the wall. "Oh, I thought you were my aunt."

"I've been mistaken for one or two people in my life, but never someone's aunt." Ellis closed the door behind him and stepped out onto the patio. "Mary saw you crossing the field and started to worry when you didn't come in."

Ellis was wearing the same clothes from this morning, but now he looked more relaxed. More confident. She had to wonder if the invitation to stay a few days gave him that confidence, or was it her father's willingness to take the blood test? "Are you all settled in?" If there was a slight edge to her question, she hoped he would chalk it up to a busy and tiring afternoon at the nursery.

"It's a lovely room, Sydney." Ellis moved out of the circle of light and into the growing shadows around the edge of the patio. "If my staying here is making you uncomfortable, I'll leave."

"It doesn't matter how I feel about it." She wanted Ellis to know she wasn't going to be as easily accommodating as her father. They needed to set some ground rules.

"It's how Thomas feels, right?"

She had to give Ellis credit for being on the ball. "Right."

"I'm sure your father wouldn't want you to be uneasy with a stranger in the house."

"I'm sure he wouldn't either. But for some reason he wants you to stay, so stay you shall." Being an officer of the law for thirty-one years had honed her father's perception of people to a fine skill. She had never once seen or known of her father misjudging a person. Thomas St. Claire trusted Ellis enough to invite him into their home for several nights. She just hoped that when her father lost his sight, he hadn't lost his perception.

"Whatever Thomas wants?"

"My father gets." It was that plain and simple. She wouldn't and couldn't go against her father on this. Thomas St. Claire had his reasons and at this point in their lives she couldn't defy her father. Then again, she'd never defied her father before the accident. She had always been a good girl.

"In case it makes you sleep better, let me assure you I'm not an ax murderer or anything. I'm not here to harm you or your father."

She stood up and chuckled uneasily as she reached for the pile of folders on the bench. She didn't like the coincidence that they both had thought up the ax murderer bit. It was unnerving. He might not be there to harm them, but there was a very good possibility that he could rip apart what was left of her family.

She glanced down at her dirt-streaked jeans and cringed. They were in worse shape than her sweatshirt. All in all, she was a mess and not in any mood for company. What she desperately needed was a shower. A long hot shower might ease some of the tension in her shoulders and possibly help the headache forming behind her eyes. As for the pain in her heart, she didn't think that would ever go away.

"I have to give you fair warning, Ellis." She stepped over to the door and placed her hand on the brass knob. She wasn't about to let Ellis think he had infiltrated her family so easily. Thomas might trust him, but her vote wasn't in yet.

"About what?" Ellis had stepped back into the circle of light. Even in the gloom of dusk and under the glare of a forty-watt bulb he looked handsome as all hell.

"If you do turn out to have any murderous inclinations, I do know how to protect what's mine. My father taught me how to shoot his thirty-eight." She smiled sweetly as if blowing big holes into things gave her great pleasure. "I've been told I'm an excellent shot and I will guarantee you that I will hit what I'm aiming at." Ellis managed to look both impressed and apprehensive. *Good, let him chew on that one for a while.* She turned around, opened the door and stepped into the warm inviting kitchen.

Ellis felt a little strange being all nestled up, kind of cozy like in the den, with Thomas St. Claire and his daughter. The evening news was on television, but turned down low and no one was paying much attention to it. Everyone was more intent on digesting the meal they had just shared.

Thomas had seemed friendly and open about his curiosity regarding Catherine Carlisle. All through dinner Thomas asked questions, none of them really bordering on being too personal. But not once did Ellis get the impression Thomas was interrogating him. And the older man had expertly broken up the questions with an array of stories about a young, seemingly shy Catherine.

Thomas didn't act as if he had anything to hide and had been quite open with his answers to the few questions Ellis had asked. Nor did Thomas act like a man who just had his unwanted thirty-two-year-old son show up on his doorstep demanding a blood sample. Thomas seemed relaxed and confident that he could prove he wasn't Ellis's father.

Ellis had come to Coalsburg prepared to hate the man whom his mother had claimed fathered him and then abandoned them both. But he had been prepared to hide his hate and bargain with the devil himself to give his son a chance. He was finding it awfully hard to keep his hatred toward Thomas alive.

The one thing he did notice about Thomas was that he ate very little of his dinner. It seemed a shame when Thomas's sister, Mary, left to go home to her husband instead of staying to enjoy the meal with them. She was an excellent cook and he couldn't remember ever enjoying a meal more. Taste wasn't the problem, but maybe Thomas's appetite was. The man appeared to be dwindling away. Of course, losing his sight might also have something to do with it. He had always considered taste and smell the two most important senses when it came to eating. But then he'd never thought about what it must feel like to be totally blind. If he was surrounded by darkness and had to eat in a black void, there was a good chance he would lose his appetite too.

His first pangs of sympathy for Thomas had come and gone over dinner. He had hardened his heart. He wasn't staying here to feel sorry for the man. He was here to discover Thomas's price to become Trevor's bone marrow donor. Thomas's one and only weakness, he had discovered so far, was his beautiful yet wary daughter, Sydney.

Ellis glanced over at the other end of the couch where Sydney was poring over a computer printout and a small mountain of paperwork. Piles were neatly stacked on the coffee table in front of her. Two piles were on the floor, and a couple of folders were next to her on the couch. She seemed totally engrossed in the surrounding paperwork, but his gut was telling him she was very much aware of him and Thomas.

Sydney St. Claire was becoming quite a distraction with that pair of glasses perched on her cute little nose. It made his fingers itch to pull off those round wire glasses and give her something more interesting to study besides dull computer printouts. Something like the human anatomy.

His anatomy in particular.

Sydney was an intriguing puzzle and suddenly he was wondering what it would feel like if he became a puzzle master. At first, he's simply seen her as the protective and loving daughter of Thomas St. Claire. She was also, he'd learned from Thomas this afternoon, the sole owner of Ever Green Nursery since her mother had died.

When he'd stepped onto the back patio earlier, he thought she'd smelled a little ripe, but hadn't been positive until she had walked into the kitchen and Mary had laughingly shooed her upstairs to take a shower before dinner. Thomas had sat silently at the kitchen table until Mary had gently patted his hand. Only then did Thomas admit that the strange odor reminded him of his departed wife, Julia. At first Ellis hadn't considered that a compliment, but then he remembered that Julia St. Claire had started the nursery. Julia and Sydney had stepped, worked or played in the same foul-smelling stuff. In his opinion it definitely took a different type of woman than what he was used to, to willingly smell like horse manure. His ex-wife, Ginny, had never even left their bedroom without dousing herself with French perfume. He shuddered to think what Ginny would have thought of Sydney's choice of fragrances.

The one thing he could say definitely about Sydney was she sure cleaned up nice. Real nice. She had replaced her work clothes after her shower with the same short-sleeved emerald green sweater she'd had on that morning, but this time she paired it with a flowing skirt of green-and-gold swirls. The silky skirt teased her calves and offered him an enticing peek of her long slim legs and her nicely shaped ankles. It made a man want to speculate what the rest of her looked like beneath all that silk.

The last thing he needed was to be thinking about what Sydney would look like beneath the silk skirt, or denim jeans, or the emerald green sweater that clung so nicely to all the right curves. He surely didn't need the dream he'd had last night, where her hair had been spread out across his pillow, her lips made swollen and red by his kisses and her legs wrapped around his hips. His overactive imagination, where Sydney was concerned, didn't need any more visual stimulation.

Sydney wasn't the reason he was sitting in the same room with the man who had fathered him. Trevor was. Sydney was a dangerous distraction.

"Did you get in touch with your son today?" Thomas's voice broke the silence of the room.

Ellis turned to Thomas, and looked away from the beautiful woman sitting on the opposite end of the couch. "Yes. I talked to him around lunchtime."

"He doesn't mind you staying a couple of days?"

He didn't want to admit that his son's voice had cracked with tears when he'd told him about the delay. He had felt so guilty for not being there for Trev, even though the boy was in the excellent and loving hands of Mrs. McCall. He didn't know how to explain to his son how important this was. He could have gone back to Jenkintown and stayed with Trevor until the results of Thomas's blood test were in. But if the miracle happened, and Thomas did match and then for some unknown reason decided not to be Trevor's donor, his hands would have been tied. He wouldn't have known enough about Thomas to know what kind of leverage he could use to convince him to change his mind. If Thomas was the kind of man to get an eighteen-year-old girl pregnant and then abandon her and the child without guilt, then who was to say he would go through with the transplant? Ellis couldn't chance it. He wasn't leaving Thomas's side until the results of the test were in.

Ellis shifted in the soft couch and remembered the bribe he had thrown his son. "Trevor was a little upset, but I promised him I would look for an orangutan."

"An orangutan?"

"Trevor is in the middle of collecting what seems like a warehouse full of jungle animals. I was informed this morning he was still missing an orangutan." He had Mrs. McCall to thank for pointing that one out to Trevor. "He has a gorilla and a chimpanzee, but no orangutan."

Thomas laughed. "Sounds like it's a real zoo around your place."

"You have no idea. Some of the guys I work with heard about Trev's collection and bought him a five-foot-long stuffed alligator. The damn thing sleeps in the bathtub because there's no room left in Trev's room. Scares the living tar out of me every time I turn on the light."

Sydney seemed to stare at her father for a long time before joining in the laughter. "Tell me, what does a five-foot-long alligator eat?"

"Anything it wants." He liked Sydney's laugh. It was low and throaty and made his gut tighten just a little bit. He gave her a slow smile. "There's usually some cute fuzzy teddy bear clamped between its vicious jaws."

"Does your son name his animals?" Sydney pulled her reading glasses off her nose and dropped them on the printout she had been reading. "I used to name all my animals when I was little." He watched in wonder as her features softened into a warm, loving smile directed solely at her father. He knew instantly that she hadn't heard her father laugh in a long time. A very long time.

"She gave them all sissy names like Lulu and Priscilla," Thomas said. "Boys give their animals tough, mean names." Thomas scratched his jaw and grinned. "I bet he named the alligator Killer or Terminator or something equally as revolting."

"I'm afraid not, Thomas. Trevor does name every one of his animals, but he believes all animals must have people names. The teddy-bear mangler is affectionately known as Fred."

"Fred," sputtered Sydney. "Where did he come up with that one?"

"Me." Ellis shrugged. "Hey, I was running out of names. There's Wilson the elephant, Lawrence the giraffe and Richard the lion." He had to shake his head at the complexities of raising a five-year-old. Trevor had stumped his mind on more than one occasion. Like why is cheese yellow and how come real stars don't look like the ones everyone draws? "It's not easy naming an entire jungle."

"Minus one orangutan." Thomas pushed his recliner back and raised his feet. "I don't envy you, Ellis. Orangutans are pretty scarce in Coalsburg nowadays." Thomas rubbed his chin. "Last time I saw one was in eighty-two. Or was it eighty-three?"

Ellis shook his head at Thomas's attempt at humor. He didn't need Thomas to tell him how difficult it was locating a certain breed of animal Trevor had set his mind on. Lawrence, the four-foot-high giraffe, had been Federal Expressed from a catalog company based in California. It was a real shame he didn't have the catalog with him. There might have been an orangutan in the potpourri of pets that the company carried. "Thanks, I'll remember that tomorrow when I'm out on the safari."

"Try Two-By-Two on Main Street," Sydney said. "They carry just about every animal under the sun."

"Two-By-Two?"

"It's a toy store named in honor of Noah's Ark. Georgette Gentry owns it. If she doesn't have an orangutan in stock, she can order you one."

"I forgot about Georgette's place," Thomas said. "It's right there at the intersection of Main and Oak Streets. Heck, Ellis, you could probably find a half-dozen species of jungle animals you don't even know about."

"So what you are telling me is that I'll be going back home with more than an orangutan in the back seat."

"Count on it." Sydney slipped on her glasses and picked up the folder sitting beside her. "Georgette has everything." Her smile held pure mischief. "I bet she'll even have a mate for Fred."

"That's just what I need. Two alligators startling years off my life and mating in the tub." If Trevor ever found out about Two-By-Two, Ellis would have to build an addition onto the boy's bedroom. Maybe that isn't such a bad idea, he thought. He could build Fred his own cage and maybe Trevor would be able to fit his collection all in one room so the occasional monkey or tiger scattered throughout the house would eventually find its way back home.

"I have a suggestion. Why don't you bring Trevor out here?" Thomas asked. "He's more than welcome to stay here, we have plenty of room for him and one or two of his favorite animals."

He was tempted to take Thomas up on his offer. He really was tempted. He missed Trevor beyond belief and the daily phone calls to his son weren't even coming close to filling the hole in his heart. But he couldn't allow himself to give in to that temptation. As rotten as it sounded after accepting Thomas's hospitality, he still didn't trust the man. He would never put his son in a situation where he might be hurt.

Trevor craved a bigger extended family. Ginny and her family had disappeared from Trevor's life when he was only six weeks old. As far as Trevor knew, he had no mother, no aunts, uncles or grandparents and he had developed the innocent tendency, born of youth, to latch on to the people who entered his life. Trevor had been heartbroken when he had to leave the hospital and the extended family he had made of the doctors and nurses.

Integrating Trevor's life with doctors and nurses was unavoidable, but purposely thrusting Thomas and Sydney into his son's life would be inexcusable no matter how much he missed the little boy. "Thanks for the offer, but it will only be for a few days, until the test results are back. I wouldn't want to bring havoc to your home. It's unbelievable what a five-year-old can do to one house." He managed to smile as if he meant it. "Besides, I wouldn't want to deprive Ma Bell of all the extra revenue she'll be making in that time."

"The offer is still open if you change your mind. This old house could use some excitement." Thomas settled more deeply into the chair. "I've been after Sydney for years to get married and give me some grandchildren to spoil."

Thomas's voice had been teasing, but Ellis picked up a note of seriousness beneath the gentle kidding.

A flush of embarrassment swept over Sydney's face. "I really don't think it would be appropriate for me to get married and have a couple of babies just so you would have grandchildren."

Ellis felt sorry for Sydney. If Thomas hadn't abandoned Catherine Carlisle and their unborn child, he would have been a grandfather five years ago. "Sydney's right, Thomas. Having a child to make someone else happy usually never works out."

Ginny had gotten pregnant with Trevor because she saw the end of their marriage looming on the horizon. She hadn't wanted to lose the way of life she had grown accustomed to. She had thought a baby would hold the marriage together, and she was partly right. Ellis never would have divorced the mother of his child. He believed firmly that a child needed a mother, and since he needed and wanted his child, the marriage was staying together. Ginny had been the one to initiate the divorce and the very substantial hole in his bank account. He hadn't minded too much. He figured he had gotten the better part of the deal. He had gotten Trevor.

"Oh, I know that, Ellis." Thomas turned his head in Sydney's direction. "My daughter knows I'm kidding, but sometimes I do wish she wasn't so damn picky."

"Picky?" sputtered Sydney.

He nearly chuckled at the look of outrage on Sydney's face. "Now, Thomas, a woman has the right to be a little picky when it comes to choosing a husband and a father for her children."

"I really don't appreciate your help, Mr. Carlisle, on the subject." Sydney glared at her father, and he was positive that if Thomas could have seen her look he would have dived for cover. "I also don't appreciate it, Dad, that you would bring up the subject of my lack of a husband and children in front of a stranger."

"Ellis isn't a stranger. He's Cathy's boy." Thomas puffed out his chest in pride. "Besides, you already had two fine catches, but for some unknown reason you let them both go."

He was positive Sydney was praying for the floor to open up and swallow her whole. Maybe he should be thankful that Thomas hadn't taken an active part in his upbringing.

"Dad, I don't believe in *catching* men or letting them go." Sydney gathered up her papers and not so subtly slammed the folders down on top of each other. "Since you seem to want to talk sports, I'll leave you and Ellis to converse to your hearts' content." She picked up the paperwork and headed for the door. "I'll check in on you, Dad, before I go to bed." She glanced at Ellis. "Give me a call if you need anything, Mr. Carlisle. Good night."

Thomas gave a low whistle and a soft chuckle as soon as Sydney left the room and her footsteps could be heard going up the stairs. "That girl has a mind of her own."

Ellis had already learned that much about her. Now he was learning more about her. "I think she was a little upset with you, Thomas." He had a feeling she was more than just a little upset. Sydney had not only been embarrassed, she had been furious.

Thomas sat back in his chair and smiled. "That was the whole point, Ellis."

"You actually wanted Sydney mad at you?" Maybe the doctors had been wrong. Maybe the accident had scrambled Thomas's brain. Why would he want his daughter upset with him? From what he could tell, Sydney had been caring for her father since the accident. What in the world would Thomas have done without Sydney's help all these months?

"No, I don't want her mad at me. But I do want her to show a little emotion. Ever since the accident she's been treating me like an invalid and tiptoeing around me as if I would break."

Thomas had a point. Sydney did overprotect her father. But Sydney also had a reason for being so sheltering. "Can I make a comment as an impartial observer?"

"Shoot."

Any man who goaded his daughter into showing some type of emotion should be strong enough to handle the truth. It really shouldn't have mattered to him, but he had seen Sydney's face when she had stormed out of the room. Thomas had hurt her, and hurt her deeply. "If you don't want Sydney hovering around you like an invalid, stop acting like an invalid."

Chapter 4

Sydney glanced from the closed door of the police station to the sky, searching for an answer. She squinted against the brightness of the sun, but didn't receive any heavenly message. Somewhere between last night in the den, when she had left in a snit, and this morning, she had lost a page of life, or had missed some boat that she didn't even know had been docking.

Her father had changed with the sunrise.

It was as though Thomas St. Claire had awakened to the world around him and decided it was time to get on with his life. Someone, or something, had snapped some spirit into him. Her instincts were telling her it had been Ellis. But how? What in the world could Ellis have said that she hadn't already? She knew her father better than anyone. What could a stranger have said or done that would have pushed one of her father's buttons?

All morning long she had been suffering from this

really queasy feeling in the pit of her stomach. Maybe it had been Ellis's presence that had motivated her father into rejoining the living. But why? There had only been one reasonable explanation. Ellis was her father's son and Thomas knew it. Thomas had discovered his real son, his real flesh-and-blood child, and decided life was indeed once again worth living.

Made perfect sense to her, except for one small fact. This morning while they were at the medical lab giving their blood samples, her father had requested that Ellis also give a small sample so that a test could be done to prove he was not Ellis's father. She had a feeling Ellis's reluctant agreement came more out of fear her father wouldn't have gone through with the blood sample needed for his son than from his own curiosity.

So she was back to square one, standing on the sidewalk outside the police station, where she had just escorted her father so he could visit the "guys." It was the first time he had stepped foot into the brick building since the accident. She had seen the shocked yet smiling faces of men who were not only former colleagues but friends as well. Everyone had greeted Thomas with open hearts, offers of coffee and the teasing refrains about the world coming to an end. She had felt her father's momentary surprise at such a greeting and then she had seen his smile. Satisfied, she had left him sitting in a place of honor, surrounded by friends and cradling a cup of coffee.

She should be delighted. So why wasn't she? Her gaze shot up the street and landed on the dark green Mercedes. Ellis's car. Ellis had insisted on driving to the medical lab, three towns over. He had then offered to drop Thomas off at the police station and hang around town to do some shopping while her father visited with his friends. But she had declined his offer, feeling as if she were being pushed farther and farther out of her father's life.

Instead of taking the few unexpected free hours to catch up on some work, she had insisted on coming to town with them. She was Thomas St. Claire's daughter and if anyone was going to help him negotiate the sidewalks of Main Street it was going to be her, not Ellis.

She headed in the direction of Ellis's car and noticed it was empty. He hadn't waited for her to come back out of the police station. She hadn't expected him to, so why did she feel so dejected? Ellis surely didn't need her to show him where everything was in town. Everything a person could want or need was on Main Street. From the local bank, to Marclay's Market, to the beer distributor. It was all there on one tree-lined street.

With a heavy heart that knew monumental changes were once again happening in her life and that she was helpless to stop or alter them, she entered the pharmacy to do her own shopping. She grabbed a red plastic basket and headed for the aisle containing shampoo.

She got as far as the second aisle. Her feet faltered at the sight of Ellis staring at a rack jam-packed with coloring books. The look of anguish on his face pierced her heart and touched her soul. It was the look of a father missing his son, his critically ill son. She watched as his hand slowly raised and touched the glossy cover featuring Winnie-the-Pooh. The trembling of his fingers tore at her anger and shredded it to pieces. How could she hold whatever was happening in her relationship with her father against Ellis? He was only trying to save his son's life.

Her feet barely made a sound as she walked down the aisle and stood beside him. Ellis didn't hear her as he continued staring at the coloring book. She could tell he wasn't even seeing the brightly colored books. She had to say something to dissolve the sadness of his memories. "My favorite has always been Tigger."

Ellis blinked, as if coming out of a dream, and glanced at her. A sad little smile touched the corner of his mouth. "Trevor received a stuffed Winnie-the-Pooh from Santa when he was two. He still has the bear, and most nights Winnie's one of the lucky ones who gets to sleep in his bed. The rule is, no more than three animals in bed at the same time."

She smiled at the picture of a little boy snuggled under the blankets surrounded by an army of his favorite stuffed animals. "I'm sure it must be a hard decision for him to make every night."

"It's near impossible most nights." Ellis reached and picked up the coloring book. "He now has a time limit on how long he has to decide." The coloring book behind the one he had just taken had a picture of Tigger and some sad-looking donkey, whose name she couldn't remember. Ellis reached for that one too. "Why Tigger?"

"Why not Tigger?" She wasn't really up to date on the adventures of Pooh and his friends in the hundred-acre woods and knew she couldn't compete with the parent of a five-year-old. In some distant corner of her mind she just knew she had always liked Tigger better. A couple of her friends who had children were walking encyclopedias when it came to cartoon characters and television shows.

"I've always been partial to Eeyore, myself."

Her memory kicked in; Eeyore was the name of the sad-looking donkey. "The grumpy donkey who eats thistles? Now that's a strange choice." She glanced at the two books in his hand. "Are you buying them for your son?"

"I'll stop at the post office and overnight them to him. It will give him something to do instead of driving Mrs. McCall crazy all day. Trevor likes to keep busy." Ellis selected a box of crayons and added them to his basket. "Did your father have any trouble getting settled in with his friends?"

"No, he's over there acting like he's been crowned king for the day." She noticed that Ellis had called Thomas her father and not *their* father. She was dying to know what had gone on in the den after she left last night. It had been around eleven when she heard both her father and Ellis come upstairs. The room Ellis was using was directly next to hers and she had heard him moving around for hours after he shut the bedroom door. Ellis obviously didn't require a lot of sleep. "Can I ask you a question?"

He gave her a curious look. "Sure, ask away."

She noticed that he didn't say he would answer it, just that she could ask. "What did you and my father talk about last night after I left?"

"Different things." Ellis took a couple of steps to his right and studied a shelf of children's books. "My mother mostly."

She studied his hands as he flipped through the books to the ones at the back. He had strong, capable-looking hands. His fingers were long and slender with neatly trimmed fingernails. He had the hands of a pianist. He had the hands of a lover. She wondered what they would feel like sliding over her skin. With an involuntary gasp at such an outlandish vision, she jerked her gaze away from his hands and down to the bottom rack of books.

Ellis gave her a strange look before turning back to a book about the circus he had uncovered. "Why do you ask?"

She willed the blush staining her cheeks to fade. "I couldn't help noticing my father has a different outlook on life this morning. He hasn't been in town since the accident. After six months of refusing all visitors at the house, he decides he wants to visit his friends at the station. Seems a little sudden to me."

Her gaze caught the edge of a book hiding behind a copy of *Auto Mechanic Monthly*. She pulled it out and smiled at the cover. It was titled *The ABC's of Jungle Animals. From Apes to Zebras*. It sounded perfect for Ellis's son. She hugged the book to her chest. "Did you happen to say anything to my father that might have motivated him to go visiting today?"

Ellis's gaze landed on the book she was clutching to her chest. His gaze seemed to linger there for an awfully long time before he raised it to her face. "There might have been something said."

She raised an eyebrow. "Like what?"

"Your father seemed a little concerned about how you are treating him."

"Treating him! What do you mean, how I am treating him?" As far as she knew, she hadn't mistreated her father. She had been bending over backward to make sure his life was as comfortable as humanly possible. Thomas St. Claire didn't even have to think about something before she had gotten it for him. "What exactly did he say?"

"Relax, Sydney, your father just felt as if you were treating him like an invalid."

"An invalid?" She hadn't been treating him like an invalid. She had been handling him with love, a daughter's love. "What did you tell him?"

"I told him if he didn't want to be treated like an invalid, he should stop acting like one."

"You didn't!" Who did Ellis think he was, telling her father he was acting like an invalid? Thomas St. Claire *was* an invalid. He could act any way he wanted. If anyone ever had just cause for acting a little needy, it was her father. "Who gave you the right to say such a thing to my father?"

"He did, when he asked for my opinion. Your father doesn't leave the house, except for an occasional doctor's appointment or when you force him to sit out back on the patio. He refuses to see any visitors or to talk on the telephone. All he does is shuffle from bedroom to kitchen to den all day long. Your father acts like an invalid, thus you treat him as such."

"He's blind! How would you treat him?" It was obvious that her father and Ellis had done some serious talking last night. Talking that hadn't included her. She was angry about being excluded from their conversation, but more importantly she was hurt. Her father had talked to Ellis, a complete stranger, about how his daughter treated him.

Ellis replaced the circus book and frowned at the pitifully small assortment of children's books. "*If* I had a father who I loved as much as you obviously love yours, I would probably treat him the same way you are treating Thomas. I would be overly protective and afraid to allow him to take any chances in case he got hurt."

"Is that how you treat your son?" She had heard his words, but she had also heard the experience behind them.

"Your father is a full-grown intelligent man. He's not a five-year-old little boy."

She heard the truth behind his words. Her father and Trevor were two totally different people, with totally different needs. Her father obviously wanted her to stop being so protective. She could do that. It would be hard, but she could do it. His first step toward independence was this trip to the police station. She was sure there were going to be more to follow. It was time for her father to regain control over his life.

The book she clutched to her chest dug in at a tender spot. She lowered her gaze. "My father needs to start facing life again while little five-year-old boys need to learn their ABC's." She smiled and handed Ellis the book. "I believe your son would enjoy this one."

Ellis reached for the book, read the title and smiled. "Thank you, Sydney. Trevor will love it."

His smile did strange and frightening things to her heart. A small spark of warmth had started in the middle of her chest and slowly spread its way outward. How was it possible for the flexing of a few facial muscles to affect her heart so?

"Of course you realize that he will compare these animals to the ones he already has cluttering his room." Ellis waved the book at her, but he continued to grin. "Lord help me if there's an animal he doesn't already have. I could be spending months tracking down a stuffed warthog or some other ghastly beast."

The heat in her chest spread farther. "Speaking of tracking down animals, do you want some company on your maiden voyage into the ark? The Two-By-Two shop can be a frightening experience for those weak at heart." She had seen more than one poor parent or grandparent struggling out the door weighted down with creatures twice their size.

"My heart's not weak, but you're invited to join me." He tossed the ABC Jungle book into his basket. "If the shop is as good as you and Thomas said, I just might need your help carrying Trevor's haul."

"It's as good as we said." She shook her head at his basket that was already half-full of stuff for Trevor. "I just hope your MasterCard is gold."

Ellis stood in the middle of the Two-By-Two shop and stared at the display that took up half of the left side of the store. Six fake trees, surrounded by twice as many stuffed animals, crowded the area. The bark and branches of the trees were made out of brown plastic and the leaves were mostly silk, but a few appeared to be plastic. Hanging by one hand from a large branch of a fake mahogany tree was the reason for his visit. A hairy reddish-brown orangutan with shiny black eyes stared back at him.

He was the perfect orangutan.

Trevor would go nuts when he added this magnificent specimen to his collection.

There was only one problem. Next to his son's perfect present hung his Mrs., complete with a darling little baby orangutan clinging to her back. He didn't know if he had the courage to break up the family.

He glanced around the shop. Surely a place that appeared to contain every animal known to man would have another orangutan. A single fellow without the added responsibility of a wife and baby. His gaze skidded over the animals and landed on Sydney. She was standing by the front door slowly running her hand up and down the long slender neck of a giraffe. The silent, lucky fellow stood a good foot taller than Sydney's five-and-a-half-foot height.

Sydney had surprised him when she invited herself along to the toy store. She had been surprising him a lot. He knew why she had insisted on coming along into town; she was afraid he was pushing her out of Thomas's life. But she was wrong. The only reason he had offered Thomas the lift was that he had to do some shopping anyway, and by the fatigue bagging beneath Sydney's eyes he figured she could use the break. Sydney had been upset with him, and by her thinking, rightly so. So why offer to accompany him to the toy store? Why start up a conversation with him in the pharmacy in the first place? She could have done her shopping and he might not even have known she had been there.

Last night, after he retired to his room, he had listened to her move around in her room for hours. The faint sounds coming from behind the wall that separated their two bedrooms had played havoc on his concentration. He had booted up his laptop and started working up a proposal for a major manufacturer when the first muffled sounds had reached his ears. He had stared at that cream-colored wall of the guest bedroom for a long time, wondering what she was doing. His imagination kicked into high gear as he started to think about what a woman like Sydney would wear to bed. His brain told him it was none of his business while his libido screamed "nothing." Needless to say, the proposal he was supposed to be working on never made it past the first page.

What little sleep he did get had been filled with dreams of a mahogany-haired beauty with soft green eyes and a welcoming smile that promised a man paradise. Sydney St. Claire had even controlled his dreams. The last thing he had needed this morning was to come down the stairs and find her filling out a pair of jeans to perfection and flipping delicious-smelling pancakes. He had felt himself start to drool, and for the life of him he hadn't been sure which sight had caused that reaction. After a near-sleepless night he had been primed to devour something, and food hadn't been his first priority.

Thomas's presence at the kitchen table had prevented him from making a fool of himself by seeing if Sydney's mouth tasted as good in person as it had in his dreams. The pancakes, on the other hand, had been light, fluffy and delicious. As for her kisses, he had made a silent vow that he would taste at least one before he headed back to Jenkintown and his son.

He walked over to Sydney and nodded at the giraffe. "Found a friend?" He watched as her hand trailed once more down the slender neck. Sydney had the shortest fingernails he had ever seen on a woman. They were rounded, clean and coated with clear polish that reflected the sunlight streaming in through the window. They were the kind of nails a man would want his lover to have. Two-inch bloodred claws made him nervous. He wanted the skin on his back to stay there and not be shredded off in the heat of passion.

"The tag says his name is Gerald." Sydney gave Gerald's rump a friendly pat. "I would kill for eyelashes like his."

He glanced at Gerald's thick, long and dark eyelashes. He chuckled. "They might complement his big dark eyes, but they're sissy lashes." He turned his head and studied her green eyes, which were filled with laughter and surrounded by dark lush lashes of her own. "I like your lashes better. They don't look like spider legs."

Her "Oh" sounded breathless and slightly confused as if she wasn't sure if she'd just received a compliment or not. It took her a moment to recover, and then she blinked rapidly and pulled her gaze away from his. "Did you find your orangutan?"

He grinned. He liked making her flustered. She was beautiful when she was flustered. She was beautiful even when she wasn't flustered. "Worse."

"Worse?"

He nodded in the direction of the mahogany tree and its swinging primates. "I found a complete family of orangutans." He gave a shrug. "I'm not into breaking up families." He hoped his words put her at ease. He wasn't in Coalsburg to break up her family and take Thomas away from her. He was here looking for a miracle.

Sydney followed his gaze and smiled at the swinging trio. "They're adorable. Your son would love them." She walked closer and stroked the baby orangutan's back. "Of course you can't split them up. They're a family."

Ellis noticed that her hands did more talking than her mouth. Syndey was a "touchy" kind of person. He had to wonder what kind of lover she would make. His gut told him a fantastic one. Sydney's hands alone would drive a man over the edge, time and time again. He forced his gaze away from her stroking fingers and took a deep breath.

"Help me look for a single orangutan. One that wouldn't take up an entire seat in the car." Two-By-Two seemed to carry its share of huge, nearly life-size animals. There was barely any room left in Trevor's room for a beanie-baby orangutan, let alone a daddy orangutan who looked to be a good forty inches tall.

Sydney chuckled as she stepped away from the fake trees. "Georgette should have something a bit smaller." Glancing at the woman behind the counter who was waiting on a young couple purchasing a small table-and-chair set, she waved.

The woman smiled in recognition and waved back. He couldn't help noticing the wonderful table set. The table was hand-painted with a scene of Noah's Ark and an assortment of animals. Each of the four chairs had a different back in the shape of an animal. There was an elephant, giraffe, tiger and monkey chair. Trevor would love it. He looked around the crowded shop and sighed. He was in trouble. Trevor would love just about everything in the shop.

Ellis wasn't surprised when an hour later he and Sydney drove to the police station to collect her father with the entire orangutan family taking up half the back seat of his car. Two-By-Two didn't have any single, unattached orangutans. The pleasant and most accommodating owner, Georgette, had assured him she could order him one and that it would be there by the end of the week. He had decided not to wait and ended up with the entire family instead.

He knew Trevor would love them all, but he also

knew he was appeasing his own guilt for being away from his son. He couldn't help it. He needed to be near Thomas St. Claire until the results came back. There was no law that could force Thomas to become his son's bone marrow donor if there happened to be a match.

Sydney had teased him unmercifully about being a marshmallow the entire time he was paying for his purchases. But she had been the one to insist on helping him carry the hairy creatures to his car. They had received more than one knowing yet sympathetic look on the way down the street to where he had parked.

The post office had been their next stop. He took two minutes to write Trevor a little note and then mailed him a package containing the two coloring books, crayons and the ABC Jungle book. It also contained two other books he had picked up at Two-By-Two.

He had offered to wait in the car while Sydney went into the station to get her father. She had refused his offer and urged him to accompany her. It seemed their little shopping expedition had put her more at ease. He wasn't sure if it was because she now considered him a marshmallow or if it had been his charming personality.

He pulled open the heavy brick-red-colored door and allowed Sydney to precede him into the station. He hadn't been picturing what the inside of the station would look like. If he had, Mayberry's jail from "The Andy Griffith Show" would have sprung to mind. He wouldn't have been far off.

Coalsburg's police station was the modern equivalent, only on a larger scale. The desks were huge battleships of gunmetal gray and each one was equipped with a computer terminal. A fax machine sat on top of an antique oak file cabinet, competing for the space with an overgrown plant. The floor was checkered in black-and-white tiles worn thin along the heavier-traveled paths. Tucked against the back wall were two cells that were empty. No Otis character was sleeping off his previous night's excesses.

Gathered around one of the scarred desks were three police officers, Thomas and two elderly citizens, all competing to get a word in edgewise during the animated conversation. By the smile stretching Thomas's mouth, he would say this morning's visit was a success.

"Hey, Sydney, your dad says he's been a good patient, hardly giving you any trouble. Is that true?" yelled one of the officers.

"Every word of it." Sydney hurried forward. "I'm back, Dad."

"So I've heard." Thomas glared for a moment in the direction of the officer who had just yelled before turning back to the direction from which her voice had come. "Is Ellis with you?"

"I'm here, Thomas." He stood next to Sydney and nodded to the men in the room. Each one of them was giving him a suspicious look, as if trying to figure out not only who he was but what he was doing here with Sydney. He wasn't going to satisfy their curiosity. His business in Coalsburg was personal as well as private.

"Hey, Pete and Harvey, think back a good thirty years." Thomas was directing his question to the two older men dressed in regular clothes. "Remember Cathy Carlisle? She was the minister's daughter who took off right after she graduated from high school."

"Cute little thing, but shy, right?" answered one of the men.

The other man snapped his fingers. "Now I remember

her. She was a looker, in a quiet sort of way." The man's smile slowly faded. "Her parents were real protective of her, if I recall. I remember my younger brother, Paul, had a crush on her bad in high school, but her parents wouldn't let her go out on a date."

Thomas waved his hand in Ellis's direction. "Well, Harvey, this is Ellis Carlisle, Cathy's son."

"Really, wow!" said the man whose younger brother had had a thing for his mother. "She got married and had a kid? That's good. How is your mother, Ellis?"

"She passed away twelve years ago." Didn't the man pick up on the fact that his mother had never married? After all, his last name was still Carlisle. When the two men spoke about his mother as a girl, they didn't tell him anything he hadn't already known. He knew his mother had been beautiful when she was young. But he didn't know Harvey's younger brother had been denied a date with her. It was a strange feeling to think about his mother as an object of unrequited love. It was strange to even imagine her dating.

"Sorry to hear that, son," Harvey said. Pete echoed his words.

"Yes, well..." He didn't know how to respond to their expressed sympathy. His mother never once mentioned their names, or even Paul's. He just hoped Sydney or Thomas didn't reveal the reason for this visit. "She once told me about living in Coalsburg and she mentioned Thomas's name, so when I found myself in the area with a few days off, I figured I'd drop in on him."

"Mentioned Thomas's name, did she?" Pete chuckled and elbowed Harvey in the side.

"They lived right next door to each other, didn't they, Pete?" Harvey said.

Thomas looked flustered as some of the officers started to chuckle. "Hey, that's the boy's departed mother you're chuckling about. Show some respect," snapped Thomas in a tone of voice that demanded instant obedience.

The knowing smirks died immediately. "Sorry," mumbled a few of the officers as they all seemed to study the tips of their shoes.

He was thankful, yet wasn't surprised by Thomas's support. He was beginning to know the man and with that knowledge grew crushing doubts. The Thomas St. Claire sitting in the police station defending his mother's name wasn't the type of man to get an innocent eighteen-year-old girl pregnant and then force her and their unborn child out of his life. It was a devastating thought. One he couldn't bear to think on.

He glanced at the officers. "No problem." All of the officers were too young to have even known his mother. Not a one of them could have been born when his mother lived in Coalsburg.

"Did you find what you were looking for, Ellis?" asked Thomas, who seemed to know that he didn't want to discuss his mother or the past any longer.

"Not only did he find one, Dad, he found an entire family." Sydney moved over to stand next to her father and lightly placed her hand on his shoulder. "The three of them take up half of his back seat and the baby clings so sweetly to the mother." Sydney's hand squeezed his shoulder gently.

"Three of what?" asked Harvey.

"Orangutans," replied Thomas with a straight face.

"Orangutans?" sputtered Pete.

Ellis willed himself not to laugh and spoil the moment. Thomas and Sydney had set it up perfectly. The police officers looked ready to pull their guns. Pete's eyes grew to twice their normal size and Harvey appeared to be having a hard time saying whatever word was still lodged in his throat. He met Pete's gaze and slowly nodded. "Yes, orangutans. A male, a female and their offspring."

"Holy sh—" The baby-faced officer glanced at Sydney and flushed a dull red. "I mean, holy cow! You got real orangutans in your car?"

"It's a Mercedes," muttered Thomas as if that was the real shocker.

By the expression on the men's faces, Ellis would have to say Thomas had indeed outshocked them. Having three orangutans in a car was one thing, but having them in a Mercedes was totally something else.

"A real Mercedes?" squeaked a young officer.

Ellis had to chuckle at that one. He'd never heard of a fake Mercedes. "Yes it's a real Mercedes."

"No way," said another officer, who was dressed in a light blue shirt instead of a navy one like the other two officers. Ellis guessed he was the chief, though he still looked a little wet behind the ears. "No one in his right mind would put three orangutans in a car, let alone a Mercedes. Plus, there's the other obvious fact."

"What's that, John?" asked Thomas.

Ellis got the feeling he'd just stepped into the middle of a pop quiz, and he had to wonder if that had been Thomas's intention all along.

"The nearest orangutans are probably in the Philadelphia Zoo and there was no way Sydney had time to drive there and back since she dropped you off." John puffed out his chest and grinned like a little boy who had just aced his history exam.

"So where did he get the orangutans?" Thomas's questions weren't done yet.

"He never said they were real orangutans." John squinted his eyes at him. The man reminded him of a twelve-year-old boy trying to imitate Clint Eastwood. Any moment now John was going to pull his gun and growl, *"Go ahead, make my day."* "I'll say they are stuffed orangutans and he bought them from Georgette's store."

He smiled and nodded his head at the chief's deductions. They were right on the money. "Very good." Thomas beamed like a proud father. "Of course, I taught him everything he knows." Thomas reached up and covered Sydney's hand.

The other officers looked slightly embarrassed for believing the story in the first place. The younger of the two said, "We knew they couldn't have been real monkeys."

Pete and Harvey rolled their eyes while the chief shook his head and tried to boost his men's morale. "I know you didn't, but even if you did, it can be expected. We don't get too many monkey cases around these parts. Once in a while we get a dog bite or a cat stuck up in a tree, but never monkeys riding around in a Mercedes."

While everyone chuckled at the young chief's attempt to console his fellow officers, Thomas patted Sydney's hand once more. "Are you ready to take me home now?"

"Sure, Dad." Sydney glanced at the chief and silently mouthed the words *thank you*.

John shook his head and glanced at Thomas as he

stood up. "Now that you're out and about, Tom, are you going to stop in for a visit from time to time? You know you are always welcome."

"I might just do that," Thomas said as he took hold of Sydney's elbow and said his goodbyes to the other men.

"Good." John walked with them to the door. "You used to use me as a sounding board, remember?"

"Two heads are usually better than one." Thomas chuckled at some distant memory.

"I could use that second head around here on plenty of occasions, Tom." John reached out and touched Thomas's arm. "I miss you around here. Don't be a stranger, okay?"

Thomas seemed taken aback by John's offer. "You wouldn't mind some blind old fool sitting in on some cases?"

"You are blind, Tom. I can't argue that," John said. "As for age, I guess that depends on who's looking at you. To a five-year-old, I'm old. As for being a fool? I never once thought you were a fool." John's voice cracked. "The department could still use you here, Tom." John's voice broke completely on his next sentence. "I still need you around here."

Thomas nodded twice before turning and walking out into the sunlight.

Ellis was moved by the touching scene, but not as much as Sydney had been. He watched her face as tears streamed down her cheeks. But she didn't sniffle or make a sound as she escorted her father to the car. Instead, her straight white teeth sank into her lower lip.

He stood silently by as he opened the door and Thomas got into the front seat of the Mercedes. Sydney hastily wiped at her tears as soon as her father was settled. She stood back as he reached for the door to the rear seat. But instead of opening the door, he stood there and waited until she raised her questioning gaze to him.

Soft green eyes brimming with emotion stared up at him. He felt as if someone had placed his heart within a vise. He had no words of comfort for her. The tears she was shedding were partly in joy, not sorrow. Tears would do her good. But the one thing he couldn't stand was to see her anguish as she gnawed her lovely mouth.

Without saying a word, he reached out with the tip of his finger and slowly smoothed the rough indentations on her lower lip. Heat sparked in his fingertips. He watched as her eyes widened and her breath seemed to hitch in the back of her throat. She felt it too. Whatever was happening between them wasn't one-sided.

It was all he needed to know for now. He was a patient man. He knew how to wait for what he wanted. He wanted Sydney, and he wanted her bad.

With a touch as light as a summer breeze, he stroked her moist lip one last time and promised himself that the next time he reached for he mouth, it would be with his own.

Chapter 5

Sydney looked at the pictures of Trevor spread out across the kitchen table and grinned. Ellis carried a complete chronological photo record of his son in his wallet. The pictures started when Trevor was one day old and as bald as a cue ball and ended at an endearing photo of him with Mickey Mouse taken last month at Walt Disney World. She could follow his growth from his first tooth, to his first steps, to his first bike ride without the help of training wheels.

With each new photo she felt the strings attached to her heart yank a little tighter. Trevor was absolutely adorable and to think this big-brown-eyed boy had a potentially fatal disease was unimaginable. But it was true. All she had to see was the anguish in Ellis's eyes to know it was true.

She glanced across the table to Ellis. "He's adorable."

It was eleven o'clock and her father had already retired for the evening. Between the morning appointment at the medical lab and then the visit to the police station, Thomas had done more today than he had in the past six months. Her father had looked tired, but it had been a healthy kind of tired. Despite her concerns about Ellis's presence in their lives she was thankful to him for shaking some life back into her father even though she wholeheartedly disapproved of his method.

Ellis smiled. "Thanks." One of his long fingers tapped the picture taken at Walt Disney World. It was a full color portrait of Trevor, his brown hair falling over his forehead, laughter in his eyes, and a space between his two front teeth. "He has his mother's coloring."

She didn't need a degree in genetics to figure that one out. "He has your chin and nose though." She could see a lot of Ellis in the small boy. Trevor Carlisle will be a heartbreaker when he grows up. *If he grows up.* She could feel the moisture start to build around her eyes. "He doesn't look sick."

Ellis stiffened and started to gather up the pictures. He meticulously made sure they were in chronological order before inserting them back into his wallet. "When he got sick, pulling out a camera was the last thing I thought about." Ellis stood up and slipped the wallet into the back pocket of his jeans before sitting back down. "I don't know of any parent who would want to carry around a picture of their child when they had been sick."

She could tell by his tone of voice that she had just offended Ellis. "I didn't mean I expected to see pictures of Trevor lying in a hospital bed hooked up to machines or anything, Ellis. It's just that...I don't know." She nervously toyed with the silver cross hanging around her neck, a gift from her mother and father.

"I'm out of my league here, Ellis. I know more about begonias than I do kids." She wanted him to know she hadn't meant any disrespect. "When you offered to show me Trevor's picture, I guess I was expecting to see a critically ill child, because that's how I've been thinking of him. I didn't expect to see this laughing little boy on the back of a pony or exploring Walt Disney World."

The stiffness in Ellis's back lessened. "You don't have to apologize, Sydney. I understand." His fingers started to crush the pleated border of the place mat sitting in front of him. "To too many people who knew Trevor, he stopped being a little boy and became an illness. To those who just met him, they learned of his illness first and almost never got to see beyond that."

"But..."

"I know, Sydney. You haven't had a chance to meet Trevor, so I'm not criticizing you. It's only natural that you would think of Trevor as some sickly child, not as a little boy who wants a pony, macaroni and cheese for dinner every night of the week and a bedtime story before he goes to sleep."

There was so much pain behind his words. So much love. So much fear. "You love him very much, don't you?" She already knew the answer to that question, but she wanted Ellis to talk about Trevor some more. He needed to talk about his son, not about his son's illness. She knew Trevor's mother wasn't in the picture any longer. She also knew Ellis's mother had passed away and that he had no brothers or sisters. It made her wonder whom Ellis talked to when his fears became monsters in the night. Her heart was telling her no one. Ellis and Trevor were alone in the world.

Ellis gave her a funny little look as if to say her question didn't deserve an answer. "The night he was born the doctors placed him all scrunched up, blotchy and bawling into my arms and suddenly my world was whole. He stopped crying the moment I held him and stared up at me with these big, really dark blue eyes." Ellis shook his head in wonder as if it had just happened yesterday. "I thought his eyes were going to stay that color, but they didn't. In a few weeks they were brown. A deep rich brown so full of life and promise that at times I swore he knew the answers to all the questions in the universe."

She smiled at the picture he had painted. She could almost see him standing there in hospital-green scrubs with his chest all puffed out with pride and wonder, holding his little son in his big capable arms. "Name one of your favorite things about Trevor. What's the one thing he does so well?"

"His hugs." Ellis's voice cracked with emotion, "No one can hug like Trev."

She pictured little-boy's arms wrapped around Ellis's neck and squeezing as tight as they could. Darn, the tears were forming again. She hadn't expected that answer. She thought Ellis would have said knowing his ABC's, or tying his shoes, or coloring inside the lines. She hadn't been expecting him to say hugs.

Hugs were intimate. No two people hugged the same. Hugs between a father and his son were special. Shared hugs between Ellis and his son were probably more special than most. "You miss him terribly, don't you?"

"More than I would miss my next breath." Ellis

didn't seem embarrassed by his honest yet sentimental answer.

"Did you call him earlier?" When they returned from their trip to town, she had left Ellis with her father and had headed over to the nursery to get some work done. She had managed to put in six hours today and the pile of paperwork she had carried home with her had been only half as big as yesterday's.

"Twice. I told him to expect a package tomorrow morning and that I'll be bringing home a surprise with me."

"You didn't tell him about the family of orangutans that had taken over your back seat?" Had Trevor been her son, she honestly didn't think she could keep them a secret.

"No, it would be too cruel to tell him I bought him the monkeys and then tell him he can't play with them until I get home. This way he knows it's a surprise and half the fun will be anticipating and guessing what I'm bringing home." Ellis relaxed and slouched back into the chair. "He probably drove Rita crazy all evening guessing what it might be."

"Rita?" Maybe Ellis and Trevor weren't as alone as she thought.

"My housekeeper and Trevor's surrogate mother. I hired her when Ginny and Trevor came home from the hospital. Ginny wasn't feeling up to handling a newborn so I employed Rita until such time that she was. Ginny left and Rita stayed on to take care of Trevor and the house."

She remembered him mentioning a Mrs. McCall before.

"Rita keeps my home life running smoothly," he

went on, "so I can concentrate on the business end of my life."

"You mentioned that you were in transportation." Ellis hadn't mentioned too much about what he did for a living. "Something to do with trucking, right?"

"I put myself through college by driving an eighteen-wheeler all summer and during the holidays. When I graduated, I bought my own rig."

"You're a truck driver?" She had never met a truck driver who drove a Mercedes, wore expensive Italian shoes or carried around his own top-of-the-line laptop computer.

"Was a truck driver. I don't drive any longer. Within five years of buying my first rig, I purchased a small fleet of trucks, hired on my own drivers and started my own trucking company, O.I.B.L."

"One If By Land?" My Lord, Ellis owned O.I.B.L.! A person would have to live under a rock sixty miles away from any interstate not to have heard or seen any of the distinctive-looking trucks with a portrait on the side of Paul Revere holding a lantern. "I see your trucks all the time. Heck, we even have some deliveries made by them at the nursery."

"Thank you."

Ellis Carlisle was rich! He was beyond rich, he was stinking filthy rich. Now the laptop and the luxury Mercedes made a lot more sense. Ellis could buy the town of Coalsburg seven times over without feeling the pinch and yet, with all his money, he might not be able to save his own son. It would have been ironic if it wasn't so sad. "I'm sure you can answer the question that always pops into my mind whenever I see one of your trucks."

"What's that?"

"Is there a Two If By Sea?"

"T.I.B.S. was deep in the developmental stage when Trevor was diagnosed with leukemia. I put everything on hold and concentrated all my energy on my son's health." Ellis stood up, walked over to the sink and stared out into the night. "Getting my son well is more important to me than some new business venture."

The tension in his shoulders told her there was a lot more to the story than he was telling. How does one just "put on hold" something as global as a shipping fleet? "I think you made the right decision." She had to wonder if anyone ever told him that. Ellis was a businessman, and a damn good one, going by the achievements he had made over the past ten years. Everyone in business probably told him he was crazy to possibly lose such a venture.

Ellis chuckled softly and turned around to look at her. "I *know* I did."

She liked his warm rough laugh. It made her feel all soft and light inside. It made her believe that everything would work out and Trevor would find his match. It made her want to believe in happily-ever-afters. Something she hadn't believed in for a very long time, if ever. "What happens if there's a match?"

"If Thomas is a match and he is willing to be the donor, he would have to stay overnight in the hospital. His bone marrow would be taken from his hip and he'd be sore or tender there for a couple of days. That's it." Ellis paced in front of the sink. "I would handle all his medical expenses and make sure he's as comfortable as possible."

"I know my father's role would be minimal. I was

more concerned about Trevor and what he'd be going through."

"Trevor will have to be admitted into the hospital two weeks before the transplant. He would be given large doses of chemotherapy, maybe some total body radiation, to destroy his own bone marrow and blood cells as well as the cancer cells. Once he was 'conditioned,' he would be given your father's purified marrow intravenously. That part will take about two hours, but it will take two to three weeks before his marrow finds its way to the proper place in the interior of Trevor's major bones and starts producing new and normal blood cells. If everything is fine, Trevor can go home about seven weeks after the transplant. He'll be closely followed. Six months after the transplant he will be able to start school, but it usually takes up to a year for total convalescence."

Sydney felt her heart lurch with each word he spoke. "He'll be in the hospital for over two months?"

"Two months is a small price to pay for living, Sydney."

She knew that, but still, Trevor was only five years old. "What happens if there isn't a match?" She needed to know it all.

"If your father doesn't match and a match can't be found before Trevor comes out of remission, then there is no hope."

She had thought the description of the actual transplant was terrifying. It was nothing compared to the words *there is no hope*. She stood up and walked over to Ellis and placed her hand on his forearm. "I'm praying for Trevor and for you that my father will be a match. Even if it means he won't be my father any longer, he would be yours."

"That's where you are wrong. Thomas St. Claire will always be your father, not mine." Ellis reached out and gently cupped her cheek. She felt the heat of his palm against her cool skin. "One thing I have learned over the past five years of being a dad is that it takes more than genetics to be a father, it takes love. Thomas St. Claire loves you, Sydney, that's plain enough even for this stranger to see."

"But if you're his son..." The tip of his finger pressed against her moving lips and stopped her next words from coming.

"I will never be his son." The pad of his index finger slowly and sensually stroked her lower lip, just as he had done this morning while standing next to his car on Main Street. "I don't want your father, Sydney. I don't want a father at all. All I want is a donor and a chance for my son."

She felt the heat coil low in her stomach and wind its way to the core of her being. She wanted Ellis. It was that plain and that simple. That basic. Need, unlike anything she had ever experienced, surged its way upward. "Then we both want the same thing." She was talking about a lot more than just Trevor. Ellis's lightest touch made her want. Made her need.

Ellis's finger stopped its torturous journey across her mouth and a spark of heat blazed in his gaze. His gray eyes turned molten with need and his breathing grew uneven. His voice contained jagged edges of desire that sliced their way down her spine. "Do we, Sydney? Do we both want the same thing?"

She knew they were no longer discussing Trevor. They were talking about this heat that had flared up unsuspectingly between them. Heat that shouldn't have been there. Her gaze lowered to his mouth. Oh yes, they both wanted the same thing. She had had two lovers in her life. Neither had ever inspired this instantaneous...lust.

Was that what she was feeling, lust? Or was there something more? How could there be more?

She slowly reached out and placed her hand upon his chest. The rapid beating of his heart came through the soft cotton of his shirt and vibrated against her palm. She could feel his warmth seep into her fingers and spread up her arm. Her gaze lowered to where her fingers pressed against his chest before shooting back up to his face. Ellis was going to kiss her, she could see it in his eyes. She wanted that kiss. "Yes, I do believe we want the same thing."

With a rough growl, Ellis pulled her into his arms and covered her mouth with his own.

Sydney welcomed his kiss but was unprepared for the overwhelming desire that assaulted her body. Firm lips seduced her mouth into deepening the kiss and she went willingly. She wrapped her arms around his neck and pressed herself closer. Her tongue met and danced with his as her world tilted to the left and then slowly righted itself to a more perfect position than it had ever been before.

Ellis tasted like coffee, cherry pie and need. Or maybe she was tasting herself. She had had the same late-night snack, and she was definitely feeling the need.

His hair was soft beneath her searching fingers and his mouth hard and demanding where it meshed with hers. Ellis kissed like a man who was used to getting what he wanted. By the way he was kissing the breath right out of her, she would have to say Ellis wanted her. Probably as much as she wanted him.

The edge of the counter dug into the small of her back, forcing her to arch her hips forward. The low groan that rumbled up his chest told her she was pressing against a very sensitive part of his anatomy. A part of his body that was reacting to the kiss. The hard column of his arousal bulged behind his zipper.

Where he was turning hard and wanting, she was turning soft and accepting. Opposites that were meant to be joined since the beginning of time.

With a ragged groan Ellis cupped her hips and put a few needed inches between them. He broke the kiss and stared down into her face. His eyes churned with so many emotions she couldn't name them all. There were glimpses of surprise and hunger beneath the burning need. She wanted to answer that need. She was ready to answer that need.

Ellis took in an uneven breath and lightly touched her mouth with the tip of his finger. "We either stop now, Sydney, or we won't be stopping until we're both naked, satisfied and totally exhausted."

She almost smiled. Did he think he was scaring her off? Naked, satisfied and totally exhausted sounded like paradise to her. Last year, last month or even last week she would have been totally appalled had someone told her she would be contemplating going to bed with a man she had met three days before. It sounded silly to say she wasn't *that* kind of girl, when she was just discovering everyone was *that* kind of girl when the right man came along. Her instincts were telling her Ellis was the right man.

She did smile then. Right against his finger. "Sounds like a plan to me."

Ellis groaned louder and put a few more inches between their bodies and lowered his hand. "I think we both might be a little bit vulnerable right now, Sydney."

Vulnerable! "What in the world are you talking about?" She wasn't vulnerable. The last time she had been vulnerable was when she was ten years old and stuck in a foster home with a foster father who had made her extremely nervous. She was never going to be vulnerable again.

Ellis took another step backward. "To be honest with you, I haven't been with a woman in a very long time." His gaze skimmed the front of her blouse before jerking to a spot somewhere over her left shoulder. "Between Trevor and my business, I really haven't had time for a relationship."

She slowly nodded as if she was understanding what he was saying. She didn't. "Are you trying to tell me you aren't involved with anyone at this time?"

"No, that's not what I'm trying to say, but for the record I'm not."

She was glad to hear that. She didn't know what she would do if Ellis had a lover tucked safely back in Jenkintown. "So what exactly are you trying to say?"

"I consider myself a pretty good judge of character."

"If that were so, you would know my father was telling you the truth about him and your mother." She refused to feel guilty for some of her own doubts. They weren't talking about her, they were talking about Ellis.

Ellis shrugged that comment off. "What I meant was, I don't think you are the type of woman who jumps into bed with every man who might be interested. If that was true, your feet would never touch the floor."

"Was that suppose to be a compliment?" Lord, she hoped not, for if it was, then Ellis needed more than a quick Emily Post refresher course.

"Yes," snapped Ellis, sounding frustrated. In a move so totally uncharacteristic of the confident and calm man she had come to know, he thrust his fingers through his hair. An unruly cowlick sprang up. "What I'm trying to say in a very backward and awkward way is that I can't stay, Sydney. In a few days, as soon as the results are in, I'll be gone. I'll have to go. Trevor needs me at home."

Now she knew why Ellis had called a halt to their kisses. He was afraid of hurting her when he went back home to his son and his business. Not only was his gesture incredibly sweet, he was right. She would have been hurt. Ellis Carlisle had been touching more than her body, he had touched her heart. She didn't know if she had it in her to make love to a man and then sit quietly by as he walked out the door and got on with his life. She didn't think she did.

"I see your reasoning." She saw more than that, but she didn't comment on any of the heartbreak that might have been in her future. Instead, she stepped to the side and tucked in her gold blouse where it had been pulled free of the waistband in her jeans by Ellis's stroking hands. There wasn't going to be any heartbreak because there wasn't going to be anything to cause it. She stared at the toe of his shoe. "The kiss was a mistake, Ellis, it won't happen again." Self-control was such a terrible virtue at times.

"Kissing you wasn't a mistake, Sydney." Ellis

reached out and touched a curl teasing her shoulder. "Making love with you and then leaving you would be a mistake. You deserve a man who would stick around for more than a few days."

"How do you know what I deserve?" She took another step away from him. Ellis didn't know her at all. If he did, he would have never kissed her. Deep down inside her soul where the dark things lived, she was praying with all her might that Thomas wasn't his father. Her prayers had nothing to do with Trevor and his chance for a bone marrow transplant. She hoped Ellis would find his biological parent and be able to save his son's life—as long as that parent wasn't Thomas.

Her prayers had more to do with her own fears. All her life she had never been good enough. Her biological parents hadn't been killed in some freak accident or died from some mysterious disease as she had been led to believe. They gave her away to the state. They signed a piece of paper and away she went. It was the horrible truth and she had faced it many years ago. Ever since she'd learned her adoption history, she'd been left with the belief that she had to have done something terribly wrong for her parents just to sign her away like that. She hadn't been good enough. The string of foster homes she had managed to work herself through only reinforced that knowledge. When Thomas and Julia took her in and legally adopted her, she had been the happiest little girl except for the doubt that was still planted deep inside her. She always expected that one day her new family would discover she wasn't good enough to be their daughter and send her on her way.

It had been decided a long time ago that she didn't deserve anything special in life.

"I can only guess that you deserve something more than I could give you, Syd. I would rather be wrong than to see you get hurt."

She could see a lot more written in his eyes than the fact that he would be heading home in a couple of days. She knew he was thinking about the future and praying for a miracle. Ellis was worried how she would react if they did become lovers and then it was proven he really was Thomas's son. He had the right to be worried about that, because she didn't know how she would react. Thomas had never lied to her before.

"It's okay, Ellis. I understand." She moved to the doorway. Her escape to the stairs and the privacy of her bedroom was only a couple of yards away. She needed to get away so she could work out the conflict of emotions assaulting her mind. "Turn off the lights when you are done in here. I've already locked the doors."

She made it out the doorway, but not to the stairs before his voice stopped her. "Sydney?"

"What?"

Ellis stepped out of the kitchen and joined her in the living room. "I said it would be a mistake if we became lovers." He gave her a small smile that strained the corner of his mouth. "I didn't say anything about not kissing you again."

She felt a traitorous flush of pleasure stealing up her cheeks and hurried toward the stairs. The cad still wanted her kisses, even though they weren't going to be making love. It was outrageous. It was scandalous. So why was a rush of excitement sweeping through her body and making her feel lighthearted? She felt his intense gaze on her as she climbed each step. She couldn't resist stopping at the top of the stairs and softly calling down, "We'll see about that, Ellis. We'll just see." Without waiting for his response, she turned and walked to her bedroom.

Ellis glanced around the main building of the Ever Green Nursery in wonder. Sydney owned all of this! The place was amazing. It was truly magnificent. It was so colorful that it nearly hurt his eyes. The main building consisted of the cash registers, rows of colorful flowerpots, clay pots and windowsill planters. There were miniature mountains of potting soil, wreaths, birdhouses, hoses and so many brilliant silk flowers that a person would need half a day to inspect them all. Two huge greenhouses filled with row after row of tables overflowing with trays of flowers joined the main building on the east and the west.

The south side of the building opened into another greenhouse. This one was decorated with working fountains, garden statues, palms, plants and outdoor furniture. It made a person want to relax and just soak up the atmosphere. It made him think about adding a sunroom to his own house. Of course it would be on a much smaller scale and he would have to be very insistent with Trevor not to leave his animals all around the room. It could be done, but he would want a fountain of some sort in it. One that could hold some goldfish. Trevor would love the fish.

"May I help you, sir?" asked a young saleswoman.

He glanced at the name tag pinned to the woman's dark green smock with the Ever Green Nursery logo embroidered above it. A yellow silk daffodil and a pink curly ribbon was pinned behind her name. "Hello, Cindy. I'm looking for Sydney St. Claire."

"She's busy right now. Maybe I could help you?"

Cindy, an average-looking blonde with a sunny smile and sparkling blue eyes, appeared quite enthused about helping him. Helping him what, he didn't know. In fact, he didn't want to know. "I'm Ellis Carlisle. I'm staying a few days with Sydney and her father."

"So you're Ellis." Cindy's gaze skimmed him from the top of his head to the tips of his shoes. Her gaze measured, sorted and categorized him in a matter of seconds. "You're not what I expected."

"What were you expecting?" He liked Cindy's honesty and he was especially thrilled that Sydney had apparently mentioned him to one of her employees. He just prayed Sydney hadn't said something too horrible about him.

"I don't know. Someone who's a cross between a movie star and a millionaire. I was picturing a cross between Tom Cruise and John F. Kennedy Jr."

He felt as if someone had just slammed him in the gut. "Excuse me, but why would you think that?"

"Syd said you drove a brand-new top-of-the-line Mercedes and that you were gorgeous." Cindy grinned. "I just put the two of them together."

Sydney thought he was gorgeous! He was stunned. Pleasantly stunned, but stunned nevertheless. "So which part didn't meet up to your standards, me being rich or me being gorgeous?"

"It was the rich part that threw me. You don't look rich."

Ellis glanced down at the loafers, jeans and old Villanova sweatshirt he had on and grinned. No, he didn't fit into any millionaire category that he knew of. He didn't care because he wasn't just some millionaire. Sydney thought he was gorgeous. "Are you going to allow me to see her?"

"Sure. She's out in greenhouse number five." Cindy pointed out a set of doors and down a gravel path to a row of greenhouses. "There's a five above the door, you can't miss it."

"Thanks." Ellis headed out the doors and down the path.

Stones crunched beneath his feet. He spotted Sydney through the glass before he saw the red enamel five hanging above the door. She appeared to be alone so he opened the door and stepped inside the greenhouse. He now understood why she had taken off the sweater she had been wearing this morning. It was warm in the greenhouse, extremely warm.

Sydney glanced up from the mound of potting soil and cuttings she was planting. "Ellis! Is something wrong with my father?"

"No, your father is just fine." He stepped farther into the greenhouse. "Stop worrying, Sydney. Thomas can take care of himself."

"He's blind." Sydney brushed her filthy hands down the front of her thighs.

"I know he's blind. You know he's blind. He knows he's blind." Ellis smiled at the picture she created all sweaty-looking and streaked with dirt. "Your father has lost his ability to see, not his ability to think."

"You left him alone at home?"

"Yes, I did." He liked the fire that sparked in her eyes. He especially liked it when it had been caused by his kisses. Those hot kisses they had shared had driven him near-insane all through the night. "He said he'd be fine and I believed him. I asked if he wanted to take a walk over to the nursery and he said no but suggested that I go ahead without him. I couldn't think of a reason why I shouldn't, without making him seem incapable of fending for himself for a while. So here I am. Do you have a few spare minutes to give me a quick tour?"

"You want to see the nursery?"

"No."

"No? If you didn't want to see the nursery, why did you bother coming?"

He took another step and was close enough to touch her. "I wanted to see you, Sydney."

"Me?"

"Now that I've seen you, I want something else." Uncertainty was clouding her soft green eyes, drowning out the fire that had been there moments before. He wanted that fire back. He took another step closer and smiled as she backed up against the wooden table behind her.

"What?"

His hand reached out and instead of touching her mouth as he wanted to do, he followed a streak of dirt across her cheek and down her jaw. "A kiss, Sydney. Nothing more than a kiss."

"You don't kiss like a man who wants nothing more than a kiss."

"It takes two to kiss. What does that say about you, Sydney?" He moved in nearer. There was barely an inch between their bodies. He could hear the unevenness of her breath, and see the soft parting of her mouth. Readying itself for his kiss.

"I don't want to know." Sydney's mouth instinctively reached for his.

He saw the fire spark anew in the depths of her eyes and welcomed her, dirt and all, into his arms.

Chapter 6

Two days later Sydney stood in the kitchen preparing dinner, feeling as if she was walking on eggshells. Her world felt very fragile with the two men in her life pulling her in opposite directions.

Her father was living in his own dark, little world, unaware of the conflicts surrounding him. He was unsuspecting of the fact that she had her doubts about his claim of not being Ellis's natural father. The one nagging question remained: why would Catherine name Thomas if he *hadn't* fathered her child?

Ellis tormented her with a whole other arsenal of emotions. Since the morning he had shown up at the nursery wanting a quick tour, she had been besieged with stolen kisses and her senses were now at a frustration level guaranteed to drive every sane thought she had ever possessed straight out of her mind. Ellis had been true to his word. Never once had he tried to take their kisses to the next step. He had otherwise been the perfect gentleman, and she hated it.

She finished peeling and quartering the last potato and tossed it into the pot. The meat loaf she had thrown together after she had gotten home from work was already in the oven cooking. Dinner would be later than normal, but at least she was handling it today. The past two nights Ellis had cooked. He was a wonderful cook, and she really appreciated coming home to find dinner on the table, but she was beginning to feel useless. Ellis had stepped into their home and before she knew it, he had taken over.

It was the same thing with her father. In the five days Ellis had been living here, he had done more good with her father than she had the previous six months. It was maddening. There was no obvious explanation for it. She should have been the one to turn her father around, not some stranger. But she couldn't begrudge Ellis for it. Her father *was* doing better.

She walked over to the freezer and started rummaging through the contents looking for a bag of corn. Her father liked corn. As for Ellis, she really didn't care if he liked corn or not. The man had no right to kiss her the way he did and not follow through with anything! She was so constantly frustrated and aroused that if Ellis talked dirty to her she would probably shatter at his feet.

"Are you sure I can't help with something." Ellis's voice came from directly behind her and caused her to lose her grip on the bag of corn she had just pulled out.

She caught the bag, backed away from the freezer and closed the door. There was something he could help with, but preparing dinner wasn't it. "No thank you, Ellis. I've got dinner under control." It was about the only thing she had under control and she wasn't going to let him take it from her.

"How about if I help set the table?" Ellis tried to back her against the refrigerator, but she managed to slip past him.

She saw another frustrating kiss coming and wanted no part of it. "I thought you were discussing the upcoming baseball season with my father?" That had been a close one. One more step and he would have had her blocked and she knew firsthand what Ellis did whenever he had her cornered. He tortured her with his mouth and promises of ecstasy that never came.

"I was, but I heard you puttering around in here and thought to offer my assistance." He moved up behind her as she stood by the sink. "You're acting awfully edgy tonight, Syd. Is anything wrong?" His hands gripped the counter on either side of her, but thankfully he didn't touch her.

Short of climbing up onto the countertop, she was indeed trapped. She shuddered as one of his fingers reached out and stroked its way down her cheek, over her jawline and down the arch of her neck. It was an intimate gesture; one designed to drive her over the edge. At this point, it wouldn't take much.

"I don't want you kissing me anymore."

Ellis dropped his hand immediately and backed up a step. All the teasing that had been in his eyes slowly faded. "Can I ask why?"

"Your kisses make me want too much." Her gaze dropped to the floor between them.

Ellis stopped his retreat. "Want what?"

"You." She raised her eyes and studied his strong jaw, the endearing bump on the bridge of his nose and the confusion shadowed in his eyes. "The kisses aren't enough any longer and we both know there can't be anything more."

"Do we, Syd? Tell me again why there can't be anything more. I know I was the one to set the boundaries, but somehow I can't remember why." He reached out a finger and stroked her lower lip.

She felt his finger tremble against her mouth and closed her eyes. He knew exactly where to touch to make her want. There were reasons, good reasons, why they shouldn't become lovers. She just couldn't remember a single one of them when he was touching her.

The sound of her father's cane tapping against the entryway into the kitchen caused her to jerk away from Ellis.

"Is dinner almost ready?" Thomas asked as he made his way into the room.

She knew a blush was sweeping up her cheeks, but she couldn't prevent it. Thomas was her father, and even though she and Ellis hadn't been doing anything wrong, it still made her feel awkward to have her father walk into the room when she and Ellis had been so close. It didn't matter one iota that her father was blind and wouldn't have known if they had been dancing naked on the counters. *She* had known.

Sydney couldn't bring herself to look at Ellis as she took another step away from him. "Dinner won't be for another half hour, Dad. Why don't you and Ellis go sit on the patio and enjoy the evening air. It's not too chilly out tonight. A light jacket should be enough."

She noticed her father was starting to use the cane the hospital had given him. He was getting around the house much better and he was even using it on the short walks he and Ellis were taking lately. The nursery's fields provided her father with exercise, sunshine and fresh country air. Yesterday she had had one of her employees travel every path throughout the property making sure there weren't any ankle-breaking holes that her father might trip in. Thomas's independence was returning by leaps and bounds. She guessed it was one more thing she had to thank Ellis for.

"That sounds like a good idea." Thomas tilted his head, but continued to face where she was standing. "What do you say, Ellis? Are you up for some fresh air?"

She felt the flush staining her cheeks turn bright brilliant red. Her father had known all along where Ellis was, and exactly how close they had been. She reached for a pot and busied herself by dumping in the frozen corn as Ellis and her father put on their jackets and left the kitchen through the back door.

An hour later dinner was done and the cleanup was nearly completed. Having Ellis share their meal had brought a range of topics to the conversation that had been missing for quite a while. Six months to be precise. At least Ellis's presence guaranteed some form of conversation. Her father had even begun to ask her about her day, the nursery and some of the employees he knew. Thomas hadn't talked about the nursery since his wife died. It was a painful subject for him because her mother's whole life had revolved around her family and her business. Julia had loved the nursery.

Thomas also was an endless well of stories about the town and people who knew Ellis's mother. He told countless tales about Catherine but said very little about her parents. Sydney suspected that Catherine's parents might not have been very loving and that her father was trying to spare Ellis any unnecessary pain. As for Ellis, he appeared to soak up every word her father uttered about the young, beautiful and shy Catherine Carlisle.

"Are you sure you won't mind, Ellis?" Thomas was relaxing and digesting his dinner over his second cup of coffee. "I told the guys that I could only stay for an hour or two."

"Stay as long as you like, Thomas." Ellis, who had already finished his second cup of coffee, winked at her. "I can run you into town and then come back here and get some work done."

Sydney dried the last pot and put it away. Ellis had been winking at her all through dinner. Each and every time he did, she blushed. It was a stupid schoolgirl reaction, one she vowed not to happen again. The vow was shattered the next time he winked. "I can drop you off, Dad." It annoyed her how her father asked Ellis instead of her to drive him into town so he could spend some time at the station with his friends. It was nice of Ellis to instantly agree, but it still bothered her.

"You have the nursery to run, Syd. I've kept you away from it long enough." Thomas pushed his cup into the center of the table. "Ellis doesn't mind, do you?"

"Not at all." Ellis turned to her and smiled.

Her comment was cut off by the ringing of the phone. With a glare toward Ellis she walked over to the wall phone and picked it up. "St. Claire residence."

A male voice that was deep and pleasant came over the line. "May I speak to Ellis Carlisle, please."

"Whom shall I say is calling?" Ellis had had only two phone calls while she had been home. Both were from his housekeeper, Rita McCall, and both times Trevor had wanted to speak to his dad. She glanced over at Ellis, who returned her look with one of curiosity.

"This is Frank Nesbitt from Alpha Laboratories."

Suddenly, she felt as if the rug were being pulled from under her feet and she rested her gaze on Ellis. Alpha Laboratories was the lab Ellis was using to see if there was a match for Trevor's bone marrow transplant—the lab that would determine if Thomas was Ellis's biological father. The results were in. "One moment, please."

Something in her look must have tipped Ellis off because he was on his feet before she even spoke. She held the phone toward him as he walked across the room. "It's Alpha Laboratories."

Ellis took the phone, turned his back and said, "This is Ellis Carlisle." The strain in his usually beautiful voice echoed throughout the room.

Sydney had noticed how his hands trembled when he reached for the phone but she didn't blame him for turning his back. Ellis needed some measure of privacy. She was surprised that he hadn't taken the call in the other room. If it had been her child's life riding on the results, she would have.

"Yes, I see." Ellis's voice turned bland now as he spoke to the lab technician.

This was it. This was what they had been waiting for. She walked over to her father and gently placed her hand upon his shoulder. Thomas's hand was strong and warm as it reached up and covered hers. She stared at Ellis's back and tried to read his body language. She couldn't. His shoulders didn't slump, nor was he punching the air in a show of success.

"Yes, of course." There was a long pause before Ellis

concluded the call with, "Yes, thank you very much for staying late to give me the results." Another pause, and then a simple, "I will."

She watched as Ellis lowered the phone. As she studied his back, which he kept carefully turned toward them, she realized the results hadn't been what Ellis had been hoping for. She gave her father's shoulder a light squeeze and waited for Ellis to tell them what the lab technician had said.

Ellis stood there for a good two minutes with the phone dangling from his hand before he spoke. "There was no match." Ellis stared at the cabinet door in front of him. "You were right, Thomas. You aren't my father. My mother lied on the birth certificate."

Sydney felt the tears run down her face. Trevor's miracle wasn't going to happen.

Thomas fumbled across the table, located the napkins and handed her one. "I'm sorry, Ellis. What can we do to help you and your son?"

She wiped at her tears and swallowed the lump that had formed in her throat. "Yes, Ellis, what can we do? What's your next step?"

Ellis's head slowly went back and forth and his shoulders finally slumped beneath the disappointment. "There is no next step. This was it. This was my last hope."

She refused to believe it. Ellis couldn't give up now. "There has to be something else we can do."

Ellis did turn around then. His pain and anguish was clearly etched across his face. "Thomas's part is done. As for you, Sydney, I gave them permission to add your name and blood to the national donor list. Who knows, maybe you'll match someone else." Ellis slowly replaced the phone. "As for me, I'm heading home. It will take me twenty minutes to pack and then I'll be out of here."

She didn't like the way he looked. His voice was raw, yet his eyes were perfectly dry. Ellis had the look of a man who had been defeated. Her heart was breaking. "I..."

"Let me finish, Syd. I want to thank both of you for your amazing hospitality and generosity under the circumstances."

"Ellis, I don't think it's a good idea for you to be traveling right now." Thomas pushed his chair back and stood up. "I might be blind, but I can still see certain things. You're in no condition to drive after receiving that news. There's no use rushing home to your son, he will be asleep before you even get there. Why don't you wait until morning before heading home?"

"You've been kind enough, Thomas. I really don't want to impose any longer."

"We never thought you were imposing, Ellis. You are the son of a dear childhood friend." Thomas picked up his cane and maneuvered himself around a chair and toward the entryway. "In my line of work I've seen what upset people do behind the wheel, Ellis. It's not a pretty sight. Ask yourself who would take care of Trevor should you wrap yourself around a telephone pole because you were too distressed to handle a car properly." Thomas stopped in the entryway. "I'll see you both at breakfast."

With a heavy heart, Sydney watched her father leave. The man who had caused the accident the night her mother died had been upset because his wife had just left him for another man. He also had been legally drunk.

It had been an deadly combination. One her father knew all too well.

She glanced over at the man who had slipped into her heart without her permission. The thought of him wrapping his car around a pole as her father had said made her tremble inside. "Will you please stay? If you leave early enough, you can still have breakfast with Trevor."

"I'll stay, Sydney, stop worrying." Ellis reached for his jacket that was hanging by the back door. "I need some fresh air."

Sydney watched him go. He wasn't going to drive while he was so upset, which was what she and her father had wanted. He was hurting, yet he hadn't asked her to comfort him. She shouldn't allow Ellis's need to be alone hurt her, but it did. She and Ellis weren't lovers. She liked to think they could have been friends if the circumstances had been different. They were just two people who were attracted to each other and who had shared a few feverish kisses. There was no reason why Ellis would need her shoulder to lean on. No reason at all.

How could she offer Ellis comfort when in the dark places in her heart she had been praying that Thomas wasn't really his father? Her tears were for Trevor and his lost miracle. The pain in her heart was for a man she'd come to care for. The man she longed to help.

Outside, Ellis studied the stars as he walked the paths through the fields behind Thomas's house. He and Thomas had walked these same paths many times in the past several days. Now he walked them and railed against the heavens, the Fates and the injustice of it all. Thomas was right. He was in no shape to get behind the wheel and speed home to his son. His arrival home wasn't going to change a thing. There was no miracle for Trevor.

Past experience told him the tears would come after the anger. He had to work through the anger, but he didn't know if he could this time. Tears left him weak, while anger gave him strength. He had always used that strength to fight another day, but this time it was different. He knew what he was fighting for, he just didn't know who to fight any longer. He was out of enemies, out of options and out of hope.

He shouldn't have left Sydney like that. She had been upset and crying, but he couldn't stay. He needed her too much. For the first time since his son's illness was diagnosed, he wanted someone to comfort him. Someone to lean on and rail against the Fates with him. He wanted that person to be Sydney.

He couldn't ask it of her. He was leaving in the morning. Trevor was his first responsibility. There was no room in his life for a woman like Sydney. It wouldn't be fair to her, or any other woman, to take on what he would be facing in the future. Her look of distress when he had finally turned around to face her and Thomas told him how much she already cared. Sydney's heart was already involved, but he had no love to spare. Trevor needed all his attention, all his love.

Ellis walked for another hour over the same paths. He used the light of the full moon to guide him, and his anger to speed him on. Slowly but surely the anger abated and he made his way to the patio outside the kitchen door. The lights inside the house were burning. He knew Sydney was still up, probably waiting for him.

He couldn't face her now. He would be too tempted

to find comfort in her arms and in her bed. He had to make it through one more night in the same house with her before he could leave with a clear conscience.

Ellis lowered himself to the small bench beneath the light. Sydney had used the same bench to take off her work boots the first night he was here. He leaned his head against the clapboard siding of the house and closed his eyes. He needed a plan. Any plan to help Trevor. He needed to do something. He needed to keep busy.

His usually active and creative mind drew a blank. A dark scary blank. He didn't know which way to turn. Every avenue had a Dead End sign posted on it. He tried one path after another and got the same results. Nothing but darkness.

He felt tears slip down his face but kept trying another path, any path. His son needed him. Trevor was counting on him to pull a miracle out of some imaginary hat. The tears came faster as another Dead End sign loomed in front of him. He had promised his son everything would be all right and he had never once broken a promise to him.

He heard the back door open, but didn't open his eyes. He knew it was Sydney. He could feel her warmth and smell the soft floral fragrance of her perfume. The bench gave a small creak as she silently sat down beside him. He prayed that she wouldn't say anything. He was teetering on the edge. The tears rolling down his face were just the beginning. The dam surrounding his heart was beginning to crack.

Sydney didn't make a sound or move for five minutes. He was meticulously shoring up the dam only to have the whole thing crumble with the simplest of gestures—

when she reached out and took his one hand in hers. The tremble in her fingers pushed him over the edge.

With a rough groan he pulled Sydney into his arms, buried his face in her hair and sobbed his heart out.

Sydney paced the kitchen like some expectant father in a maternity ward. She had heard Ellis moving around in his room earlier, and by the sounds she knew he had been packing. Any minute now he was going to be coming down to say goodbye. She had one chance left to offer Ellis and Trevor hope. Even if it was only a small sliver of hope.

When she had come down earlier to put on some coffee, she had found her father sitting at the table in the predawn darkness. He looked as if he had spent a sleepless night too. She had kissed her father's cheek and told him she had a plan. Thomas had wanted to know what it was, but she'd told him he would have to wait until Ellis came down.

Last night when Ellis broke down in her arms, she knew she had to think of something. Ellis had been crying for his son and the miracle that hadn't happened. Her tears had been for the little boy she'd never met and Ellis. She had held Ellis for a good forty minutes before they came into the house and went to their separate bedrooms. There had been no heated kisses to torment her night.

She had spent the night curled in a chair in front of the window, staring out into the night and thinking. The plan came to her around four in the morning. It wasn't a foolproof plan, but it was something. She could offer the man she had come to care for at least one thing. She could offer him hope.

The sound of Ellis coming down the stairs stopped her pacing. When he stepped into the kitchen, she could tell he hadn't slept, either.

She tried to smile at Ellis. "I just made some coffee, would you care for some?"

"No thank you, Sydney. I want to get an early start. I'll pick up a cup when I stop for gas."

So much for pleasantries. She wasn't going to get Ellis to sit down. "I've been thinking a lot about your situation and I think I know a solution. At least it might be an answer if my father agrees to help out."

"Of course I'll help," Thomas said. "Just tell me what to do."

Ellis looked unconvinced. "I know you both want to help, but there isn't anything you can do unless you talk to everyone you know and get them to give a blood sample and to become registered on the National Marrow Donor Program. If more people volunteer to become donors, there's a better chance that a match will be found."

"We'll do that gladly, but that wasn't what I was thinking." Sydney took the last sip of her coffee and placed the empty cup on the counter. "The one question that has been bugging me is why your mother named Thomas St. Claire as the father of her baby. I think I now know why she did that."

"Why?" Ellis's curiosity was at least piqued.

"For some reason she didn't want to name your real father...possibly she was afraid, I just don't know. Catherine knew she would be raising you alone and that if something should happen to her, the state would check the birth certificate and notify your father. Your mother and my father had been neighbors and good friends. She trusted Thomas, so she used his name as a safeguard. She knew my father, who always loved children, would take you in and raise you as his own." She stopped next to her father's chair and placed her hand on his shoulder. "And she was right to think so. If he took me into his home, a complete stranger, he would have taken Catherine Carlisle's son."

"My mother had no idea that Thomas would have taken me in or not," Ellis countered. "Thomas was only twenty-one years old when she listed him as my father."

"Catherine knew I would have taken you in and raised you as my own, Ellis." Thomas slowly nodded his head as if he was finally understanding something.

"How?"

"I told her."

"What?" Ellis appeared just as startled as she was by that confession. "What do you mean you told her? You knew she was pregnant?"

"No, I didn't know she was pregnant at the time. Looking back, I guess I should have known." Thomas wearily rubbed his unshaven jaw. "One of the last conversations we had was about children and the future. She asked me if I ever wanted any children and I told her I wanted a houseful. I remember telling her I wanted Thanksgiving dinner to be so crowded that it would take a twenty-five-pound turkey and a kids' table set up in the living room to handle it all." Thomas seemed saddened by the memory. "She asked me what I would do if my wife and I couldn't have any children of our own. I told her we'd adopt. I said there were plenty of children who needed a good loving home who wouldn't mind being crowded when eating Thanksgiving dinner."

She was right. Catherine had used Thomas as a safeguard against the uncertain future. Her father had thought about adoption long before she had shown up on the scene. She had to wonder why he hadn't adopted any kids before she had come along or even after she had arrived on the scene. She'd think about that one later. For now, she had to convince Ellis to give her idea a try.

Ellis appeared momentarily moved by the story before shrugging it off. "I still don't see the connection to the current situation."

"Thomas St. Claire isn't your father, Ellis, agreed?"

"Agreed."

"So that means your real biological father is still out there somewhere."

"It's a real big world out there, Sydney. There's more than two hundred and fifty million people in the United States alone. How do you suppose I find him?"

"Coalsburg is a pretty small town. Not too many people leave it."

"My mother left it."

"Yes, she did. She also never came back. Not even for a visit."

"Ellis, Sydney's right." Thomas sat up straight and all signs of fatigue were gone. "Catherine might not have come back for fear of running into your real father. She knew he would still be here."

"Maybe she was afraid of running into her parents."

"Could be, but if Sydney's right about her being scared of naming your real father, then my money's on her being afraid of running into him. Your father has to be from this town, Ellis. Catherine was in high school back then and she rarely left town except for a few church trips that I remember."

"There's still a chance, Ellis." Sydney didn't want to build up his hopes just to watch them come crashing down, but he needed to explore every opportunity. "Trevor's grandfather still might be living in town. We could find him."

"How?"

"That's where we need my father's help." She reached out and touched her father's hand. He turned his palm over and linked fingers with her. "My father knows everyone in town, and he knows who was around thirty-three years ago." She gave her father a loving smile and squeezed his hand. "With his help we could find Trevor's grandfather."

Ellis thought about it for a moment then released a heavy sigh. "I would greatly appreciate anything you two might uncover, but I still have to head on home. Trevor needs me right now and he's too young to understand why I'm not with him. I've been away too long as it is. I can't stay any longer."

"We understand, Ellis, and we certainly don't want to cause Trevor any more distress," Thomas said.

"I think the only solution would be if you brought Trevor out here to stay." Sydney squeezed her father's hand once again. "While my father's mind might be a steel trap, he is going to need someone to do his legwork for him. If you bring Trevor to stay with us, there would be two of us to do the running. Plus you would be with your son. There's plenty of room in the house and I know both my father and I would love to meet him."

"You won't mind?"

"Mind having Catherine's grandson under my roof?" Thomas said. "It would be my pleasure, Ellis. Catherine thought enough of me to name me as the father of her child. The least I can do is help her son and grandson out. She would have wanted me to." Thomas stood up and reached for his cane. "I'm going to the den to start working on my strategy. Thirty-three-year-old mysteries can be tricky." Thomas left the room.

Sydney didn't watch her father leave. She was too busy watching the emotions sweep across Ellis's face. Doubt was slowly being replaced with hope. She prayed she was doing the right thing and not setting Ellis up for another fall. "You know there is a chance your father might have left town or won't admit to impregnating your mother and then abandoning her."

"I know, Sydney. Your little scheme has a very slim chance of working, and even if it does there's no guarantee that Trevor's grandfather would take the test and agree to become a donor. Then there's the slim-to-nothing chance there would be an actual match." The frown on Ellis's face lifted slightly. "Then again, if I headed home, there would be no chance at all, would there?"

"Trevor would love springtime in the country."

"Five-year-old boys can be a handful. The house will be stuck in perpetual chaos."

"I'm sure the chaos will be outweighed by the love he will bring."

"The only thing that would outweigh the chaos is the number of stuffed animals he is going to insist on bringing with him." Ellis chuckled as he shook his head at the thought. "I have a hell of a time saying no to him."

Sydney answered his chuckle with one of her own. The love Ellis felt for his son was obvious even to her untrained eye. "Five-foot-long alligators in the tub would definitely liven things up around here."

Ellis's laugh slowly faded and a gleam of hunger leaped into his eyes. "You know that if I come back we're going to become lovers." His finger reached out and touched the corner of her mouth. "I can't fight the desire any longer, Sydney. I want you too much to spend another night under the same roof as you without touching you. Tasting you. Knowing all of you. This time I won't be stopping with kisses. This time there won't be any stopping at all."

Sydney felt the heat of his gaze burn into her soul and the touch of his finger singe her heart. Ellis was telling her the truth. There wouldn't be any stopping when he returned.

Ellis lowered his hand. "I'll ask you one last time, Syd. Do you want me to come back with my son to look for his grandfather?"

She knew what he was saying. They would become lovers, but eventually he would have to leave again. Ellis's home wasn't in the small coal town of Coalsburg. Trevor needed advanced medical treatment that only big urban hospitals could provide. Even Ellis's business was based in Philadelphia. Everything was stacked against a happy-ever-after ending. She told herself she could live with that as long as she knew it from the beginning. Making love with Ellis wasn't a desire. It was a necessity.

She stepped closer to him and gave him temporary custody of her heart. "Come back, Ellis. I want you too much to fight it any longer."

Ellis's mouth crushed hers beneath his with the promise of both fulfillment and the pleasure that was soon to come. Real soon.

Chapter 7

Sydney glanced around the living room in awe. She had just figured out a new mathematical equation. One little boy times three hours equaled total chaos. Ellis had been right. She really hadn't doubted him for a moment. She just thought he had been exaggerating a bit.

The room that had once been her mother's pride and joy had been turned into a zoo. The huge overstuffed sofa that was upholstered in a soft cream with huge pink cabbage roses was overrun with lions and tigers. The matching chair held an elephant and a six-foot-long rubber snake. The orangutan family had claimed the Queen Anne chair. She had to chuckle at the scene.

Trevor had followed the one rule she had set down. Nothing was to go on the floor, where her father might trip over it. The floor was spotless, except for the expensive wool area rug her mother had purchased last year. It was the rest of the room that was in disarray. A charming disarray that would have panicked her mother and made her father laugh if he could see it.

Thomas had fallen in love with Trevor within twenty minutes of the boy's arrival. She was positive the feeling was mutual. Ellis had obviously explained to Trevor about Thomas and the fact that he was blind. Trevor had accepted her father's blindness without any awkward silences or questions.

Her father had been more nervous about the first meeting than the little boy. Trevor, who had been clutching one of the orangutans, had immediately gone into some long explanation on what the hairy apes ate. After being duly impressed, Thomas had asked to hold the monkey so he could "see" with his hands. Trevor, intrigued by this new way of "seeing," had instantly shown Thomas every animal he had brought with him. The back seat of Ellis's Mercedes had been full when they had pulled up earlier.

"I did try to warn you." Ellis's voice came from directly behind her and held a hint of laughter.

"Yes, you did." She felt the flutter of excitement dance in her stomach at his nearness. Ellis was back. They were going to become lovers. She could see it in his eyes and hear it in his voice. She glanced over her shoulder and gave him a warm smile. "I can see why you have trouble saying no to Trevor. He's not only adorable, he does things quietly. He doesn't go around demanding things and throwing tantrums when he doesn't get his way, does he?"

A couple of her friends had small children and she had experienced firsthand what some of them could do when they didn't get their way. Heck, she had heard the noise they could create when things *were* going their way. She hadn't really known what to expect with Trevor, but quiet hadn't even entered her mind.

"Trevor has never thrown a tantrum in his life. With everything he has been through, no one would blame him for throwing more than a tantrum or two." Ellis reached out and lightly touched a curl that had escaped the ponytail she had pulled her hair into earlier. "I've missed you."

"You only were gone seven hours." *Seven hours and fourteen minutes, but who was counting?*

"That's the part that scared me."

Since he had walked out the door and driven away this morning, she had been half-afraid he wouldn't return, while the other half of her was anxious that he would. The decision was already made, they were going to become lovers. She turned her face and pressed her cheek into his warm palm. "I know that feeling well."

Ellis had only been here less than a week and the house had seemed empty when he left. What was she going to do when he was gone for good? She'd face that future when she had to. For now, him being there was all that mattered.

She moved a step closer and watched as the heat of desire flared in his eyes. She felt his hand cupping her cheek, pulling her closer still. Closer to his warmth. Closer to his mouth.

She could feel the forthcoming kiss that was already electrifying the air between their mouths. She wanted this kiss. She had been dreaming of this kiss for seven hours and fourteen minutes. With a light sigh she closed her eyes and reached for him.

"Dad, can we have dinner soon. I'm hungry." Trevor's voice came from the area around her thigh.

Sydney jerked back and nearly collided with the chair holding the orangutan family. She glanced down at Trevor, who had entered the room unnoticed and was standing less than a foot away from his dad. A quarter of an inch more and Trevor would have caught them kissing. It was an unsettling thought. A flush darkened her cheeks as she glanced at Ellis.

Ellis's gaze seem to stare longingly at her mouth while he ruffled his son's brown hair. "I'm sure dinner will be soon. I'm feeling mighty hungry myself."

She knew exactly what Ellis was hungry for, and it wasn't the roast she had slipped into the oven over an hour ago. "Dinner will be in about twenty minutes, Trevor. Can you wait that long?" Somewhere in the kitchen there had to be something the boy could munch on without ruining his dinner. Trevor was on the thin side. An extra calorie here and there wouldn't hurt him.

"How many's that, Dad?"

"Twenty minutes, Trev. You know how to count to twenty." Ellis appeared quite proud of that fact.

"Yeah, but how long's that?"

"Enough time for you to have one cookie and help me set the table." She gave Trevor a friendly smile. "I baked a batch of chocolate-chip cookies while your father went to get you. He told me they were your favorite." She wanted Trevor to know he was welcome in their home and she had needed something to do while Ellis was gone. It had been a toss-up between food shopping, stopping in at the nursery, baking cookies and fixing dinner or having her very first anxiety attack. She had chosen to bake.

Trevor pulled on his father's hand. "Can I, Dad?"

"What, have a cookie or help Miss St. Claire set the

table?" Ellis smiled down at his son. All the love he felt for the child was clearly visible in that smile.

"Both, Dad, please." Trevor tried not to appear excited about the prospect of getting a cookie before dinner.

"I guess it's all right just this once." Ellis gave her a probing look. "As long as you don't make a habit of eating cookies before every meal."

"I won't." Trevor gave her a hopeful look.

She smiled down at the boy and held out her hand. "Follow me, Trev, and I'll show you the way to the cookie jar." Trevor's little hand felt so fragile and warm when it reached for her outstretched hand. He grabbed her hand without a moment's hesitation and the trust he handed her with his tiny hand nearly overwhelmed her heart. Trevor had given her his trust. She turned and headed for the kitchen before Ellis or Trevor saw the tears forming in her eyes.

The red stool, positioned near the phone on the wall, caught her eye. When she was a little girl, her mother always pulled it over to the counter for her. She used to sit on it and watch or help with whatever her mother was doing. Many fond memories were connected with that stool.

Without releasing Trevor's hand, she pulled the step stool over near the counter and motioned for him to climb on up. The stool had two little steps and had seen its share of action whenever she or her mother had needed something from the back of one of the top shelves.

Trevor scampered up the steps and perched himself on the seat as if he were king. "Mrs. McCall lets me set the table at home."

"I bet you're pretty good at it, aren't you?" She reached for the white ceramic cookie jar with red geraniums painted on it and lifted the lid. The aroma of freshly baked cookies whiffed out and tantalized even her senses. Amazingly, she had not sampled any of the cookies as they lay cooling on the wire rack. Her father was another story. She had to shoo him out of the kitchen before there wasn't any left for Trevor.

She held the jar out to the little boy. "Remember, only one."

Trevor took a cookie and smiled. "Thank you."

"You're welcome." She held the jar out to Ellis who had followed her into the kitchen and was leaning against the counter watching the exchange between her and his son. "Only one for you too. I don't want you ruining your dinner."

Ellis took a cookie and grinned at his son and winked. "Thanks, Trev. Without you here, she never would have let me have a cookie before dinner."

She picked a cookie for herself and replaced the cookie jar. "Just don't tell my father."

"Don't tell your father what?" Thomas had entered the kitchen just as the words came out of her mouth.

Ellis chuckled and Trevor bit into his cookie. She shook her head at the cookie clutched in her hand and knew she couldn't hide the truth from her father. Thomas had probably smelled the cookies the instant she took the lid off the jar. "They aren't allowed to tell you we're sneaking cookies before dinner."

One of Thomas's eyebrows raised behind his dark glasses. "Cookies?"

"Trevor was hungry." She smiled at the boy and bit into her own cookie.

Thomas walked farther into the room and tried to sniff out the direction of the cookie jar. "Can't have the boy go hungry, can we?"

Once again she reached for the cookie jar and gently bumped it against her father's hand. Thomas immediately snatched up a cookie and grinned. "What do you think, Trev, are the cookies any good?"

"They're real good, Mr. St. Claire. They're almost as good as Mrs. McCall's."

Almost! Almost as good as Mrs. McCall's! She frowned at the cookie—minus one big bite—in her hand. What did he mean *almost* as good as Mrs. McCall's?

Her father tried, but wasn't successful in covering up his chuckle before he turned his attention to eating his cookie.

"A high compliment indeed." Ellis gave her a reassuring smile. "Trevor is totally smitten with Rita and everything she does."

She nearly blushed with pleasure as Ellis tried to soften his son's words. It was very sweet of him to reassure her. Then again, she was the one cooking their dinner tonight.

"What's smitten?" Trevor asked.

"It means you really like Mrs. McCall." Ellis ruffled his son's hair as he polished off the rest of his cookie.

"I love her, Dad." Trevor frowned for a moment. "Kyle came over to play zoo with me yesterday and he told me he has two grandmoms and that I didn't have any. Mrs. McCall said I wasn't to worry none because she'll be my grandmom anytime I want."

The look on Ellis's face as he gazed at his son not only tugged at her heart, it hauled it across her chest and jammed it into her throat. Trevor wasn't belittling her cookies, he was being loyal to his "grandmother" Rita. The woman earned more than a raise in salary. She deserved a nomination into sainthood.

Ellis walked into the den and immediately glanced at Sydney. She was curled up on the couch with her nose buried in the mounds of paperwork surrounding her. Guilt assaulted him again. Because of him, and now Trevor, she had once again missed out on going to the nursery and doing the paperwork there. Instead, she would spend half the night doing it. He knew what it took to run a business. Whatever energy of his that Trevor didn't use up, One If By Land did.

Sydney was in the same boat. Her father was now solely dependent on her, at least physically. As for financially, he didn't know how Thomas was set, before or after the accident. He had considered it too personal to have him investigated that way. It hadn't mattered to him how well off Thomas had been. All that had concerned him was the components in his blood. Now he was glad he hadn't had the man's financial status investigated. Thomas wasn't his biological father after all.

The television was turned on low and Thomas seemed to be listening to it.

Sydney turned her head and glanced at him the moment he walked into the room. "Is Trevor asleep?"

"He made it through one book, but conked out on me in the middle of the second." He had started the habit of reading to Trevor at night years ago. His son had grown up with a love for books and words. "He now knows at least eight more jungle animals that he doesn't have in his collection."

"The boy sure knows his animals," Thomas said with

a chuckle. "Maybe he'll be a veterinarian when he grows up."

Ellis felt his heart jerk at Thomas's words *when he grows up*. He knew Thomas hadn't meant to hurt him, but the pain was there nevertheless. It was an innocent slip of the tongue. Just like the other day when he inadvertently said to Thomas, *Wait until you see...* A heavy silence filled the room.

"Lord, I'm sorry, Ellis." Thomas hit a button on the remote and the television went off.

Sydney busied herself with restacking her piles into one mound and placing it on the coffee table. "Are you sure Trevor will be okay up there alone?"

"He's fine. He hardly ever wakes up in the middle of the night and if he should, I brought his night-light from home. The door's cracked and the hall light's on. Trevor's used to sleeping in strange places." Seven hospital stays in nine months could do that to a kid. "Besides, he has an entire roomful of animals to protect him."

He had left his son snuggled in the middle of the double bed in the guest bedroom clutching his baby blanket with its ratty edges. Winnie-the-Pooh was on one side of him and the baby orangutan was on the other. When he went to bed later, he would have to move Trevor and his friends over to make some room for himself.

"Is that what all the animals are for, protection?" asked Sydney.

"Partly." He was tired of trying to figure out all the psychological explanations for everything Trevor did or said. He had decided six months ago to let Trevor lead, as much as possible, the normal life of a five-year-old. Most parents didn't go around psychoanalyzing everything their five-year-old did. "Some of it is security, surrounding himself with something of his own. The other part is because he likes animals."

"That he does." Thomas chuckled. "Did you manage to fit them all in the guest room?"

Sydney, Trevor and he had carried up the wild assortment of animals earlier and scattered them throughout the room. Now that Trevor was settling into the guest room, he would leave the majority of the animals up there during the day and only bring down one or two of them at a time. "Yes, Trevor's very happy at how they all fit, and I do believe he hinted that there might be room for one or two more."

Thomas chuckled again. "Georgette down at Two-By-Two will be mighty happy to hear that."

Ellis shook his head knowingly and sat down on the other end of the couch. "Georgette will probably be able to retire to Palm Beach, Florida, by the time we head home." He glanced at Sydney and frowned when she wouldn't meet his gaze. Was she having second thoughts about them becoming lovers?

Thomas settled more comfortably in his chair and faced the couch. "I've been giving the matter of your father some thought." Thomas rubbed his chin. "Well, it's been more than just some thought."

Ellis's attention immediately went to Thomas. Trevor, and possibly finding a donor, had to be his first concern. He would question Sydney later. "What did you come up with?" As far as he could figure, finding his biological father would be like finding the proverbial needle in a haystack.

"The more I think on it, the more I have to agree with Sydney. I think your father is still in town, or at least he had been up to twelve years ago. Catherine had some good decent friends in Coalsburg. I think she would have eventually come home, if only for a visit."

"There's what, eight thousand, ten thousand residents in Coalsburg? That's a lot of people, Thomas."

"I'm not just referring to the city limits, Ellis. We need to look at the surrounding area, too. Catherine was in high school when she got pregnant. There are four other towns whose students are bused in to the school. The other towns have their own elementary schools, but everyone uses Coalsburg Middle School and Coalsburg Senior High School."

"So we're talking what, forty thousand people now?"

"More like fifty thousand."

He leaned his head back and closed his eyes. Fifty thousand people! The needle in the haystack had just been shrunk to the size of a pin. Hell, four angels could be dancing on the head of that pin and he still wouldn't be able to find it.

"It's not that bad, Ellis. Roughly half those people are women."

"Oh joy, now we're only talking about twenty-five thousand people."

"Then we eliminate anyone under the age of forty-eight," continued Thomas as if he hadn't heard his last comment.

"Why forty-eight?"

"Catherine was eighteen at the time. She might have...let's use the words *paired up* with a boy who was only seventeen, but I'm going to include sixteen-year-olds in there, too, just to be on the safe side."

Ellis didn't want to think about his mother and some sixteen-year-old kid. Hell, he didn't want to think about his mother being "paired up" with anyone. "What about the other end of the spectrum? Are we going to cut off the age limit at fifty-two? That would have made my father twenty at the time."

Thomas rubbed his chin for a long moment. "I think we should broaden that figure, Ellis. I don't mean any disrespect toward Catherine, but there are a lot of girls who get their heads turned by a much older, more mature man."

"How mature are we talking about? Could he have been thirty?"

"I was going to suggest cutting off the age group around fifty."

"Fifty! My mother was only eighteen at the time." A fifty-year-old man and an eighteen-year-old girl! "I thought you were my mother's friend?"

"Ellis..." Sydney reached out and gently touched his hand. "It's possible that your mother could have fallen for some charming, debonair man in his forties, early forties."

"A man in his forties could father a child," added Thomas gently.

"Hell, a man in his seventies could father a child. Shouldn't we include them too?"

"That would make him roughly one hundred and two today, Ellis." Thomas shook his head. "I think we should concentrate first on the boys who were in her school at the time and maybe a year or two older than her who were still in town at the time."

"What about her teachers?" asked Sydney.

"Teachers? You want to ask her teachers if they remember seeing my mother with a certain boy?" Made sense to him. It could be a starting point.

"No, I was thinking maybe your mother...had an affair with one of her teachers."

He stared at Sydney in disbelief. "This is my mother you're talking about."

"I know, and I'm sorry if I'm offending her memory, but many girls have crushes on their teachers, especially young male teachers. Maybe your mother's feelings went beyond the crush stage?"

"She's got a point there, Ellis. If you want to find your father you are going to have to put sentiment aside. Catherine must have loved you very much to do what she did. Back thirty-two years ago a girl could have arranged to have a back-room abortion, or it was more common to leave town for a while and visit an aunt or an uncle out of state for a couple of months and put the baby up for adoption. Not too many chose to keep the child out of wedlock."

"I know that, Thomas." He knew how hard it had been for his mother to raise him on her own. Seeing her daily struggle had given him the ambition to do well in school and to make something of himself. He had planned on making his mother's life easier. She had died before he was able to do that.

"Catherine would have loved Trevor, just as much as she loved you."

"I know that, too." He remembered the wistful look on his mother's face whenever someone from the neighborhood had a baby. His mother had wanted more children.

"Then trust me when I say Catherine would want you to do everything within your power to save Trevor's life. Even if it meant unburying the truth about who your real father was."

Thomas was right. If his mother were alive today, she would tell him the truth. He didn't mind turning over stones to find out who his father was. What did bother him was turning over those stones to find out a very personal and intimate secret of his mother's—who she had slept with. He had to push those reservations aside and concentrate on Trevor.

"Okay, Thomas. We do it your way. How do we find out who she went to school with?"

"Yearbooks." Thomas relaxed now that things were going his way. "My wife, Julia's, yearbook and mine are both in the attic somewhere. Julia and your mother both graduated in the same year. I graduated two years before them. Tomorrow morning you and Sydney go up to the attic and see if you can locate the yearbooks. I'm pretty sure they're in an old black steamer trunk up there."

"What about the other years? The two years after she graduated and the one before." Sydney started taking notes and glanced up from the pad on her lap.

"I'll make a few phone calls and see if I can round them up." A flush of excitement tinted Thomas's cheeks. "I'm going to need a pair of eyes to read me the names in the books."

"I'll do it." Sydney volunteered.

"No, I'll do it." Ellis had already caused Sydney to lose enough time at work. "After we locate the yearbooks, you go to the nursery. Trevor and I will keep your father company and fix dinner. I don't want you home until six." He knew the nursery closed at five, but Thomas had told him that before the accident she never got home before six.

"But I want to help." Sydney didn't look upset that

he was dictating to her. She looked mad as hell. "This whole plan was my idea."

"I know, Syd, and I thank you." He reached over and covered her hand with his own. "You've been missing a lot of work lately because of me." *And your father,* but he didn't voice that. Sydney didn't need to hear it and Thomas already knew it. She also had been missing a lot of sleep, but he didn't think he was the sole reason for that, either. "Tomorrow night, after Trevor's tucked in, we can have another brainstorming session to see where we stand." He gave her hand a gentle squeeze. "We are going to need you for legwork later, but for now, I can read your father the names of the boys in the yearbooks and take notes."

"Ellis is right, Sydney. We are going to need you later. Go to work before your employees decide to fire you." Thomas stood up and stretched. "I think we're done for the night. I don't know about you two, but Trevor wore me out with all his questions. I think I'll head for bed."

He carefully watched the way Thomas stretched and yawned. It was an act. Thomas hadn't been worn-out by his son, as he had feared. Sydney's father was discreetly leaving the two of them alone. Not for the first time, he had to wonder if Thomas sensed what was going on under his roof. He doubted it. Thomas didn't strike him as a man who would leave his daughter, his own precious and beloved daughter, alone with a wolf. Tonight he was definitely feeling like a wolf. A big, bad and extremely hungry wolf.

"Night, Dad." Sydney watched as her father made his way out of the room.

Thomas used his cane to tap against the doorjamb.

A moment later Ellis could detect the light tapping of the cane as Thomas made his way up the stairs.

Silence filled the room.

He turned, looked at Sydney and wondered what made her so different from the countless other women he met every day. Sydney was beautiful, that was an undisputed fact, but he had known more glamorous women who had expressed an interest in him. He rarely, if ever, returned their interest. Sydney had a body that curved in all the right places and made him think of cool sheets and hot sex. None of the other women had inspired such instantaneous lust, not even Ginny, when he was married to her.

His thoughts turned to Trevor. His son had taken a liking to both Sydney and Thomas. When he was helping Trevor to get ready for bed, the boy had asked if Sydney was his girlfriend. He had been taken aback by such a question, until Trev explained that Kyle's daddy had a girlfriend. Kyle's parents were in the middle of a messy divorce and poor Kyle and his little sister had been drawn into the center of the fight. He had asked Trev how he would feel if he did have a girlfriend. His son had once again astounded him by telling him it would be okay because Sydney baked great cookies.

During his drive back to Jenkintown this morning, he had been worried about Trevor becoming too fond of Sydney and Thomas. Now he realized how trivial that seemed when one looked at the whole picture. He had more important things to worry about. His son's health had to be his top priority. Besides, Trevor couldn't have picked a better surrogate family than Thomas and Sydney.

Sydney glanced up from the pad of paper on her lap.

He met Sydney's curious glance and smiled. Yeah, Trevor was right, her cookies weren't half-bad.

"What are you grinning at?" Sydney self-consciously checked her hair and frowned.

"You." He moved close enough to smell the light floral scent she always wore. "You made quite an impression on Trevor today."

"I did?" Sydney tossed the notepad onto the coffee table with the rest of her paperwork and turned to face him. "What did he say?"

"He wanted to know if you're my girlfriend." Sydney looked adorable with her feet tucked up under her bottom, so anxious to hear what his son had said.

"He didn't!" Sydney looked horrified at the thought.

"He did." Sydney didn't have to appear that startled and distressed by the prospect of being his girlfriend. "You're not doing wonders for my ego here, Syd."

"What did you tell him?"

So much for his ego. If he was really lucky, he might be able to scrape what was left of it off the floor and tuck it back into that pocket marked Pride before he went to bed. "Since I'm not in the habit of bringing women home with me and introducing them as my girlfriends, I was more curious about how he knew about daddies having them." He inched close enough to press his jean-covered thigh against her knee. "Turns out the little boy from up the street, who plays with him occasionally, parents are going through a messy divorce. Kyle's dad has a girlfriend, and I believe that's what initiated the divorce in the first place."

"Lovely, and their little boy knows about it?"

"Oh yeah. Kyle knows, the neighborhood knows and the dueling lawyers know. Hell, everyone knows, including my son." He had been disgusted by the whole sordid affair, but he couldn't have done anything about it. He had been so concerned about protecting Trevor from medical jargon and the possible outcome of his illness that he hadn't even thought about what the neighbors were up to.

"Did you discuss this with him?"

"Somewhat." His heart hadn't been in the mood for a deep heavy conversation with his son while he was giving him a bath in the St. Claires' tub. He saved the intense emotions for when the doctors gave him news to pass on to Trevor. "The topic of divorce didn't seem to go with his bathtime buddies." Trevor had packed a small bag of his favorite tub toys and brought it with him.

"Divorce must be a very painful topic for him, considering the situation between you and his mother."

"Trevor doesn't know we're divorced. He doesn't remember his mother at all. Ginny and I thought it was best that way." He had made sure that his son wouldn't be pulled in two different directions. He had witnessed firsthand some of his employees going through messy divorces and somehow the kids always ended up in the middle of them all. He had seen fights over holidays, birthdays and who was paying the orthodontist bill. He hadn't been about to drag his son into that battle. "Ginny wasn't cut out to be a mother."

"So why did she have Trevor?"

"Our marriage was in deep trouble, and Ginny thought a baby would help hold it together. About four months into her pregnancy she knew she had made a mistake."

"She considered Trevor a mistake?" Sydney not only looked appalled, she sounded it.

"No, for all Ginny's faults, she loved Trevor enough to let him go." It might have cost him a small fortune in divorce court, but she kept her end of the bargain. "She was also the first to get her blood tested to see if she'd match."

"So what did you tell Trevor about his mother?"

"Nothing really. He just knows he doesn't have one." He knew in the future he and his son would have to have a father-to-son talk about Ginny.

"His mother hasn't seen him at all, even when he was sick?"

"No. It may sound cruel, but I believe it's easier on everyone this way." He knew Sydney had been adopted when she was ten. Trevor's not knowing his biological mother was probably a real issue for her, and he could understand that. But Trevor was his son and Ginny was his spoiled and selfish ex-wife. Sydney, who opened her home and her heart to his son, deserved to hear some of the truth.

"I believe it's better for Trevor to think he doesn't have a mother than to know his mother tricked me into getting her pregnant to hold on to a crumbling marriage and an open-ended checkbook. Once she realized that being pregnant didn't help the marriage or make her glowing or radiant, she wanted to terminate the pregnancy. Whatever had been between Ginny and me was gone. For five months I paid dearly, until Trevor was born. I allowed Ginny to stay until she had recuperated from what she referred to as 'the ordeal' and then she was on her way."

Sydney stared at him for a long time before she said,

"I think you might be right, Ellis." She glanced down at his hands resting on his thighs. "One day you're going to have to tell him, though."

"I know, but not yet." He opened one of his hands and held it out to her. Sydney's warm palm connected with his palm as her fingers entwined themselves around his. "He has a lot on his plate for now."

"It doesn't seem fair, does it?"

The sorrow in her gaze pulled at his heart. "No, it doesn't." He tugged on her hand and drew her closer. He loved his son with all his heart and was doing everything within his power, and beyond, to help Trevor. But now, right now, this very minute, he needed something more than a sympathetic ear and an understanding heart.

He needed Sydney.

"Know what really doesn't seem fair?" He drew her closer and watched her soft green eyes widen with perception and a touch of desire.

"What?" Sydney's gaze fastened onto his mouth.

"That I haven't gotten to kiss you once since I arrived." He released her hand and wrapped his arms around her waist.

Sydney's arms had nowhere to go but around his neck. "You noticed that, too?" Sydney smiled at his mouth before placing her lips against his.

Chapter 8

Sydney couldn't resist the temptation of Ellis's mouth a moment longer. By the scorching look in his eyes she would have to say he had reached the end of his tolerance too. With the touch of his mouth and the sweep of his tongue, heat assaulted her body like an inferno.

Strong arms pulled her closer and she uncurled from her position in the corner of the couch to practically stretch out on top of Ellis as he twisted sideways and lay back, taking her with him. Her arms clung to his neck as she continued to meet the thrust of his tongue with slow swipes of her own and breathless abandonment.

Someone moaned, and she couldn't tell if it was Ellis or herself. It didn't matter. The only thing that did matter was the feel, the taste of Ellis. She had never wanted like this in her life. His mouth was promising her things she had never dared dream.

She shifted her hips and felt his arousal, long and hard, press against her thigh. This time she was positive it was Ellis who groaned. The tip of her tongue traced his upper lip before her teeth gently nipped at his fuller lower one. His arms tightened around her. She raised her head and, using her arms to support herself, she stared down at him. The look in his gray eyes had gone from scorching to predatory.

He reached up and buried his fingers in her hair. "Witch."

She pressed her head against his fingertips and arched her neck. She felt his mouth skim down her throat. "Was that a compliment?" The way the word *witch* had tumbled off his lips it had sounded like a cross between a prayer and a curse.

Ellis arched his hips against her thigh, letting her know exactly what condition he was in. "Only a witch could make me ache so badly after one kiss." His fingers slipped to the base of her skull and his thumbs moved to below her jawbone and tilted her face upward, giving his searching mouth wider access to her throat.

She matched him ache for ache, only hers was a soft warm liquid ache pooling at the junction of her thighs. Wanting him to know that he wasn't the only one who felt painfully aroused, she said, "That would make you what...a warlock?"

Ellis pulled back from tracing the V at the base of her throat with his tongue to glance up at her. "Are you aching, Sydney?"

She closed her eyes. She had never before asked a man to make love to her. The all too few times she had been with a man it had just seemed to happen. Ellis wasn't going to allow her to casually slip into a relationship with him. He was going to demand her full undivided attention. "If I tell you I am, will you make it go away?"

"Eventually." Ellis chuckled softly against her throat as he released her jaw and lowered his hands to her waist. "But first I'm going to make you ache some more." With a tender tug he jerked her farther up his body, until his mouth was in a direct line to her breast. "You want to ache some more, don't you, Syd?"

She kept her eyes closed as she felt his warm fingers start to undo the buttons running down the front of her blouse. Her breasts grew heavy with anticipation and her nipples hardened against the lace of her bra. Ellis had never touched her there. The warmth of his fingers brushed against the curve of her breast, making her tremble. "Oh, I want all right." She wanted so badly, she was about to shatter into a million pieces.

The last of her buttons came undone and Ellis pulled the blouse from the waistband of her jeans. The silky material fell to each side of his chest, giving him a clear view of her breasts covered in an emerald green bra. Strong, blunt-tipped fingers reached up and toyed with the front clasp on the bra. "You're going to have to open your eyes, Syd."

"Why?" She didn't want Ellis to see the need that would be clearly visible in them. Wanting him was one thing. Needing him was something totally different.

His fingers traced the edges of the lace across the top of her breasts. "I want you to see me take my first taste of you." His fingers took another path, this time they skimmed her nipples, causing her to jerk back.

Her eyes flew open in shock and she glanced down. Her gaze slammed into Ellis's. He had been watching her face, not her breasts which were suspended in her bra not six inches away from his mouth. His face looked taut and flushed with desire, yet he hadn't really touched her. He wanted her to watch him as he touched her.

Her whisper trembled with excitement and embarrassment. "You want me to watch?" She had never watched before. Satisfying the urges of one's body was done under the covers and in the dark, not with two seventy-five-watt bulbs burning on either end of the couch and without a blanket in sight.

Ellis locked gazes with her as he lifted his fingers once more and released the front clasp of her bra. "I need you to watch."

She felt her breasts swing free, the lace tugging on her swollen and hard nipples. She swallowed the sharp cry that filled her mouth. Her arms trembled as she held herself above his waiting mouth.

Ellis's hands were tender as they brushed aside the lace and cupped the two pale mounds. Rough thumbs grazed her nipples, making them quiver in need. His breath bathed her skin in its warmth. "You're beautiful, Sydney." His lips reached for one of the nubs. "Are they ready for me to taste them?"

She gazed at him in anticipation. Ellis wanted her to watch and she was drawn more by the excitement of his request than the need to close her eyes in embarrassment. "I..."

He reached up and captured the nub deep in his mouth.

She felt herself jerk and she arched her back, thrusting herself deeper into his mouth. Her eyes closed in ecstasy as Ellis's teeth tenderly pulled on the bud.

"Open your eyes, Sydney." Ellis's thigh inserted itself between her legs.

The hardness of his thigh between her legs caused a moan to rumble deep in her throat as her hips slid against him. "Why?" A tingle of pure pleasure shimmied from her nipple down to the wet junction between her thighs.

Nimble fingers unsnapped her jeans. The rhythm of her hips matched the gentle tugging of his mouth on her nipple. Everything seemed connected. Her pounding heart echoed his breathing. His soft groans reverberated the rhythm of her hips. Why hadn't she realized before that making love was a well-orchestrated dance?

The heat of his palm pressed against her abdomen and slowly slipped beneath the waistband of her jeans and her silk panties. Fingers burrowed through curls and stroked her moist center.

Ellis released her nipple from between his lips. "Sydney, look at me."

A trembling "Why?" was torn from her throat before she clamped down on her lower lip with her teeth. She opened her eyes and glanced down at him because she was fearful that he would stop the wonderful, marvelous things he was doing to her body. His eyes were no longer gray. They were burning silver.

Ellis increased the rhythm of his fingers as her thighs moved farther apart. The tip of one of his fingers slipped inside and out of her with every thrust of her hips. "I'm going to be watching your eyes when you climax."

She never heard of such a thing. Why would he want to watch her as she climaxed? "I don't understand."

"You don't have to, Sydney, just feel." Ellis cupped her one breast with his free hand and squeezed the nipple between his thumb and forefinger. When her hips arched in response, his finger slipped all the way inside, making her want more.

Much more.

She felt the tension coil and twist as she thrust her hips faster and harder against his hand. She had reached the center of the vortex Ellis had brought her to, yet she couldn't look away from his eyes. He held her gaze as the storm within her broke and she was hurled over the edge. Deep within her she could feel the tiny contractions signaling her release, gripping him tightly.

As the last of her climax faded she closed her eyes in mortification and allowed herself to finally collapse against Ellis's chest, burying her face in his shirt. Humiliation didn't even begin to describe what she felt.

Ellis had just given her the most mind-shattering sexual experience of her life and he was still fully clothed. Not one button on his shirt was undone. His shoes were off, but that was because he had taken them off before he had given Trevor his bath. If she was able to move, she would find some deep dark hole to climb into.

"Are you okay?" Ellis's voice was raspy and uneven as it feathered against her ear.

Both of his hands were slowly rubbing her back as if she were fragile and would shatter at any moment. She had news for him—she had already shattered and he had witnessed it all within her eyes. With her ear flattened against his chest she heard the thundering of his rapid heartbeat. His arousal, which surely had to be past the aching point, was still pressed into her hipbone. No, she wasn't okay. She was humiliated. Two of his buttons pressed against her cheek as she mumbled into a third one, "I'm sorry."

Ellis's hands stopped in midstroke. "For what?"

"For...you know..." She couldn't bear to look at him, so she weakly waved one of her hands into the air. Her experience with men might not be what most twenty-eight-year-old women's were, but she knew Ellis should have been with her on that incredible journey he had just taken her on.

He reached down, cupped her chin and forced her to look at him. "No, I don't know, Sydney. Explain."

Mortification flooded her cheeks. If she had the energy, she would have fled the room. As it was, she still couldn't feel her knees, let alone stand up and run. Her hand fluttered helplessly once again into the air. "You know, you didn't..." She couldn't think of a proper way of completing that sentence.

"I didn't what?" Ellis refused to allow her to bury her face back into his shirt.

"You know..." The flood of embarrassment heated her face as Ellis continued to stare at her. He was waiting for an answer and by hell he was going to get one. "You weren't...satisfied." She nodded her head as if she was some slow-witted pupil who just thought of the right answer. "You know what I mean...."

Ellis chuckled until she glared at him. It took him a moment to catch his breath and then he asked, "Is that what you were sorry for?"

"What did you think I was sorry for?" Ellis wasn't slow or thickheaded. What else could she possibly be sorry for?

"Old insecurities die hard, Sydney, that's all." Ellis cupped her face and kissed the tip of her nose.

"What old insecurities?"

This time his kiss landed at the corner of her mouth. "Later, my love. I'll tell you later."

My love! Ellis had called her his love! When he tried to kiss the other corner of her mouth, she turned her head and landed a direct kiss of her own.

He chuckled. "You didn't think we were finished, did you?"

"Finished?"

Ellis gave her a kiss that not only rekindled a couple of the sparks she had thought were fading, but lit a few new ones as well. "Sydney, Sydney, Sydney." Warm and insistent lips placed tiny little kisses all over her face. "That was only the first inning."

"First inning?" She tried to capture his roaming mouth, but he was too quick for her.

"You know what they say about first innings." Ellis's teeth playfully nipped at her earlobe.

"What?"

"There's eight more to follow."

An hour later, Sydney stood under the warm pounding spray of the shower and tried to relax. She couldn't. She was still waiting for the second inning to begin. Ellis obviously wasn't in a hurry to restart the game. Or maybe the anticipation was part of his game plan.

He had teased away her embarrassment with gentle kisses that hinted at even greater pleasures yet to come as he had refastened her bra and redone her buttons. They had locked up the house together and climbed the steps hand in hand. He had walked her to her bedroom door, kissed her until she nearly melted at his feet and then asked her if there was a lock on her door. She had skidded her fingers down the buttons on his shirt and told him yes, but she wasn't planning on using it—at least not to keep him out. He had captured her wandering fingers, opened her bedroom door and gently nudged her inside with the promise of joining her soon.

She had nervously paced her room, listening to the sound of Ellis taking a shower across the hall. Mental images of him standing under a pounding spray had had her nearly hyperventilating. She had pictured broad shoulders, muscular thighs and a chest worthy of her undivided attention, for at least an hour or two. Suds and water had been running in rivers down his body.

A stirring of heat had had her cursing both her imagination and Ellis. She had turned into a wanton woman.

As soon as he left the bathroom and returned to his room, she had dashed across the hall praying that a bracing shower would cool her down.

Her prayer had been in vain. She wasn't cool. Heck, she wasn't even warm. She was hot and aching.

With a rueful shake of her head she grabbed the pink netted shower puff and squirted it with the bottle of shower gel. The scent of raspberries filled the steamy air as she started to lather her body. She jerked in surprise as the net brushed against her still hardened nipples and heat rushed through her. What in the world had Ellis done to her body?

With warmth coiling its way deep within her abdomen and slowly settling at the junction of her thighs, she quickly finished washing and stepped out of the tub. The thick yellow towel was soft against her skin but she hardly noticed. What held her attention was the scent of Ellis's aftershave still clinging to the air and the sight of his small travel case sitting on the back of the toilet.

The black leather case was opened and she could see the various items he had brought. His aftershave bore an expensive designer name. Shaving gel, razor, toothbrush and toothpaste were common brands. They were all masculine things and it reminded her that Ellis was the first man to share this bathroom with her. Her father had a bath connected to his room and this had always been her private domain, except during the occasional visit from Aunt Rose. There was something so intimate about Ellis sharing her space.

She raised her leg to the rim of the tub and rubbed it with the towel. There was something else that caught her eye in Ellis's bag. A bottle of no-tears baby shampoo, a tube of bubble-gum flavored toothpaste and a small toothbrush with Bugs Bunny on the handle. Trevor's things. Ellis wasn't the only new male in the house.

Seeing Trevor's personal items reminded her that Ellis's first and foremost reason for being here was his son.

She slowly hung up the towel and slipped into the white chenille robe that hung on the back of the door. With fingers that shook, she tied the belt, took off the shower cap she had donned to keep her hair dry and hung it on the hook by the tub. Sighing heavily, she turned and faced the mirror.

Steam condensed on the reflective surface, but it wasn't enough to obscure the view. Suddenly she saw what she had been afraid to see—a woman on the brink of falling in love. The wonder and excitement were clearly in her eyes. So was the pain to come.

She picked up her hairbrush, turned from the mirror and left the room. She glanced down the hall to where her father's room was and then back to the closed door of the guest bedroom. Ellis and Trevor's room. She paused, then walked firmly down the hall to her own room. The one thing she had learned from the accident that had taken her mother and blinded her father was to live for today, for tomorrow might never come.

The thought of spending all of her savings or charging up her credit cards just because tomorrow might never be was ridiculous. But the thought of taking a lover and savoring every moment with him was something else entirely. Ellis would be heading home soon enough. For now, she wanted to make each day and every night a memory.

She stepped into her bedroom and closed the door behind her. Ellis would come. He said he would come later and she believed him.

Her hand holding her brush was raised and halfway through its first stroke when his low voice startled her. "You look like a little girl all barefoot and in that oversize robe."

Her gaze shot to the big comfortable chair she had positioned in front of the window. Dressed in a T-shirt and boxers, Ellis slouched down and sank into the chair's depths, hidden in the shadows created by the small light on her bureau.

She forced her hand to complete the stroke of the brush and start another one. She had seen what her wild and curly hair looked like in the mirror in the bathroom—as if she had jammed it all under a plastic shower cap, which she had. She was surprised he hadn't run in horror when she had entered the room.

"I'm not a little girl, Ellis." She wanted to dispel any notions he might have on that score because she definitely didn't feel like a little girl. In fact, she was having some big-girl fantasies where he was concerned.

Ellis grinned as he stood up and walked toward her. "I know."

The heat in his gaze confirmed that statement as he gently took the brush out of her hand. "I like it when you leave your hair down." He took her by the shoulders and turned her around.

She was surprised when he started running the brush through her tangled hair. "I—I put it up in a ponytail because it's easier when I work," she said, stammering nervously. She never had anyone besides her mother or a hairstylist brush her hair. It felt strange in a good way. It was a very intimate gesture.

Ellis's hands were gentle as he worked the brush through her curls. "It looks dark now, but when the sun hits it I can see the red highlights."

She glanced over her shoulder and crinkled her nose at him. "Don't remind me. It's a lot calmer now than when I was a little girl."

Strong fingers wove their way through the wavy curls as if he were memorizing the texture. His gaze followed his fingers. "What, the curls or the color?"

"Both, but mostly the color." The intensity of his gaze caused her to take the brush out of his hand and back away. She didn't want Ellis to see what she saw when she had looked into the mirror. She placed the brush on top of the bureau and moved away from the light. "Is Trevor okay?"

"Trevor's sleeping fine." Ellis followed her into the shadows. When she turned toward him once again, he reached out and cupped her cheek. "Second thoughts, Syd?"

She pressed her cheek into his warmth. "No." The only other person who dared to shorten her name to the ridiculous-sounding Syd was Cindy. Sydney had gone through puberty and into adulthood with her best friend by her side and so Cindy had earned the privilege of calling her just about anything she wanted. When Ellis used the shortened version he made it sound intimate and special.

"Nervous?"

That was the understatement of the year. "What, you can't see my knees knocking?"

Ellis glanced down and grinned. "No offense, Syd, but dressed in that thing I can't see anything but trim ankles, cute feet and painted pink toenails." Ellis's thumb stroked her jaw. "I shudder to think what kind of pajamas you are wearing under it."

She glanced down and frowned. Ellis had a point there. Any woman who wore more material than a bedspread for a robe was apt to wear flannel pj's and kneesocks to bed. She didn't own a pair of flannel pajamas, and the few pairs of kneesocks she owned were meant to be worn with jeans and work boots. She was one of those people in the world who preferred to sleep in the nude—she had been since she graduated from college. The feel of material wrapped around her arms or legs while under the covers made her feel claustrophobic.

Sydney met Ellis's gaze and tried for a casual shrug. "I'm not wearing any pajamas."

Ellis lowered his gaze to the front of Sydney's robe and he had to swallow twice before he could unglue his tongue from the roof of his mouth. "What exactly are you wearing under that tent?"

"A blush." Sydney's hand reached out and held the lapels together.

Sydney was naked beneath the robe! He noticed the slight trembling of her fingers and wondered if it had to do with embarrassment or desire. The blush she was referring to was sweeping up her throat and tinting her cheeks a lovely shade of red. He would have given everything in his wallet to know exactly where that blush had started from. "You look adorable when you blush. Your face nearly matches your hair when the sun catches it." He reached out and touched her heated cheek. "But I wish you wouldn't do it."

"Why?"

"Because it's telling me that you're embarrassed or something I said made you uncomfortable." The confusion in her eyes pulled at his heart. It was very obvious to him that Sydney wasn't used to entertaining men in her bedroom. That fact made tonight that much more special to him. "Tell me what you are thinking, Syd."

"I didn't dress like this because of you." Sydney appeared more mortified at her words. "I mean...I never wear pajamas."

He let out the breath he had been holding and relaxed. Sydney had been embarrassed or uncomfortable about her normal lack of sleeping attire, not because of him. "It doesn't matter."

"It doesn't?"

"Nope." He shook his head and tugged her closer. "I would have taken them off anyway."

Sydney whispered a soft "Oh," and came willingly into his arms.

He captured her soft whisper with his mouth, wrapping his arms around her and pressing her close against his aroused body. Desire boiled through his blood and turned into pulsating need. His tongue swept into her mouth. A low groan ripped through his chest as her tongue met his advance with sweet little stabs.

Sydney's hands caressed his back, pulling him closer

and deepening the kiss. Pleasing musical purrs rumbled up her throat and mated with the kiss. He loved that sweet sound she made when they kissed, and silently vowed to discover if she would still be making it when her thighs were wrapped around his hips and he was deep inside her.

He broke the kiss as Sydney tugged his shirt up and over his head. His fingers toyed with the belt on her robe. "You smell like raspberries." He nipped the enticing curve of her neck, where the robe had slipped a bit. "Will you taste like them too?"

Sydney trembled within his arms. "No, it's not edible. The manufacturer only guarantees that I'll smell like raspberries after a shower, not taste like them."

"Write them in the morning." His mouth brushed aside the soft white robe and trailed a string of kisses to the curve of her shoulder. "Tell them to start research on making it taste like raspberries and that you'll take the first case of the stuff off the line." He gave her shoulder a tender nip. "I love raspberries."

His mouth skimmed downward as the robe slipped farther. The seductive curve of her pale full breast caused him to groan as he savored the soft flesh. "Scratch that last comment."

"What comment?" Sydney's hands stroked the quivering muscles in his back as he restrained himself from picking her up, tossing her onto the bed and sinking so far into her it would take an act of Congress to get him out. He could feel each of her fingers quiver against his skin.

"About tasting like raspberries." The tip of his tongue followed the low sweeping line of the robe against her skin. "No manufacturer could ever duplicate your taste." He lifted his head and met her gaze. Sliding his tongue slowly across his upper lip, he reveled in her flavor. "You taste like hot silk and sinful pleasures."

A blush started to sweep up Sydney's cheeks once again, but he could see that this time she mastered it beautifully. Her hot gaze singed his chest as she smiled slowly. "What do you taste like, Ellis?" Sydney's fingers teased their way through the scattering of curls arrowing their way down his chest.

He captured her hand just as it reached the waistband of his boxers. "I'm going to taste like humiliation if you go any lower." His arousal was painfully obvious. If she so much as touched him, he was going to embarrass himself beyond belief.

He had wanted their first time together to be slow and sweet. He wanted to touch, taste and savor every inch of her body and make her feel things she had never thought possible. When he had to return home, he wanted to leave with Sydney knowing she had been loved, and loved well.

Now he wasn't even sure if he could last until they made it to the bed. The little prologue to their loving that had taken place in the den had nearly done him in. He had held her and watched as she had climaxed at his touch. He thought it was the most beautiful thing he had ever seen. The next time she climaxed, he not only wanted to be deep inside her, he wanted to be with her all the way.

If he had any hope of achieving that goal, he had better do something about it, and fast. Ellis reached for the belt on her robe and gently tugged.

Sydney stood still as the robe gaped and slipped farther off her shoulders.

He swallowed hard as his gaze followed the pale line of skin from between her breasts to the dark nest of curls at the junction of her thighs. The air in his lungs turned blistering as he forgot to breathe.

Sydney lowered her hands and shrugged.

The robe slid to her feet like a white puffy cloud. He knew she was beautiful, he just hadn't realized how beautiful. Sydney looked like an angel. Twin mounds with jutting pink nipples begged for his mouth. A waist, so slim he could span it with his hands, pleaded for his touch. Legs that were both long and curved ended in rounded hips. And the thatch of dark curls guarding her secrets implored him to explore farther.

He reached out and traced her collarbone with the tip of one of his fingers. "You're beautiful, Sydney." He felt her tremble beneath his touch and smiled. This time he knew she shook with desire. He could see it in her eyes.

Eyes that were normally soft green burned with a fire as hot as his own. Sydney wanted him. His finger trailed lower and slowly circled one of her protruding nipples.

Sydney swayed toward him and he needed no further response. She was his. With a quick movement he gathered her up into his arms and carried her to the bed. The comforter was swept onto the floor before he lay her across the mattress.

Sydney held out her arms to him and softly whispered, "Please."

He shook his head and stepped away from her tempting arms. "Soon." Slowly he pulled a foil packet from his pocket and tossed it onto the bed before pushing down his boxers and stepping out of them. He couldn't afford for her to touch him now. He would never last. He was beyond aching.

Sydney shivered as he placed a kiss on the inside of her ankle. She reached for him, her voice filled with the same aching quality that he was feeling. "Ellis, please."

His mouth caressed her calf and teased the sensitive spot behind her knee. He gave her other leg the same slow treatment before kissing his way up her trembling thighs.

Strong fingers pulled at his shoulders, forcing him to move away from his intended target. He didn't mind. There would be other opportunities later for that particular kind of loving. His fingers trailed up the inside of her thigh as he kissed his way to the taut peaks of her breasts. His teeth lightly nipped a tight bud the same instant his finger slipped deep inside her moist and welcoming opening.

Sydney arched her hips upward, pressing against his hand. The harsh quality of her breathing told him what he already knew. He released her and reached for the foil pack he had tossed onto the bed. "You're ready for me, aren't you?"

"I've been ready." Sydney reached for him, only he was quicker. He grabbed her hand and avoided her touch. Sydney glanced at their clasped hands and then at his arousal already sheathed in protection. "Why?"

"If you touch me, Syd, it's all over before it even begins." He moved up her body, letting her breasts press against his chest. Berry-hard peaks poked their way into the hair covering his chest.

The tip of his arousal pressed against her slick opening and she immediately wrapped her legs around his hips, dragging a low and powerful groan through his body.

He felt himself sinking into her warmth and captured her mouth as he lost the battle against his control and plunged as deep as she could take him. The tight hot walls cradling his shaft sent him higher and higher. He pulled back and plunged again.

Sydney matched his every thrust, sending him to the brink. He might be losing the battle but he'd be damned before he'd lose the war. He broke the kiss and gazed down into her flushed face. "Open your eyes, love."

Eyes brighter than emeralds stared up at him. "Ellis?"

He pumped his hips faster and ground his teeth. He could see how close she was to the brink by looking in her eyes. She was teetering precariously over the abyss with him. He refused to go without her. He needed her with him.

"I..."

"Shh...I know." He thrust harder and prayed for strength. He knew what was holding her back, fear of the unknown. He couldn't blame her. This wasn't like the prologue in the den. This was something else. He had never experienced this deep-seated need before. He didn't understand it, all he knew was Sydney had to be with him when he reached the center of the vortex pulling him in.

Ellis slipped his hand in between their bodies and cupped her breast. The rigid nub pressed against his fingers and he gave it a gentle squeeze as he thrust deeply once again. He saw Sydney's climax in her eyes before he felt it in her body.

As she shattered beneath him, he gave one last thrust and allowed the maelstrom to pull him over the edge.

Chapter 9

It was late the following afternoon when Sydney glanced over at Trevor and grinned. "Are you sure you haven't done this before?" Ellis's son was helping her unload a cart of red geraniums onto a table in one of the greenhouses connected to the store. His little hands were positioning each plastic pot just so.

Trevor shyly shook his head and placed another plant onto the table. "What are these called again?"

"Geraniums." She knew he was trying to memorize the names of some of the plants so he could impress his father with all his newfound knowledge. "If you get stuck later trying to remember the names, I'll help you out."

She reached for another tray, packed with fifteen blooming plants, from the top of the cart, and transferred them to the middle of the table. The tables were too wide for Trevor to reach the middle, so he was doing the rows closest to the edge. The huge cart that was used to transfer the plants from the back greenhouses, which were off-limits to the customers, to the greenhouses connected to the store was nearly empty already.

Trevor glanced at the table behind them. "They're pansies, right?"

"Right." She couldn't help but be impressed. Trevor was indeed one very smart little boy who picked things up quickly. The sweet yellow and purple faces of hundreds of pansies nearly overflowed the table. Within the next week or so the weather would be warm enough to plant the bright flowers outside. "Next week, if you're still here, maybe you would like to help me plant some of them around the house." Her mother's gardens were mostly perennials but she had peppered them with a few of her favorite annuals. Pansies had been one of her mother's favorites.

"Really?" Trevor's dark eyes grew wide with excitement.

"Really." She reached out and ruffled the top of his head. She had seen Ellis do the same gesture and had wondered at its significance. Now she knew. Touching Trevor, even if it was only the top of his head, made her feel as if they had connected on some level. By the gleam of interest still sparkling in his eyes, Trevor appeared to be interested in gardening. Maybe it was the idea of digging in the dirt that sparked that gleam, but that was okay too. Every gardener loved to dig in the dirt. "I'm sure your dad won't mind if you get a bit dirty."

She hoped that was correct. Over lunch, Ellis had seemed a little leery of allowing her to bring Trevor to work. She could understand his overprotective attitude.

If she had a critically ill child, she would probably never let him out of her sight. It had been the bored expression on Trevor's face that made her combat Ellis's unease with assurances of his son's safety.

Trevor had watched cartoons and played with his animals the entire morning while Ellis and her father pored over the yearbooks she had brought down from the attic before she left for work. The little boy had jumped at the chance to spend the afternoon at the nursery helping out. She had enjoyed the pint-size company and the hundreds of questions that came with him.

As for the boy's father, she didn't know what to think. Ellis had her spinning so fast she still hadn't had time to catch her breath. She didn't *want* to catch her breath. She wanted to feel his touch again.

Making love with Ellis last night, not once but twice, had been the most incredible experience of her life. There was no other way to describe it. She didn't want to describe it. She wanted to experience it again.

Sometime before dawn she had fallen asleep in Ellis's arms only to wake up alone to the shrilling of her alarm clock. The sheets had still been warm from where his body had lain, but he was gone. She had missed his warmth, but she had understood his reasons. There were two reasons, and they both had names—Thomas and Trevor.

The fact that she had taken a lover while living under her father's roof told her how desperately she had wanted Ellis. She had never so much as kissed a boy while in her father's house. Ellis had been the first, and they had done a heck of a lot more than just kiss.

Her father respected her as an adult and hadn't been too happy with her when she had given up her apartment to move back home to be with him after the accident. Thomas had insisted that she needed privacy and independence. She had assured him she wasn't about to give up either and that they would both have some adjusting to do.

Taking a lover to her bed hadn't been in her plans, but that was what she had done. Ellis was now her lover.

She wasn't going to change that fact. She couldn't even if she had wanted to. What was done, was done, but it didn't mean she had to flaunt their relationship in front of her father. They could be discreet.

She didn't believe in carrying around a bag full of regrets through life. The desire that flared between herself and Ellis had to be explored. She didn't have one regret. Well...maybe one. She was dying to know what it would have felt like if Ellis would have...

"Here you two are." Ellis reached out and swung a grinning Trevor up into his arms. "I've been looking all over for you both."

The sensual vision that had been filling her head erupted into a thousand shattering pieces. The object of her fantasy was standing less than two feet away with a five-year-old boy clinging to his neck. This was Ellis the father, not Ellis the lover from last night.

He gave her a smile that curled her toes and dropped her stomach down to her knees. Maybe she was wrong about that. His smile had *lover* written all over it. She was thankful that none of her employees were in the greenhouse to see that smile. They would have known what their employer had been up to in the middle of the night.

She reached for another tray loaded with plants and busied herself arranging them onto the middle of the table. "Trevor and I are getting out the first bunch of geraniums for the year."

"First bunch?" Ellis glanced at the other three tables overflowing with white and pink geraniums. "It looks like you have enough here to beautify every house in Coalsburg."

"This will be picked nearly bare the first really nice weekend we get." She placed the empty tray back onto the cart and reached for the last full tray of plants. "Trevor's been such a big help."

Trevor scampered out of his father's arms and reached for another plant. "I did all the outside ones myself." Little fingers carefully placed the pot next to the last one he had set out.

"You did!" Ellis appeared suitably impressed. "When we go back home, how about if we take some of these plants with us? I think they might look real nice by the front door. What do you think, Trev?"

Trevor positioned his last plant before answering. "Wayne won't let me plant them." Big brown eyes stared up at her as if seeking her help. "Sydney said I could help her plant some around her house."

"Yes, I did." She placed a hand on Trevor's shoulder to reassure the boy that she hadn't changed her mind. "If you and Trevor are still here in another week or so when the danger of frost has passed, I told him he could help me in the gardens at home." She met Ellis's gaze head-on. "If that's okay with you, that is."

"It's fine by me." Ellis took the tray Trevor had just emptied and placed it on top of the other trays. "Maybe I could lend a hand and get some tips from a professional. I didn't realize Trev would be interested in flowers."

"It's not the flowers so much." She pushed the cart back out onto the wider center aisle. "It's the digging in the dirt that has him so excited about gardening." Trevor hopped onto the front of the cart as she carefully pushed it toward the doors. It was the game they had been playing all afternoon. She pushed, Trevor rode.

She glanced at Ellis as he automatically started to follow them. "Who's Wayne?" She wanted to know not only who he was, but why he wouldn't let Trevor dig in the garden.

"Wayne's the man I hired to take care of the lawn. He cuts the grass, rakes leaves and mulches." Ellis shrugged his shoulder as if he had never really given any serious thought to Wayne or the gardens at his house. "You know, stuff like that."

She frowned. *Stuff like that.* What in the world did that mean? "What kind of flowers do you have at home?" She glanced at Trevor to make sure he was holding on tight and wasn't in any danger of falling.

"Flowers?" Ellis held open the door as she pushed the cart outside and toward the greenhouse nurturing all the geraniums. "We don't have any flowers."

"You don't have any gardens?" What kind of house did Ellis and Trevor live in? She had imagined Ellis living in some great big modern home filled with expensive furniture to match his expensive car.

"Of course we have gardens." Ellis walked beside her and watched his son, who was glancing around in total awe.

"Well, if you don't have flowers, what's in them?" She stopped in front of a greenhouse and Ellis graciously opened the door.

"I don't know." Ellis followed her into the greenhouse. "Bushes and—" his arms waved into the air as if he was going to pluck the answer from the sky "—green things."

She had to duck her head to keep from laughing. Ellis had *green things* in his gardens. "I see."

"Don't you dare laugh."

She bit her lower lip and tried picturing something sad. She pictured Ellis's fancy house surrounded by gardens without a single flower in them. The *green things* sprouting were little martians with big heads and six round glowing eyes. She couldn't hold it in a minute longer. She burst out laughing.

"Sydney," Ellis warned as he took a step closer.

"I'm sorry." She glanced at his face and saw the smile twitching at the corner of his mouth. "It's just that I've never seen a house without at least one flower in the yard somewhere."

"We have flowers." Trevor hopped off the cart now that she had stopped pushing. "They're pretty yellow ones."

"We do?" Ellis looked perplexed.

"Do you know their names?" Trevor had picked up on quite a few names this afternoon. Maybe he knew what kind of flowers Ellis obviously couldn't remember owning.

"Yep, Wayne told me what kind they are."

"What kind are they?" she asked.

"Damn dandelions." Trevor appeared quite pleased with himself. "Wayne calls them damn dandelions. I remember because I like lions, but they don't look like lions."

Sydney tried to cover her laugh with a cough and failed miserably. Ellis seemed to be having the same trouble. "They're just dandelions, Trevor, and they aren't a flower. They're weeds."

Ellis reached for Trevor's hand. "I think it's time I took you back to the house so Sydney can get some work done around here."

Trevor looked ready to cry. "But, Dad..."

"I'm sorry, Trev, but you need to take a bath before we go out."

She glanced at the dirt smearing the front of Trevor's jacket and hands. A little dirt never hurt anyone. "Out? Where are you two going?" Hopefully it was someplace Trevor would like.

"It's not just the two of us, it's the four of us." Ellis smiled at his son. "Thomas wants to go out to eat, so you need a bath before dinner tonight."

"My father wants to go out to eat?" First Thomas was visiting his friends at the police station, and now he was going out for dinner: Thomas hadn't eaten in public since the accident. When she had suggested going out to eat months ago, he had declared he wasn't going to be someone's evening entertainment. When his frustrated jabbing at the plate to locate his food had settled down to a gentle probing, he had finally decided to eat something once in a while. And since Ellis's arrival, her father's appetite had improved tremendously.

"There's a steak house about twenty minutes away that's owned by a guy who went to school with my mother. Thomas called him and he said to stop in tonight and he'd not only guarantee a great meal, but he'd answer any questions your father might have."

"Do you mean Josh's Place?"

"That's the name. Josh has us down for reservations at seven."

She couldn't detect any hope in Ellis's eyes, only curiosity. "Josh's Place has the best steaks in the county." She wondered if her father wanted to talk to the restaurateur for information or if he suspected that Josh might be Ellis's father. Tonight would tell.

She smiled at Trevor, who was still holding his father's hand. "You go ahead home with your dad and get ready. I'll be there as soon as we close." She glanced at her watch and frowned. Where had the afternoon gone? It was nearly closing time. "Tomorrow if you want to help, we can start putting out some of the asters and marigolds."

"Can I, Dad, please?"

"As long as it's okay with Sydney." Ellis gave her a smile that not only thanked her for being so nice to Trevor, but promised a sweet reward later. "Let's get going so you'll have plenty of time to play in the tub. Say goodbye and thank-you to Sydney."

Trevor smiled at her. "Thank you and goodbye."

"You're welcome and I'll see you in a little while." She gave Ellis a look that she hoped conveyed what she'd be doing with *him* in a little while.

Ellis's answering smile told her he got her message, loud and clear. "Come on, Trev. On the way home I think it's time we had a man-to-man talk on appropriate language."

She watched as father and son walked out of the greenhouse and toward the path that would lead them back to the house. One day she would have to watch them walk out of her life, but not today. Not yet.

Josh was a big robust man who looked as though he should have been a cattle rancher out in Montana someplace. Instead, he was born, raised and still lived in Coalsburg. The farthest he had ever been was Atlantic City, New Jersey, and the only thing he knew about cattle was how to cook them.

Josh didn't remember a whole lot about Catherine Carlisle. He remembered her parents more because his family had been members of their church.

"Sorry, Tom, but I can't really remember too much about Cathy. She didn't hang out with the gang. Her parents wouldn't allow her to do anything that wasn't related to the church." Josh took a sip of his beer as the waitress cleared the table of the empty dishes. "She had some strict parents. Both of them used to frighten the living tar out of me. Preached about H E double L and damnation all the time." Josh smiled at Trevor, who was busy coloring another kiddie paper place mat the waitress had brought him.

Sydney knew Josh was toning down his language for Trevor's sake, even though the boy seemed totally disinterested in the conversation. It had been agreed upon that Thomas wouldn't mention that Ellis was Cathy's son unless it became necessary. Who Ellis really was would be circulating around town soon enough. Pete, Harvey and John down at the police station already knew, and she was sure the news was getting out and about. If Josh didn't connect Ellis to Catherine, then they weren't going to do it for him. They wanted honest answers. Josh might hold back some information or speculation out of respect for the departed Catherine.

And under no circumstance was Thomas to mention Trevor's illness and the reason for all the questions.

She glanced at Ellis to see how he was holding up. He seemed more interested in his coffee than in what

Josh was saying, though she knew he was listening carefully.

"Do you remember when she left town?" Thomas seemed to relax more now that dinner was done and the table in front of him was cleared.

"I don't remember when she left, but I remember the stink her parents put up." Josh sadly shook his head.

"Her parents were concerned for her safety?" Ellis suddenly appeared interested.

"Can't say that they were." Josh took another sip of his beer. "Her father preached for months about disobedience of children and breaking of the Commandments, especially the one about obeying thy father and mother. Her mother used to glare around the congregation and claim her daughter had been seduced away by the devil." Josh drained the rest of his glass. "Me, I figured the poor girl couldn't take any more and just split. Why you want to know about Cathy anyway?"

"Let's just say I'm curious." Thomas rubbed his chin with his thumb. "Do you remember if she was dating anyone back then?"

Josh shook his head. "Cathy didn't date anyone. She wasn't allowed. Quite a few of the guys asked her out, but she never went with any of them."

"What about the prom?" Sydney couldn't sit quietly by and watch Trevor's only hope vanish before her eyes. Someone had to have some idea about who Cathy had been seeing. She hadn't gotten pregnant all on her own. "Surely she had to have gone to her senior prom."

"Afraid not."

"Were you one of the guys who asked her out?" Ellis was staring directly at Josh.

Sydney glanced between the two men and couldn't imagine them being father and son.

Josh chuckled and shook his head. "You obviously never met my wife, Paula. We've been together since we were fifteen. Paula would have cut my...ah...ears off if I so much as thought about asking out another girl."

Thomas chuckled along with Josh. "How is Paula and the family?"

"Good, good. Paula's out in Pittsburgh with Bethany, our youngest of six daughters. Bethany just had her first baby last week, another granddaughter." Josh shook his head in wonder. "That makes our eleventh grandchild, and not a grandson among them. A man can get tired of buying pink frilly dresses and dolls." A big grin split his face. "But they sure are cute when you hold them."

Josh nodded to a waitress who was trying to get his attention. "I've got to go see what the problem is now." He laid a big hand on Thomas's forearm and gave it a gentle squeeze as he stood up. "It's sure good to see you getting out and about now, Tom. Don't make yourself so scarce in the future."

"Thanks." Thomas seemed moved by Josh's words.

Josh released her father's arm and smiled at her and Ellis. "It's good to see you too, Sydney. I don't know what all the questions about Cathy have been about, but I do know one thing. If she had a secret boyfriend, the boy had to be either incredibly stupid or incredibly brave. Her parents would have roasted him in Hades for just talking to her."

Sydney watched as Josh disappeared into the kitchen. He hadn't been able to shed any light on who Ellis's father might be. The only thing he had done was confirm what she had been beginning to suspect. Cathy's parents, Ellis's grandparents, hadn't been very supportive. They were dominating, severe and uncompromising. No wonder poor Cathy had fled when she had discovered she was pregnant.

"Well, that was interesting," Thomas said to no one in particular.

"What was so interesting about it?" Ellis finished his coffee. "He didn't say anything that we didn't know before."

"He confirmed what I was beginning to suspect. Your parents hid Cathy's liaison very well. Too well, in fact." Thomas's thumb continued its journey back and forth over his jaw. "I was away at Penn State during Cathy's last year in high school. I got home for summer vacation right before she graduated. I didn't remember her having a boyfriend, but it was possible I might not have heard about it."

"I still don't see what's so interesting?" Ellis looked discouraged.

"I think we might be looking in the wrong place. I don't think her *friend* was in high school with her."

"What makes you think that, Dad?" She gave Trevor a curious glance, to see if he had finally started to pay attention to the conversation. He hadn't. He reached for a blue crayon and started to color in the sky on his picture.

"I don't think they could have kept it such a secret in front of the whole school. One thing I have learned in all my years of police work is that high-school students don't keep secrets."

"What secret?" Trevor was done with the picture and

his attention was finally drawn to the adult conversation at the table.

Thomas looked startled, as if he had forgotten about Trevor's presence. Ellis looked guilty. She took pity on them both and answered Trevor's question. "The secret is dessert." Trevor didn't need to know that they had been discussing his grandparents' affair.

"Dessert?" Trevor appeared quite interested now. "What kind of dessert?"

She leaned in closer and whispered, "Do you like chocolate cake?"

Trevor licked his lips and nodded.

She forced herself not to smile. "I happen to know that this place has the best chocolate cake in the whole town."

"Really?" Trevor looked around the room at the other diners.

"Really." She moved in closer and kept her voice low. "But there's one thing you have to do when you order it."

"What?"

"You have to ask for a glass of milk with it." She licked her own lips and rolled her eyes, causing Trevor to giggle. "Trust me on this one, Trev, it just doesn't taste the same without the milk."

Trevor nodded his head, folded his hands in front of him and gave the outward appearance of being a little angel. His gaze was glued to the waitress two tables away.

Ellis chuckled and motioned for the waitress. "What are we waiting for? Let's order some chocolate cake."

"Milk too, Dad." Trevor grinned at Sydney. "Don't forget the milk."

Sydney glanced across the table and met Ellis's gaze. There was a fire burning in the depth of his eyes that had nothing to do with chocolate cake. That fire was directed solely at her and it not only warmed her blood, it warmed her heart.

She had to swallow twice before she could manage to say any words at all. Then she only managed a foolish, "Yeah, Ellis, don't forget the milk."

Ellis knew he was in trouble. Deep trouble.

He pulled the blanket up higher and tucked it under Trevor's chin and around a sad-looking Winnie-the-Pooh who was sharing a corner of his son's pillow. Trevor had fallen asleep on the way home from the restaurant and he had barely stirred when Ellis had carried him upstairs and changed him into his pajamas.

Trevor was exhausted, but it was a good kind of tired. It hadn't been caused by endless rounds to doctors and batteries of tests. His son was tired from working at the nursery with Sydney. The fresh spring air and the excitement of helping out had put a rosy glow into Trevor's usually pale cheeks. Dinner out had furthered the excitement and the huge slice of chocolate cake the waitress had placed before him had done him in. Trevor had done a remarkable job of trying to finish off the entire slice.

Ellis brushed back a lock of his son's hair and gently kissed his forehead. He loved Trevor beyond life itself and would do anything to try to save him. Right now he didn't know if he was doing the right thing or not. The odds were heavily stacked against them.

He felt sleazy and disrespectful poking around in his mother's past. He knew there had to be a very good reason she never told him about his grandparents. The more he heard about his mother's parents, the more he understood why she had chosen to raise him on her own. He was also beginning to understand why his mother never stepped foot into a church the whole time he had been growing up. The picture he was getting about her childhood wasn't pretty. But that still didn't explain why she had named Thomas St. Claire as his father.

He had DNA proof that Thomas wasn't his father, and that his mother had lied. Somewhere out there was his biological father, if the man was still alive. There was no guarantee that the man would be in good physical condition if they did locate him. The odds weren't even that good that his father would still be in town.

Then there was the fact that this man would have to step forward and claim him as his son, after thirty-three years of silence. Then this fatherhood dropout would have to agree to be tested. When Ellis added on top of all those insurmountable odds that there would have to be a match, the whole thing seemed just about hopeless.

If all that wasn't depressing enough, he had come to care for a woman—really care—at the worst possible time of his life. Just as Trevor didn't deserve this disease, Sydney, poor innocent Sydney, surely didn't deserve all the emotional baggage Ellis would be bringing into any relationship they might have.

But when he had glanced across the table at her in the restaurant, he had known he couldn't walk away from her. His heart wouldn't let him. Just as his heart wouldn't let him give up on Trevor. There was a miracle out there with his son's name on it. All he had to do was search hard enough and he would find it. Bringing

Trevor to Coalsburg showed him just how far he was willing to search.

He reached out and turned on his son's night-light by the side of the bed. He never wanted Trevor to wake to total darkness. His son might not be afraid of the dark, but *he* was, and with good reason. A couple of nights he had awoken in total darkness and was seized with such fright that he had panicked uncontrollably until he had reached his son's bed. He knew that if Trevor succumbed to the disease invading his body, the darkness would control the rest of his life.

He felt his fingers tremble as they reached out and lightly caressed his son's soft cheek. "I won't allow the darkness to touch you, Trev, I promise." He closed his eyes and silently prayed to the God his mother had shunned. No brilliant light or heavenly trumpets answered, but he did feel the strength to go back downstairs and see what else Thomas might have come up with.

Thomas had been awfully quiet both during dessert and the drive home. The man had been thinking, and thinking hard. Maybe he had come up with a new plan to locate Trevor's grandfather. If not, the trip downstairs wouldn't be wasted. Sydney was down there. He needed to see her and there lay his other problem—his growing feelings for this woman.

He had been handling Trevor's illness on his own, with the support and concern of Rita, his employees and his small circle of friends. Their support had always been enough to see him through whatever rough patch he had been facing. Now it wasn't enough anymore. He needed someone to lean on, someone to share this terrible ache within his heart. He needed Sydney.

Ellis left the bedroom door slightly ajar before heading down the stairs and for the den. Thomas was in his usual chair and, also as usual, Sydney was curled up at the end of the sofa. But tonight, instead of poring over paperwork, she was leafing through a magazine. He stepped quietly into the room and took a seat at the other end of the couch.

Thomas turned his head in his direction. "Did you get Trevor settled in for the night?"

"He never woke back up. He mumbled a couple of words about chocolate cake and dandelions, but nothing made much sense."

Thomas frowned. "We didn't tire him out too much today, did we?"

"No, Trevor's fine. It was just a busy day for him, that's all." He slid closer to Sydney and held out his hand. He wanted to touch her. Today had been a lesson in futility. He had only managed to sneak in two kisses since leaving her bed before dawn. Finding her without Thomas around had been easy. Finding her without Trevor around was proving impossible.

Sydney tossed the magazine back onto the coffee table and reached for his hand. "He did a pretty good job of trying to polish off that slice of chocolate cake."

"Can't blame the boy there," Thomas said. "It was great cake."

"Yes, it was." He squeezed her fingers and smiled a promise of things to come. Last night had only been an appetizer where Sydney was concerned. Tonight he wanted the main course.

"I've been giving this a lot of thought, Ellis," Thomas said as he made himself more comfortable in the chair. "I think we should continue going through the yearbooks eliminating everyone we can, but I also want to pursue a new avenue."

"What avenue's that?" He knew Thomas had been hatching another plan.

"The church." Thomas's thumb rubbed at his jaw. "I think her parents' church might hold the key. Everyone we've talked to so far mentioned that Cathy was only allowed to do things that were church related. It stands to reason she would have spent quite a lot of hours not only at the church, but with some of its members."

"That's true, Dad." Sydney squeezed his hand lightly. "Maybe someone from the church would remember who she might have been spending a lot of time with."

Ellis felt his own excitement level rise a notch in response to Sydney's. "How are we going to find out who went to that particular church thirty-three years ago?"

"Membership records. All churches keep membership records. All we have to do is look up the right year." Thomas rubbed his hands together as if the matter was settled. "First thing tomorrow morning we go to the church and look up the records." Thomas stood up, stretched and yawned. "Ellis, I'm going to need your eyes again."

"No problem." He was curious about the church that both his grandparents and mother had gone to. Maybe there would be some photographs of his grandparents or even one of a young Catherine Carlisle.

"Drop Trevor off at the nursery on the way." Sydney seemed to be watching her father as he made his way toward the door. "I think he enjoyed himself immensely today and all the employees fell in love with him."

Ellis sighed. Trevor was his son, his responsibility. He

didn't want to burden Sydney with watching him all morning long. Five-year-old boys contained nothing but energy and questions, especially after they had a good night's sleep. "Trevor can come with us, Sydney."

"I don't mind, Ellis. Trevor's such a big help and I don't know of one little boy who would want to spend the entire morning poring over old membership records in some stuffy church office."

"She has a point there, Ellis," Thomas said. "We'll pick Trevor up when we're done at the church and take him into town with us. I'd bet he would love to see the inside of the police station."

He knew when he was beat. Between Thomas and Sydney he didn't have a chance. "Okay, but if he becomes too much for you, Sydney, I want you to call me. I'll give you my cell-phone number."

"Good. Now that's settled I'm heading for bed myself," Thomas said. "I'm an old man and I need my beauty sleep. Good night, you two."

"Good night, Thomas."

"Night, Dad." Sydney smiled and scooted closer to Ellis as her father walked out of the room. They listened in silence as Thomas made his way up the stairs and then closed his bedroom door. Delicate fingers that were capable of planting begonias or driving him to the brink of ecstasy started to toy with the buttons on his shirt. "Alone at last."

He captured her hand before she got to the bottom button on his shirt, and every ounce of control he possessed went flying out the window. "You're a wicked women, Sydney St. Claire."

Sydney smiled a devilish grin as she brought her mouth closer. Temptingly close. "You have no idea."

He laughingly hauled her the rest of the way into his arms. "Show me how wicked you can be."

Sydney wrapped her arms around his neck and proceeded to do exactly that.

Chapter 10

Ellis glanced at his jailbird son, who was peering at him from behind thick iron bars, and grinned. Trevor waved and grinned back. The visit to the police station was a hit with Trevor, at least. As for Thomas, the jury was still out on that one.

Pete and Harvey were back, and this time they brought Harvey's younger brother, Paul, and two other men who Ellis had heard Thomas mention in conversation. He had always been under the impression that females were the ones who knew everyone and, usually, everyone's business. He was wrong. He was most humbly wrong. He should go out immediately and offer every woman who crossed his path a sincere and heartfelt apology.

Between Thomas, the two officers and the other five men, there wasn't a person, place or thing within a fifty-mile radius that wasn't known. Catherine Carlisle's life was open for discussion, at least the part of her life anyone could remember. Apparently his mother could have doubled as a wallflower.

Paul did remember asking her out once during their senior year. The young Catherine had politely declined, saying her parents wouldn't allow her to date. Though Paul had honestly seemed embarrassed about telling Ellis he had asked his mother out, he had respectfully told him that Catherine had been cute, in a different sort of way. She hadn't been allowed to wear the same type of clothes that the other girls wore. Makeup was also forbidden, and her long brown hair had always been severely pulled back away from her face.

"Hey, Charlie," Paul said, "you were in our class. Don't you remember anything about Cathy?"

Charlie, a bald man with a belly that hung over his belt, seemed startled by the question. "She was in a couple of my classes, but I don't really remember too much about her at school. She was always quiet and sat at the back of the room." Charlie gave a shrug. "She always got good grades and wore white blouses."

"White blouses?" He couldn't prevent himself from asking. He couldn't ever remember seeing his mother in a white blouse.

"Yeah, you know, the kind that buttons down the front. She wore one to school every day."

"That's right, she did," Paul said.

Charlie beamed as if he had just solved the energy problems of the world. "Most of the time she wore them to church too, but sometimes she wore other colors."

"You went to church with her, Charlie?" Thomas sat up a little straighter.

"Every Sunday." Charlie, clearly warming to the idea

of being the center of attention, leaned back against a file cabinet and balanced his chair on its back two legs. "We were in the same bible-study class on Monday nights and youth group together on Friday nights."

"You spent a lot of time with my mother, didn't you?" He looked at Charlie with renewed interest. Was it possible...?

Charlie gave a rough laugh that sounded like a bark. "I spent time in the same places as your mother, Ellis, but I was never with her. She didn't hang around anyone except for her parents and a few of the deacons and elders."

Ellis saw Thomas tilt his head in his direction, but he was already ahead of the man. He had pulled out the list of members of his grandparents' church and was skimming the names of the four deacons and the four elders. "Do you remember which deacons or elders in particular?"

"She liked Hal Remson."

"She did?" Hal Remson had been the head elder at the time. Maybe they were finally getting somewhere.

"Scratch that one, Ellis." Thomas sadly shook his head. "Hal Remson must had been what...eighty-three, eighty-four at the time. Everyone fawned over Hal. Every year the church had to take up a separate collection to buy him a new pair of dentures. Hal kept losing them."

"Yeah," remembered Charlie, "he used to have this brass walking stick."

"He did have an eye for the ladies," Harvey said.

"He wore the same suit to church for twenty years, and he never missed a Sunday." Charlie placed both his hands behind his head and stared up at the ceiling. "Yes sir, Cathy was constantly fluttering at his side. Come to think of it, so was every other woman in that church. Hal loved all that attention. Sure do miss the old coot." Charlie looked over at Harvey. "He passed away what, twenty years ago?"

"More like twenty-four."

Ellis frowned at the list in his hand. It was hopeless. They were never going to discover who his father was. Charlie had said something about elders and deacons. Maybe reading the list of names out loud would jog Charlie's memory. "What about Franklin Smythe?"

Charlie shook his head as Ellis read down the list. He had just read the last name when Charlie finally showed some interest. "Repeat that one."

"Arthur Graystone."

"Mayor Graystone?" Harvey seemed startled. "I didn't realize that he was a member of the Methodist church back then. He's some bigwig over at the Lutheran church now."

Ellis glanced back down at the paper in his hand. "He was a deacon at the Methodist church thirty-three years ago." He skimmed the list of active members. "He and his wife, Sophie, were both members."

Thomas rubbed at his jaw. "That's right. He and Sophie got married in the Methodist church when I was still in high school. Sophie's father was the richest man in town and she was his only child. They acted like it was the wedding of the century. Nearly the whole town was invited and no expense was spared. I remember thinking that the whole thing was a terrible waste of money."

Ellis glanced away from Thomas and over at Charlie.

"Do you remember seeing Catherine with Arthur Graystone?"

"Well, sure, they were together a lot because he was always at the church and so was she." Charlie leaned forward and his chair finally rested on all fours. "They used to whisper a lot."

"Whisper?" He felt his heart skip a beat. "What do you mean by whisper?"

"I don't know." Charlie shrugged. "You know, whisper."

"Do you mean they used to whisper because they were in church?" asked Thomas. "Like most people whisper in the library?"

"Naw, not that kind of whispering. They used to whisper when they thought no one was watching."

Thomas tilted his head in Ellis's direction. "Did it appear as if they were hiding something?"

"I can't remember," Charlie said. "All I can recall is seeing them whispering."

"I saw them together once," Harvey said.

"You did? Why didn't you say so?" demanded Thomas.

"I didn't think anything of it. They were out on Turkey Run Road at that roadside stand that was set up every year. They were buying pumpkins, lots of little pumpkins. I guess for the Sunday school or something."

Ellis slowly folded the list and slipped it into his pocket. Great, his mother bought pumpkins for kids in the Sunday school in the company of a member of her church and he was ready to call Arthur Graystone Dad. It just confirmed how desperate he had become. A simple outing and he was picturing his mother and some old married deacon of the church doing the wild thing in the back seat of some car surrounded by dozens of pumpkins.

Suddenly he was disgusted with himself. His mother might have lied on his birth certificate as to the identity of his father, but she didn't deserve his lascivious mind conjuring up those visions. Catherine Carlisle had been a decent, loving mother.

"I want to thank you gentlemen for traveling down memory lane for me," Ellis said. "If any of you remember anything more concrete than a pumpkin-buying expedition, I can be reached at Thomas's house for the next several days." He needed to get out of there before he fell apart. As his mother would have said, he was chasing the fog.

When he was a little boy, his mother used to take him to a park near where they lived. There had been a small creek running through the park and he loved going first thing in the morning when they had the entire place to themselves. The fog rising off the creek used to fascinate him and he used to run around trying to catch it in his little hands. Whenever he thought he had captured a fistful, he had opened his hand, only to discover the fog wasn't there.

The same disappointment that had besieged him then was surrounding him now. He needed to see Sydney. He needed to hold her and love her. Sydney had a magical way of turning his disappointments into hope. He needed that hope now more than ever.

He motioned for Trevor to come out of the cell as he reached for Thomas's hand to give him his cane. It was time to leave. There were no answers here today.

As Ellis drove to the St. Claire home three days later, he checked the rearview mirror, to make sure no one was behind him, and then applied the brakes and stopped in the middle of the street. The slight rise in the road gave him the perfect view of both the nursery and the St. Claire home. The sun was a fiery red ball, bathing the small valley in fading sunlight. The view brought a lump to his throat. As ridiculous as it sounded, he felt as if he was coming home.

His home was ninety-six miles away. At least his *house* was ninety-six miles away. But everything that was important to him was here. Trevor, Sydney, Thomas. The only one back at his house was Rita, and she wasn't even there right now. He had sent her on a well-earned, long-overdue vacation to visit her daughter and her real grandchildren. Rita hadn't left his or Trevor's side since the initial diagnosis last summer.

He never should have agreed to the business trip he had just taken. Three days and two nights away from Trevor and Sydney were too long. If it hadn't been for Sydney's gentle persuading, he never would have gone, no matter how important it had been to the company. He had excellent employees and he could name four people off the top of his head who could have handled the situation without breaking a sweat.

The negotiations in Atlanta had been a tension-filled two days with facts and figures pouring out of fax machines and sliding across mahogany tables worth more than what most people made in a year. There had been lunches, dinners, early-morning conference calls and endless hours of sitting in his solitary hotel room with his laptop up and running in front of him. The competition had been fierce but One If By Land had toppled them all. They had signed the contract over lunch.

The whole time everyone had been shaking on the deal, he had been thinking of Trevor and Sydney. He had been informed that his composure during the frantic dealing against other carriers had won him the contract. He hadn't bothered to tell his newest client that it wasn't so much composure as it was perspective. Yes, he had wanted the contract, and had wanted it badly. But he also knew that if he didn't get it, life would go on. O.I.B.L. trucks would still roll across endless highways. Trevor's illness had given him new priorities, both in business and in his life. What was a lost contract when he was losing his son?

In the week since he had brought Trevor out to the country, he had been discovering quite a bit about his son and himself. The only thing he hadn't been able to discover was who had gotten his mother pregnant and then abandoned her. His calls home both nights he had been away hadn't been encouraging in that department. Thomas had been using Sydney's eyes and talking to more people than a politician during an election year. If he hadn't checked and rechecked all the dates himself, he would have sworn his mother couldn't have been four months pregnant when she left Coalsburg.

It took two people to create a baby, and so far the most incriminating thing his mother had done was to buy a bunch of pumpkins. He had heard of babies coming from cabbage patches, but never pumpkin patches.

With an effort, he pulled his troubled thoughts away from the frustrating task of locating his father, and back onto the more pleasant topic of Sydney and his son. His gaze skimmed over the nursery below. It was already closed for the night. The parking lot out in front of the main building was empty and the security lights were lit. In the three days he had been gone, changes had occurred. Clusters of daffodils and hyacinths were now blooming. The grass was turning a deep shade of green and would be needing to be mowed soon. Dozens of trees had been brought in from the fields, filling the yard next to the main building.

Sydney had been one very busy lady. Correction, Sydney and Trevor had been busy. Each night when he had talked to his son, Trevor had filled him in on every detail of his day. His son's days began with Sydney, consisted of Sydney with a touch of Thomas thrown in for good measure, and then ended with Sydney. Even over a thousand miles of telephone lines he could hear the emotions tugging at Trevor's voice and words. His son was falling in love with Sydney. He couldn't blame the boy. Like father, like son.

His gaze left the nursery and traveled the empty path he knew Sydney walked every day. The path that led directly to her father's house. He hadn't been surprised when he learned that Sydney had given up her apartment, and her independence, to move back home with her father after the accident. Her father's house was a nice comfortable home, but somehow it didn't really fit Sydney. He would have liked to have seen her apartment.

Daffodils, hyacinths and a tulip or two were flowering in the gardens surrounding the house. The flowers added a touch of color and the promise of warmer days ahead. Atlanta had seemed to be in the middle of a heat wave, yet up in the mountains of Pennsylvania it was still chilly enough to wear a coat. He eased his foot off the brake and drove toward the house. He didn't need a coat. He had thoughts of Sydney and their private homecoming to keep him warm.

Four minutes later he was hauling his garment bag and laptop from the trunk of the car when Trevor opened the front door of the house and flew down the walkway yelling, "Dad!" Ellis dropped the garment bag, but gently lowered the laptop to the ground a second before Trevor blasted into his arms.

He held his son as he swung him around in circles. "I gather you've missed me?" Trevor's squeals of laughter not only brought a smile to his own mouth, but laughter to his heart. He was home. After receiving a half-dozen noisy kisses, he slowly lowered Trevor back to the ground and noticed Sydney standing quietly at the door.

He could tell she had just taken a shower because her curls were still on the frizzy side, which was fine with him. He liked her hair a little wild almost as much as he liked it when the sun hit it at a certain angle and it appeared to be on fire. She was dressed in dark purple pants, that fit her legs like skin, and an oversize white shirt with tiny irises embroidered on the collar and pocket. And on her lips was the warmest smile he had ever seen. It nearly matched the warmth in her eyes.

He gathered up the garment bag while Trevor picked up the laptop. His son liked to help him unload after a trip, but he wasn't big enough to handle the garment bag, so he always took the laptop. It was an awfully expensive piece of equipment to allow a five-year-old to carry into the house, but the look of pride and love brightening his son's face was well worth the risk. Computers could be replaced, the look on his son's face couldn't.

Trevor slipped past Sydney and entered the house, calling for Thomas. Ellis stopped in front of Sydney and tenderly cupped her cheek. "I've missed you." Homecomings with Trevor were filled with wild hugs, excitement and "What did you bring me?" Coming home to Sydney was filled with slow heat.

If he and Sydney had been totally alone there wouldn't be any wild hugs or frantic yelling. He would carefully peel off every article of her clothing and make slow, deep love to her. Over and over again. He would want to savor every inch of her to satisfy the hunger that had been building for days. Tonight, when Thomas and Trevor were in their own beds and he could safely join Sydney in hers, he doubted if he'd still have the patience or control to go slow. They had hours to go before he could taste her again.

Sydney turned her head and pressed a kiss into the center of his palm. "I bet you didn't miss me half as much as I missed you."

"You'd lose." He glanced into the house behind her and couldn't see either Thomas or Trevor. He leaned in closer and pressed himself against her softness. The gentle green of her eyes darkened. "Do you have any idea how badly I want you this very minute?"

Sydney arched her hips and smiled knowingly. "I have an idea."

He muttered, "Witch," before capturing her smile with his mouth. There was no way he could conceal his desire. The proof of it was pressed gently into her thigh. But that didn't mean she had to torment him even more.

He broke the kiss when she begun to wrap her arms around his neck and it started to threaten his control. Having Sydney pressed up against his aching body was just too much of a temptation. He was never going to last until tonight if he didn't put some room between them, and fast.

He forced himself to take a step back and yell over her shoulder, "Trevor?"

"What, Dad?" Trevor's voice came from the direction of the kitchen.

He glared at Sydney's knowing grin before answering his son. "Come see what I've brought you back from Atlanta." He heard Trevor's shout echo off the kitchen walls.

Sydney leaned back against the doorjamb. "You, Mr. Carlisle, are a coward."

He leaned against the other jamb and grinned. She was going to pay for the comment, and pay dearly. "It beats explaining to your father and Trevor why I'm carrying you up the stairs."

Trevor's full-speed arrival through the living room prevented Sydney from responding. But he had to admit she looked extremely receptive to the idea.

"What did you get me, Dad?" Trevor skidded to a halt three inches away from the garment bag.

He reached down, unzipped one of the outer pockets on his suitcase and pulled out a bag imprinted with the name of a famous nature-store chain. "Bugs."

"Bugs?" Trevor reached for the bag. "Real ones?"

He saw the look of horror on Sydney's face and chuckled. "No, they're made from all kinds of different things, like wood, plastic and rubber."

Trevor pulled a wooden box from the bag and showed it to Sydney. It was engraved with red letters.

"It says African Insects." Sydney looked on with interest as Trevor slowly undid the latch and opened the box.

Ellis smiled at the look of total rapture on his son's face. He had known as soon as he had spotted the insect collection that Trevor would love it. The box opened on hinges and both sides contained a dozen replicas of insects in their own compartments, neatly labeled and protected by a clear plastic cover. "There's everything from a desert locust to a tsetse fly."

"Wow, Dad, can I hold them?"

"Sure, but you have to be very careful, they're fragile." He reached down and showed his son how to undo the protective plastic cover. "Only take out one at a time so you'll remember which compartment it goes back into."

"What's this one?" Trevor pulled out a dark-colored plastic bug with gossamer wings.

"It's a termite."

"Cool, can I go show them to Thomas?"

"I...sure, go ahead." *Show them to Thomas.* Trevor knew Thomas couldn't see, so why did he want to *show* them to Thomas.

Trevor carefully replaced the termite into the appropriate compartment and took off for the kitchen. He and Sydney followed at a slower pace.

He took a step into the kitchen, but Sydney stayed in the doorway, silently watching the scene unfolding before them.

Trevor pulled up a chair next to Thomas at the kitchen table. Thomas seemed to have been enjoying a cup of coffee. There was an empty glass of milk at the place next to him. A couple of cookie crumbs dotted the table. "Wait till you see them, Thomas, they're cool." Trevor carefully opened the protective plastic and removed a large brownish grasshopper. "Hold out your hand."

Thomas immediately obeyed. "What am I holding my hand out for?"

"A bug. I'm not sure what this one's called, but he's cool." Trevor carefully placed the bug onto Thomas's palm.

Thomas sat very still as he brought his other hand over and lightly touched the bug. "It's not real."

"Of course not." Trevor chuckled. "Dad wouldn't give me real bugs. He's not that crazy."

Thomas laughed along with him. "I guess he's not." His fingers cautiously felt the bug. "This one feels like a grasshopper. What other kinds of bugs did he bring you?"

"All kinds of neat ones." Trevor replaced the desert locust and reached for another one to show Thomas.

Ellis felt his heart give a funny little lurch at the scene. His son had formed a special bond with Thomas. The older man's blindness didn't matter at all to Trevor. In his own way his son had simplified Thomas's disability. If Thomas couldn't see with his eyes, he could see with his hands.

Thomas should have been his son's grandfather.

He turned away from the touching scene and glanced at Sydney. She was mesmerized by Thomas, Trevor and a boxful of bugs. He could see the love gleaming in her green eyes, but he could also see the tears.

Thomas St. Claire was the man she called Father. The love they shared was obvious, and so was her pain. Sydney had been tossed out onto the stormy sea, just as Ellis had been. They were in different boats, fighting different waves, but they were on the same turbulent sea. He and his son were rowing against the monstrous wave called leukemia. Sydney was sitting alone in her boat watching her father row against the turbulent waves known as blindness.

It was Thomas's fight, and Sydney had the difficult task of standing back and allowing him to fight the seas. She could make her father's life comfortable and offer him her companionship, but the fight was his. The blindness was his to deal with as best he could.

He took a couple of steps to Sydney and wrapped his arm around her shoulder. He felt his heart give another funny little lurch as she leaned into him and rested her head on his shoulder while continuing to watch her father and his son with misty eyes. Sydney St. Claire was one amazing and strong woman. And he knew he was falling in love with her.

Ellis felt like a thief, sneaking out of the guest bedroom and silently tiptoeing to Sydney's room. Discretion was a key element to loving Sydney. His gut was telling him they weren't fooling Thomas for a minute. Thomas might be blind, but as Trevor demonstrated so nicely, he could still *see*.

He slipped into her room just as the shower stopped in the bathroom across the hall. Sydney was in there and the temptation to join her had been strong. Showering with Sydney was definitely one of life's experiences he was dying to try. The sound of running water had affected his body in a basic male way. A very *hard* basic male way.

He wanted Sydney. He wanted the whole woman. He not only wanted her body, he wanted her warmth and her smiles. He wanted her heart.

The small box clutched in his hand felt inadequate as a missed-you gift. He had been rushing around the hotel in Atlanta when he passed the window of a jewelry store next to the restaurant where he had just had dinner. It was an expensive shop geared to tourists and hurried businessmen and women who never saw more then the inside of the airport, taxis and the hotel. The blaze of green caught his eye and halted his feet. The shimmering emerald stud earrings that blazed with an inner fire reminded him of Sydney. The depths of her beautiful green eyes blazed with the same inner fire when he was deep inside her, loving her.

He placed the box on the top of her bureau, walked over to the window and stared out into the night. This evening when he had pulled up in front of the St Claires' home he had felt as if he was coming home. His son had been waiting with hugs and kisses. Sydney had been standing there silently with a certain gleam in her eyes. A gleam that promised a warmer welcome once they were behind closed doors. Even Thomas had seemed happy that he had returned.

Was this what a real family felt like?

The small rural town of Coalsburg had had that friendly, homey feel to it as he had driven through on his way home. John, the police chief, had waved to him. So had Georgette, who had been closing up her toy shop. Harvey, driving some big old Buick, had beeped and one of the other officers had passed him on his way out of town and tooted his horn.

He liked the warmth of the town and thought it would be a great place to raise Trevor. But it wasn't to be. Trevor's illness required the top doctors, the top hospitals, the top everything if he was going to win this battle.

The nearest hospital to Coalsburg was thirty-seven miles. He had checked. Trevor's illness had to take precedence over everything, including his own happiness.

The sound of the closing bedroom door was soft, but he heard it anyway. He needed some time to pull his emotions under control before he turned around and faced Sydney.

Less than a moment later he felt warm, gentle hands stroke his back. "Are you looking at anything in particular?" Sydney's breath feathered his ear as her hands continued their journey over his shoulders.

He felt some of the tension melt away under the heat of desire. Tomorrow would take care of itself. Tonight there was only Sydney. He pulled his gaze from the darkness and studied her reflection in the window. Sydney looked like some wanton angel. She had on her oversize white robe, her hair was a wild mass of dark curls. If an artist captured her right at this moment on canvas there could only be one title to the picture—*Tempting Angel*.

He felt the last of his strain fade as her hands slid around his waist and up his chest. "Yeah, I'm looking at an angel."

Sydney's gaze shot to the window. He could tell the instant she realized he was referring to her. She smiled a slow easy smile.

"I'd say you're suffering from jet lag." Tempting fingers made their way down his chest to toy with the drawstring of his pajama pants.

"Atlanta's in the same time zone as Pennsylvania." He felt his body come to life beneath her gentle touch.

Sydney's lips were warm and teasing as they left a

trail of kisses down the side of his neck. "So why did it feel like you were half a world away?"

He turned and hauled her up against his chest. He couldn't stand it a minute longer. With a rough expletive toward the Fates, he lowered his mouth and savored Sydney's heat.

Somehow Sydney managed to yank his T-shirt over his head and undo the tie on his pants. Her robe slid off her shoulders with a minimum of effort, which was remarkable considering he was too busy kissing every available inch of her body to pay it much attention.

The bed was soft and comfortable, but neither of them noticed. Pillows fell to the floor, protection was rolled on, and someone made a begging little plea. He wasn't sure which one of them had moaned, but it probably was himself. He was not above begging.

Within three minutes of claiming her mouth, he was deep inside her watching the emeralds once again form in her eyes.

The emerald gleam of her gaze shattered as she climaxed beneath him. He felt her body's contractions cradle him more deeply inside, forcing him to join her in that place over the edge.

Some time before dawn, emerald fire gleaming on Sydney's earlobes and he totally exhausted from her inspired and heartfelt thanks for the gift, he heard her whisper into the darkness, "Welcome home." Her words matched his sentiments exactly.

"Oh," cried Norma Hess. "No wonder the poor girl ran away. Her parents would have never approved."

Ellis looked at Norma and tried to rein in his frustration. Time was running out. He had been back from

Atlanta for two days now, and nothing new turned up. It wasn't for the lack of Thomas's efforts. The man was obsessed with finding Trevor's grandfather.

He had been afraid of that. Thomas and Trevor had become very good friends and now Thomas's desire to locate his son's grandfather had nothing to do with proving he wasn't Ellis's father. And Ellis knew it was more than just a matter of solving the mystery and keeping his police skills honed. It had to do with Trevor—only Trevor. Thomas had realized that Trevor, his new little friend, could die without that bone marrow transplant. The older man's panic had turned into an obsession, just like his had done.

At least Thomas and he were working toward the same end. The same results. Find Trevor's natural grandfather, no matter what. Of course the "what" consisted of talking to everyone who had been alive and living in the town when his mother was here. Norma and her friend Vivian were the twelfth and thirteenth persons they had talked to since he had been back from the business trip.

"Cathy's parents would have never supported her, either financially or emotionally." Vivian shook her head.

"We're sorry, Ellis, but your grandparents weren't the shining example of humanity they thought they were. They held poor Cathy up as some symbol of purity and never let her forget it." Norma appeared apologetic.

"It's all right, Vivian and Norma. You're not telling me anything I haven't known already. I knew why my mother chose to raise me on her own, and from some of the stories I've heard, I can only thank her."

"Good, good." Norma took a sip of her coffee and

nibbled on the edge of a cookie. "It was such a long time ago, you understand."

"We've got years to go before we can retire, Alzheimer's hasn't set in yet, but boy, do we feel old," added Vivian with a rusty laugh.

Thomas chuckled. "Nonsense, you two. I don't feel old, and I'm older than you both." Thomas pushed the cookie plate back into the center of the table. "So you can't remember anything about Cathy and who she might have been seeing? She left this town four months pregnant. Surely someone had to have seen her with someone."

Norma shook her head. "Cathy wasn't very social in school."

"The only time I saw her actually talk to anyone was at church. She seemed more comfortable there than at school." Vivian reached for another cookie.

"Who did she talk to at church?" Ellis asked. The crumpled list of members was tucked safely into his pocket. "Can you remember anyone in particular? Some boy from the youth group or bible-study class?"

"She didn't really talk to any boys." Vivian chewed for a moment. "I remember she used to lock up the church after we all went home. She always wore the key around her neck during youth group. It was as if her parents didn't trust her not to lose the thing."

"Who did she lock up with?"

"Arthur Graystone, he used to head the youth group back then."

"Mayor Graystone?" Thomas's voice held a certain edge to it. Ellis identified immediately with that edge. Dear old Mayor Graystone had once again popped up in connection with his mother.

Yesterday, Andy Beamer, who ran the pharmacy, remembered seeing Arthur Graystone with someone who looked like Cathy out near Lookout Point one night. But the thought of Arthur with the minister's daughter had been so absurd that Andy realized he must have seen wrong and mistaken Cathy for Graystone's wife, Sophie. It still had struck him as strange, because he couldn't for the life of him think of one good reason why Arthur and his wife would go parking. He had dismissed the whole thing from his mind years ago and hadn't remembered it until Thomas had brought up Arthur's name.

"He wasn't the mayor back then," Norma supplied another tidbit of information. "He use to drive Cathy home when the meetings were done and everyone went home."

"How old would Arthur Graystone have been back then?" No matter how hard he tried, he couldn't picture his mother and some old married man together.

"Oh, he was what, twenty-five or twenty-six?" Vivian glanced at Norma for confirmation. "But I do know he was one handsome-looking man back then. Still is for that matter."

"Oh my, yes," Norma said. "Sophie Bradshaw could have had her pick of men from miles around, but no one suited her but Arthur."

"Only the best for Sophie," echoed Vivian.

"Do either of you remember if Arthur was happy back then? I know him and Sophie are still together, but you know how sometimes marriage can be a little shaky in the beginning." Thomas was rubbing his jaw.

"Sophie was delirious. Daddy had given them that big old house as a wedding present." Norma wrinkled her nose.

"And a maid," added Vivian. "Can you imagine someone in Coalsburg receiving a maid for a wedding present?" Vivian took another sip of her coffee. "I remember the maid because quite frankly I was jealous."

"So, Sophie was rolling in newfound marital bliss." He wanted answers and he didn't give a flying fig about Sophie or how many maids she had received. "What about Arthur?"

"Arthur got what he wanted when he married Sophie. He got the manager's job at the mill with a hefty salary, a fancy sports car, a new house and Sophie. What more could the man want?" Vivian seemed to think that was all that made a man happy.

Ellis knew different. It took love. It took a family to make a man happy. "But was he happy, Vivian?"

"Yes."

"No," Norma said as she frowned down at her coffee. "In the first couple of years of his marriage, Arthur wasn't happy. He had been bought, and he knew it."

"He was one of the deacons at my grandparents' church the year I was conceived," Ellis said, glancing at Norma, who seemed to be the more perceptive of the two. "Was he a very religious man?"

"He was the deacon because that's what Sophie's father told him to be. Sam Bradshaw wanted the best for his daughter, so he was bound and determined to mold Arthur into the best." Norma slowly nodded her head. "Sam succeeded too. Today Arthur Graystone is Coalsburg's mayor and leading citizen."

"In your opinion, Norma, do you think Arthur was capable of having an affair with my mother?"

"Saints!" cried Vivian, clearly outraged by such a suggestion.

Norma handled the question with a sense of calmness. "Yes."

"Oh my." Vivian shuddered. "Do you mean to tell me you think Arthur might be your father?"

He didn't know what to think. Arthur Graystone's name didn't mean a thing to him. All he was interested in was the possibility of the man being his father. So far Graystone was the only candidate. Ellis shuddered and let Norma answer.

"He could very well be," Norma said.

"That would explain a lot of things," Thomas said. "Cathy never would have had her parents' support once the scandal of her being pregnant ripped through the town. Arthur never would have claimed the child and forfeited the golden egg he had found with Sophie. But worse yet would have been Sophie's wrath. Spoiled, pampered and rich Sophie Bradshaw Graystone would have ripped the young and innocent Cathy Carlisle to shreds and picked her perfectly capped teeth with the bones."

Vivian and Norma shuddered and whispered in unison, "Amen to that one."

Ellis leaned back in his chair and smiled. He had a name! Finally, he had a name!

Chapter 11

Ellis stopped the car at the sight of the ten-foot-tall black iron gates guarding the brick driveway leading to Arthur Graystone's home. His glance shot to the brass plaque neatly screwed into the brick wall supporting the open gates. The plaque proclaimed this was Graystone Manor. A more presumptuous display of wealth he had never seen. A *manor* in the middle of Coalsburg. He almost chuckled at the thought but he was afraid he might choke on the gesture. He was about to meet his father, or at least the man Thomas and he thought was his father.

The pieces seem to fit. Arthur Graystone and Catherine Carlisle had been seen together quite a few times. More important, they were seen together at the time she had conceived him. Arthur Graystone was the only man who had been linked to his mother, besides her own father. He had to be his father. Trevor's hope lay beyond those imposing black gates.

He glanced at Sydney, who was sitting silently beside him staring at those same black gates. She didn't have to come, but she had insisted. Not only had she set up the appointment with the mayor, she had contacted Thomas's sister, Mary, to come stay with Trevor and her father. He reached out, took her hand and skimmed his thumb over her pounding pulse. "Relax, Sydney."

Sydney gave him a look that clearly said he had lost his mind. "Aren't you nervous at all?"

"Let's say I'm anxious."

"Because you're about to meet your father for the first time?"

"No, because I'm about to find out if Trevor has a chance." He was also anxious because there was a very good chance, should Graystone admit to being his father, that he would punch the son of a bitch for what he had done to Catherine Carlisle. He would have to control that impulse until after the results of the blood test were in. That is, if Arthur agreed to taking one.

"It doesn't mean anything to you that Arthur might be your father?"

He shook his head. "Not a thing, Sydney. Just because a man has a sperm count doesn't mean he's a father. It takes a heart and a whole lot of love to be a father. Arthur Graystone obviously lacks in both of those departments." Sydney, of all people, should know that. She called Thomas, the man who couldn't be her or anyone else's natural father, Dad. His gaze returned to the open gates and the winding driveway beyond. "I'm only here because of Trevor. He's the only thing that matters." He released her hand, shifted the car into gear and headed up the driveway.

Graystone Manor was one impressive-looking house.

It was all brick with black shutters and gleaming brass everywhere. Circular marble steps led to the front door. He parked the car on the circular driveway and opened Sydney's door.

"Does he always conduct mayoral business from his house?" As far as Arthur Graystone knew, Sydney's request for an appointment had to do with the town's business. Sydney had thought, and Ellis had agreed, that the first step was to get in to see Arthur. The second step was to confront him about Catherine.

"Coalsburg can't afford to build a city hall or any kind of administrative offices. The town meetings are held in the hall at the firehouse, but Arthur prefers to do business out of his home." Sydney smoothed a wrinkle out of her skirt. "Arthur and Sophie both like to impress people with their wealth."

"Do you think Sophie is going to be home?" He didn't want to confront Arthur on his infidelity while his wife was in the room.

"No." Sydney followed him up the grandiose marble steps. "I know for a fact she's attending the monthly women's group meeting at their church. Sophie never misses a meeting. She's their president."

He reached up and tenderly touched her cheek. "Smart and beautiful."

Sydney grinned. "Remember that."

A chuckle escaped his throat as he pressed the doorbell. When he had first met Sydney, that comment would have caused her to blush. A very becoming blush that would have intrigued his senses. Sydney was now more relaxed in their relationship, more natural. The woman standing beside him now not only intrigued his senses, she captured his heart.

The door was opened by a woman wearing a plain green dress. He wouldn't class it as a uniform, but it was surely meant to be one. "Yes, may I help you?"

"My name's Sydney St. Claire. We have an appointment with the mayor." Sydney smiled pleasantly at the woman.

"Come in, please." The door opened wider as the woman took a step back. "I believe he's expecting you."

He followed Sydney into the foyer and felt his curiosity pique. A sweeping staircase curved its way to the second floor and a crystal chandelier the size of a Cadillac hung from the thirty-foot-high ceiling. Antique settees were placed at just the right spot and gilt-framed portraits followed the stairs upward. He counted three fresh-flower arrangements as the woman walked them across the foyer to a closed door.

The woman knocked lightly, opened the door and announced, "Your ten o'clock appointment is here, Mr. Graystone."

"Good, show them in, Claire." Arthur Graystone's voice emerged from the room.

Claire took a step back. "Mr. Graystone will see you now."

For some absurd reason, he felt as if he had just been granted an audience with the great Wizard of Oz. He had to wonder if all the stress he had been under was finally getting to him. He gave Sydney an encouraging nod as they both entered the room.

Arthur Graystone rose from behind his massive teak desk. "Sydney, welcome."

Sydney reached for Arthur's outstretched hand and

gave it a polite shake. "Hello, Arthur. I would like you to meet Ellis Carlisle."

He watched Arthur's face, looking for any sign of recognition to his last name. There was none. Graystone had a poker face, displaying only a small glimpse of curiosity as he shook his hand. The only gesture he could pick up on was the fact that Arthur Graystone didn't once meet his gaze. The man seemed unusually interested in Ellis's right shoulder. "Mr. Mayor."

Arthur released his hand and smiled a politician smile. "Mr. Carlisle. Won't you both have a seat." Arthur waved to the two empty chairs in front of his desk. When they were both seated, he returned to his position behind the desk and sat. "So, Sydney, what can I do for you?"

Sydney folded her hands and placed them on her lap. "I'm afraid this is of a private matter, Arthur."

"Oh?" Arthur arched one gray eyebrow but he didn't seem particularly surprised.

Sydney gave Ellis a sideways look and waited for him to step into the conversation. Her part in the meeting was done, she had supplied the introductions. The next step was up to him.

He supposed Vivian and Norma were right. Arthur Graystone could be classed as a handsome man, even at his age, which Ellis had approximated to be around fifty-eight. He was in excellent shape and though his hair was mostly gray now, Ellis could tell it had been blond in his youth. The same color as his own.

"Do you remember a young woman named Catherine Carlisle?" He was struggling not to come right out and demand if Arthur was his father. For Trevor's sake he would control both his temper and his words. Arthur started to shake his head and Ellis quickly added, "You would have to go back about thirty-three years, and she was only in high school at the time." If Arthur refused to acknowledge that he even knew his mother, he honestly didn't know what he would do. Deck the older man was his top choice.

"Catherine Carlisle?"

"She went by Cathy. Her father was the minister at the Methodist church in town. You were a deacon there at the time." He was willing to supply as much information required to help Arthur's memory kick in.

"Oh, yes, the Carlisles. I remember them now. Mr. Carlisle was a fire-and-brimstone type of preacher. Mrs. Carlisle played the organ."

"What about Cathy, their daughter?"

"Sorry, don't remember much about Cathy. She was quiet and shy. The wallflower type if I'm not mistaken."

He was on his feet and approaching the desk before he could stop himself. Only the soft pressure of Sydney's hand on his arm stopped him from climbing over the desk and throttling the man. He sucked in a deep breath and slowly released it through his nose before quietly asking, "Do you always have affairs with the wallflower type, *Mr. Graystone?*"

Arthur stood up, but his gaze never went higher than the second button on Ellis's shirt. "I don't know what you are talking about, Mr. Carlisle. But I do know that I don't appreciate the insinuation."

"Did you or did you not have an affair with Catherine Carlisle thirty-three years ago that resulted in a child?"

"No, I did not."

He knew Arthur was lying, but his hands were tied. The only way he could force the truth out of the mayor was to beat it out of him. He couldn't do that because that would kill all chances of Arthur agreeing to be tested. He had to try a different tactic. Arthur Graystone wasn't as cool and calm as he wanted them to believe. "I'm Catherine's son. The man she had an affair with, while she was still in high school, is my father."

Arthur's hands trembled violently against the desk. "I'm not that man."

He felt his frustration level topple over the edge. Trevor's miracle was dissolving before his very eyes and there was nothing he could do. If Arthur Graystone was that coldhearted not to admit to being his father, the man would never agree to be tested. "Catherine Carlisle was a good, honest woman who had to struggle daily to raise me on her own. She gave me everything I could possibly need, especially her love, until the day she died." He glared in disgust at the man hiding behind the width of his desk. "I hope to hell you are right. You aren't man enough to be connected in any way to my mother."

He had to get out of there before he did something incredibly stupid. "Let's go, Sydney. It takes a spine to admit to a past mistake. Your illustrious mayor happens not to have one." He turned and headed for the door.

Sydney's heart was breaking for Ellis and his son. There had to be a way to reach Arthur. She had been silently studying the two men and she could see the resemblance, even if they couldn't. Both Ellis and Arthur held themselves in a certain way, the color of their hair was the same, even though Arthur was now mostly gray, and the squareness of their jaws was identical. They had the look of a father and a son.

She had vaguely known Arthur since she had been ten years old, but she had learned that he was basically a very unhappy man—in his life and in his marriage. He and Sophie turned out for all the right social occasions, but they were otherwise never together. The rumor about town had been that Sophie was unable to have children, so they'd remained childless. She had seen Arthur's envious glances at young families over the years and had always wondered why they had never adopted. Arthur seemed more resolved now with his life, but maybe it was all a front. Maybe Trevor, not Ellis, was the key to breaking Arthur's silence.

She knew Ellis didn't want Trevor's illness mentioned as the main reason that he was now searching for his father. But she had to try. Instead of following Ellis to the door, she approached the desk.

Arthur looked up and met her gaze.

She wasn't startled to discover that Ellis had Arthur's eyes. They were the same shade of steel gray. She knew Ellis had stopped by the door and was waiting for her. She prayed he would forgive her. "Arthur, you have a five-year-old grandson named Trevor."

Arthur flinched, gripped the desk harder but didn't say a word.

"Trevor is critically ill. He's dying of leukemia." She narrowed her gaze and willed Arthur to respond in some way. "His best and probably only chance of survival is a bone marrow transplant. It needs to be done now, while he's in remission. Being Trevor's natural grandfather there is a chance, a very slim chance, that you could match his bone marrow and become his donor." She leaned closer and hammered in her point. "You can save your grandson's life, Arthur."

Arthur paled considerably, but remained silent.

Ellis stepped next to Sydney. "It's not for me, Graystone. I'm begging you for my son's life, your only grandchild's life."

She reached out and held Ellis's hand. The room was swimming because of her tears but she could see Arthur fighting his emotions. She silently prayed.

"Name your price, Graystone. You married Sophie for her money and everything it could buy you. I'll double it all!" Ellis thrust his fingers through his hair as his voice broke. "He's my son, Graystone, and you're my last hope. Name your price!"

Arthur's gaze studied the top of his desk. He didn't raise his head or speak a word.

Ellis couldn't stand it a moment longer. He had to get out of the room before he rearranged every feature on Arthur's face. "Let's go, Sydney. I've got to get out of here."

She watched Ellis storm to the door and open it. She started to follow only to freeze in her tracks when Arthur softly said, "I'll take the test."

Ellis didn't turn around. His knuckles turned white as they gripped the doorjamb. "Name your price."

"It's steep. I don't know if you'll be willing to pay it." Arthur's voice trembled.

"Name it!" Ellis's voice was more of a growl than a demand.

"Forgiveness for the past." Arthur slowly lowered himself into the chair behind the desk.

Ellis turned around and stared at him. Sydney couldn't read Ellis's expression. His face was a cold stark mask. It matched his voice. "Forgiveness?"

Arthur met Ellis's gaze. "I had an affair with Catherine Carlisle thirty-three years ago. I wasn't proud of that fact then, nor am I now. Cathy was forbidden fruit and just like Adam I couldn't resist the temptation."

Sydney watched as Ellis stepped back into the room.

"Your mother was eighteen, beautiful and looking for a way to rebel against her strict parents. I know you have no reason to believe me, but your mother singled me out, it wasn't the other way around. I never had the intention of seducing the minister's daughter." Arthur traced the edge of the blotter on his desk. "It was her innocence that enticed me into the affair. Cathy knew nothing about men, sin or the realities of an affair. The affair didn't last long, but the realities did. She told me she was pregnant with my child the month before she graduated from high school. Appalled by our foolishness and the consequences that irresponsibility had caused, I offered her money for an abortion."

She watched Ellis as he just stood there and stared. Her heart went out to the man before her. Here he stood facing his father after thirty-two years and the man was telling him he was never wanted in the first place.

"Cathy refused. She demanded that I leave my wife and marry her instead. She wanted to be a family." Arthur's fingers trembled against the blotter, but he continued. "I'm ashamed to admit that I laughed at her and told her I would never leave Sophie. It all seemed so simple back then." Arthur shook his head. "Cathy threatened to tell everyone who the father of her child was and I pulled a power number by saying if she so much as told a living soul, I would take her to court, prove she was unfit to be a mother and take the child and raise it as my own."

Arthur glanced at Ellis. "It was an empty threat. Cathy would never have been an unfit mother. My money, or should I say Sophie's money, threatened her, so she believed me. Two weeks after she graduated from high school she accepted a handful of my money and was gone. At first I thought she had taken my advice and had gone to get an abortion. After a couple of days I was worried, by a couple of weeks I knew she wasn't coming back." He paused. "Can I ask you a question, Ellis?"

"What?"

"Where were you born and raised?"

"Philadelphia, why?"

Arthur gave a weary sigh. "Cathy once told me if she ever left this town she wasn't stopping until she hit the Rocky Mountains. She said Colorado had a nice ring to it. When she didn't come back, I hired a private investigator to see if he could locate her in Colorado. He never could and after three years I gave up."

"Would you have gone to her if he found her and me?"

"Honestly, I don't know what I would have done. I do know one thing, if I had found her, Ellis, she wouldn't have had to struggle financially raising you. I would have provided for you."

Arthur sank deeper into the chair and appeared to have aged right before her eyes.

"The one thing in life that I have always wanted was children." Arthur gave a weak chuckle. "When Sophie and I decided to start a family and nothing happened, she blamed me. I knew she couldn't have been right but it took me years to convince her to see a doctor. Sophie couldn't conceive a child and she refused to adopt and raise someone else's. My one child in life boarded a bus with a woman who had every right to hate me and rode out of my life. You probably call it poetic justice. I prefer to look on it as the Lord's revenge."

"I now know why my mother didn't name you as my father on my birth certificate." Ellis studied Arthur with something akin to hatred burning in his eyes.

"If she did, you would have marched right up to my door the day you came to town looking for me." Arthur shifted in the seat. "I'm sorry to hear about Cathy's passing."

Sydney glanced at Ellis to see his reaction. He appeared to be just as he'd seemed when he had thought Thomas was his father.

"You're right, Graystone. Your price is too high, I can't promise forgiveness."

Arthur nodded. "I understand, but I'll take the test anyway."

"You will?" Sydney couldn't believe it. Ellis had found Trevor's grandfather and he was willing to be tested. Now the only miracle that they needed was a match.

"Yes, Sydney, I will." Arthur stood up. "I owe Cathy's memory more than I could ever repay."

Ellis drove Sydney up the winding roads to Lookout Point. Thomas told him the way the other day when they had learned that Andy, the pharmacist, had seen Arthur and Cathy up here. Thomas figured he might want to see the place where it all began. He didn't care too much about that, he was more interested in the view and in a few minutes alone with Sydney when they weren't near a bed. Put Sydney and a bed in the same room, and wham, his mind only functioned on one level. All he could think about was making love with her.

He gave her a sideways glance as he pulled into a parking space and shut off the engine. Sydney had been awfully quiet since they left Arthur Graystone's house. He couldn't blame her. It hadn't been a very pleasant experience. The only good thing to come out of the whole thing was Graystone's admission that he was Ellis's father, but more important, his agreement to take the test.

The first part of Trevor's miracle had occurred, and all because of Sydney. He had been ready to walk out the door and either give up or try another day with Graystone. Not Sydney. She had hit Graystone right where it counted. She had hit him with Trevor and his illness. As he had said earlier—she was smart and beautiful.

He glanced out of the window and noticed a winding path that skirted the parking area. Lookout Point wasn't your typical teenage hangout. It was a small park overlooking the town two thousand feet below. "Let's go for a walk."

Sydney gave him a curious glance before getting out of the car. "Okay."

He joined her at the side of the Mercedes, reached for her hand and led her down the path. A wooden picnic table sat at the side of the path and he pulled her down onto the seat next to him. Coalsburg was spread out below them like some tiny miniature village. He could see Sydney's nursery, the acres of trees that enclosed it and the tiny little square that was Thomas's house. Graystone Manor was also easy to pick out with its manicured lawn and brick wall that surrounded the place. It looked like a lonely place to live.

To the right of Main Street was the neighborhood where his mother and Thomas had lived when they were growing up. Off to the left and up several blocks was the tall white steeple of the church where his grandfather had preached. This was where it all began.

Over the past several weeks he had come to realize this was where he belonged. He belonged at this place, but more important, he belonged with this woman.

He loved Sydney and his life wouldn't be complete without her by his side. He wanted to be part of a family, a whole family.

He continued to hold Sydney's hand as they stared out at the valley below. His gut instinct told him that she felt the same way, but something was holding her back. Something was scaring her. Sydney accepted and fully participated in their physical lovemaking, but emotionally she seemed hesitant, unsure of either him or herself. *Which,* he couldn't tell.

He had questioned Thomas on Sydney's earlier upbringing and received the standard answers. Thomas had only known what Youth Services had told him. No one really knew what Sydney had gone through, except Sydney, and she didn't talk about it. At least she hadn't talked to Thomas or his wife. Maybe there was a chance she would open up with him and discuss her past.

From his perspective there were only two reasons that Sydney held back her emotions from him. Either she was afraid of being abandoned, as she had been by her parents. Or she didn't want to get too involved with him and share the enormous responsibility of a critically ill child. Who was to say it was even fair of him to ask her to take on that kind of responsibility. Trevor, after all, was his son.

"Syd?"

"Hmm..."

"How do you feel about Trevor?"

"Trevor? Well, I'm excited, anxious and partly sick to my stomach with worry Graystone won't be a match." A small smile of encouragement lifted her lips. "I have my fingers crossed, my toes crossed and even my eyes are crossed."

He knew that feeling well enough. "I know you care a great deal about his health, but I wanted to know how you felt about Trevor as a person, not as a sick child."

Sydney's hand trembled slightly. "I've fallen in love with the little tyke."

"He's easy to fall in love with." He squeezed her hand. This was good. This was very good.

"I know it sounds strange now, after all the fussing I did in the beginning, but I secretly wish that he really was my father's grandson." Her shoulders gave a helpless little shrug. "He's brought a lot of warmth and happiness back into the house."

"I didn't know your mother, Syd. But from what Thomas and you have told me about her, I don't think she would have wanted Thomas or you to stop living and enjoying life just because she's no longer here." If only half of everything Thomas had told him about his wife was true, Julia St. Claire had been one amazing woman.

"You're right. It's just been so hard on my dad. You, and especially Trevor, have given my father a reason to rejoin the living. Thank you."

"No thanks are necessary, Syd. If it hadn't been for Thomas I doubt if I ever would have tracked down Arthur Graystone as Trevor's grandfather." He pulled her closer and cupped her cheek, forcing her to look at him.

"Thank you for finding Graystone's weak spot. I was too upset at the time to think clearly."

"Call it a hunch."

He could call it many things, but nothing fit it more than "love." "Do you know Trevor asked me if we could move out here?"

"Really, he wants to move to Coalsburg? That's a first. Most kids want to move into a big city where there's plenty to do. Coalsburg is known as a hick town."

"To a five-year-old it's paradise." His fingers stroked the gentle curve of her jaw. "There's only one thing I could think of that he would love more than moving out here."

"What's that?"

He studied her eyes. "Getting a mom." He saw the distress that clouded her gaze, but he continued. "He needs a mom, Sydney, not a housekeeper."

Sydney looked away. "All kids need a mom."

He felt the warmth he had been feeling earlier start to fade and he dropped his hand. Sydney wasn't reacting quite the way he had hoped. "Trevor needs one more than most other little boys because of his illness." He had to be honest with her, no matter how much it broke his heart to say the words. "Trevor's illness will become critical if Graystone doesn't match and if we can't find another donor while Trevor's in remission." His voice was breaking with unshed tears, but he needed to tell her. "Trevor will be requiring a lot of care and loving no matter which way it goes."

He saw Sydney shake her head in denial, but pushed on. His biggest fear lay before him. He loved Sydney— he knew that now for sure. But if Sydney agreed to become his wife and Trevor's mother, she would have to share his fears for his son. "Do you know how strong a person would have to be to stand helplessly by and watch a child die?"

"Stop it!" shouted Sydney as she brushed away tears streaming down her face. "Stop talking like that!" The tears ran faster than her fingers could brush them away. "A match will be found. If Graystone doesn't match, there's the registries. People are joining the registries all the time. A match will be found if I have to go out and personally beg every person across this country and beyond to get tested."

He almost smiled at her determination. "What would you do, Syd, if you had a son with leukemia?"

"Exactly what you are doing," Sydney said, sobbing. "I'd search for a donor, and love him."

Ellis pulled her into his arms and slowly rocked her as huge sobs racked her body. Trevor wasn't the reason she held a part of herself back. He could feel the tears she was shedding for his son soak the front of his shirt. "Hush, Syd, it's going to be okay. We have to believe that."

Holding Syd as she cried for his son gave him a strange sense of comfort. He didn't understand it. Didn't want to understand. All he knew was that he wasn't alone in this horrible nightmare any longer.

Sydney slowly got herself under control and pulled out of his arms. She fumbled in her pocket for a tissue and used it to blow her nose. "I ruined your shirt."

"It will wash." He plucked a clean tissue out of her hand and gently dried the streaks of tears running down her face. "Better now?"

Sydney nodded. "Yes, thank you."

He should tell her she was welcome, but he didn't. He should be the one thanking her. He gave her a couple moments to compose herself before softly asking, "Can you tell me about your past, before the St. Claires adopted you?"

Sydney studied the crinkled tissue being crushed in her hand. "Does it make a difference?" Her voice trembled with each word and her expression was guarded.

"To me, no." He reached out and touched her cheek where the tears had been. "But I think it might make a difference to you."

Sydney slowly shook her head. The pain that clouded her eyes wasn't for Trevor any longer. It was for things that might have been, could have been and never were. Her voice was barely above a whisper when she asked, "Can you please take me home now? My father must be going out of his mind wondering how it went at Graystone's."

He studied the pain in her eyes and knew he wouldn't push the subject any further this afternoon. There was enough pain in her life and he didn't want to cause her any more. He had grown up bitter and resentful of his father, who had refused to claim him or want him. When Thomas told him about her childhood, Ellis couldn't imagine what Sydney must have felt knowing her parents abandoned her at a gas station out on the interstate at the tender age of four.

He cupped both of her cheeks and softly kissed her trembling mouth. "We'll go back now if that's what you want. But I want you to know one thing first."

"What?"

His mouth sought hers again for a quick kiss. "I'm in love with you, Sydney St. Claire."

Chapter 12

Two days later, lying in Ellis's arms, Sydney felt the heat of his kisses and the strength of his desire for her as he urged her to reach a higher pinnacle. She couldn't climb any higher. She was on the edge about to go over, but she wanted him with her. She needed him with her when she tumbled into the abyss.

Her hands reached up and stroked the trembling muscles across his back. Her rapid breath matched his and heated skin slid against heated skin. His pace was unmerciful and delicious. Each thrust sent her soaring, craving more.

She reached up and skimmed her mouth over his jaw. His jaw was smooth from his recent shave. He smelled like expensive cologne, but he tasted like heaven. A heady blend of sweat, desire and heat.

Ellis's fingers threaded their way into her hair and forced her to look at him. His voice was a low growl, "Now, Sydney."

She could see the dazed look enter his eyes and knew he had reached the limit of his endurance. He was perched on the brink with her. She tightened her legs around his hips and hung on to him as she allowed the tide of passion to sweep her over the edge. Somewhere in a distant corner of her mind she hear his hoarse cry and knew it signaled his own release.

Ten minutes later she was still trying to control the rapid pounding of her heart as she lay exhausted against Ellis's chest. His own brisk heartbeat beneath her ear told her he was suffering the same fate. The night had turned cool and Ellis had thoughtfully pulled up the blankets. It was a good thing that he did. She didn't think she had the strength to move one lone muscle, let alone the entire group of them it would require for her to reach the blankets that had been shoved to the bottom of the bed. Ellis was her hero. Her incredibly sexy and patient hero.

In the two days since his talk of moving to Coalsburg and getting a mother for Trevor, he had been charming, attentive and amazingly forward in his courtship. He sent her flowers. He sent a woman who owned her own nursery flowers! Of course she grew and sold rosebushes, not long-stemmed red roses. He teased her unmercifully in front of her father and Trevor, who saw what was happening and egged him on further. Her father seemed totally thrilled with the courtship of his one and only daughter.

Ellis had gone from a secretive lover to a very public suitor. During the day he tempted her with sweet words and smoldering glances. His nightly visits to her room were filled with passionate kisses, words that made her blush and want, and hot love.

His courtship was sweet and a great ego booster, considering they were already lovers. Ellis didn't have to court her, she was already his. Didn't he realize that she was already in love with him?

Ellis's hands gently stroked her back. "Penny for your thoughts?"

"Who has the strength to think?" Her lips pressed a light kiss to the center of his chest.

"Do that a little lower and you'd be amazed at what I have strength for." His hands skimmed her hip and tugged her closer.

She could feel his laughter rumbling deep within his chest and she grinned. This was how she had always dreamed having a lover would be like. Ellis was exciting, serious and playful. "That's mighty big talk from a man who ten minutes ago was begging."

Ellis' strong fingers danced across the small of her back and over the curve of her bottom. "So you think it's all talk, do you?"

She instinctively wiggled closer. "If I say yes, your male pride would force you to show me otherwise, wouldn't it?"

"Indubitably."

She giggled. "I've never heard anyone ever actually use that word before." She loved the way Ellis made her feel. He made her feel alive.

Strong, blunt-ended fingers were no longer teasing, they were arousing. "Obviously you've been hanging around the wrong sort of people."

"Obviously." How was it possible for him to make her full of desire again so quickly after satisfying her so completely? He was a magician. But she had already known that.

Ellis Carlisle made her want to open up her heart and declare the love she felt for him. He had already proclaimed his love for her and had even hinted at something more permanent. He talked about possibly moving to Coalsburg and how Trevor needed a mother. He whispered *"I love you"* in the heat of passion or during walks with Trevor through acres of trees. He hinted about a future that not only contained her, but her father as well.

She was on the verge of the biggest risk of her life, but she was scared to take that final step. Love, to her, was a personal thing to be clutched against her heart and held as a secret. Once the words were spoken it gave the other person power. Ellis couldn't hurt her if she didn't hand him her heart. She had been hurt so many times in the past that she was more than a little gun-shy. She was terrified of being abandoned again. Everyone she had ever loved left her. Everyone, that is, except Thomas. A shiver shook her body.

"Cold?" Ellis's hands briskly rubbed her back and hauled her closer to his warmth.

"Someone must have walked over my grave." It was a simple cliché, an easy answer. Tennyson had been wrong when he said, "'Tis better to have loved and lost than never to have loved at all." Alfred, Lord Tennyson had obviously never been abandoned in some old gas station by his parents when he was four years old.

At night sometimes she could still feel the terror. She couldn't remember what her parents had looked like, or even their names. She couldn't remember the gas station or even what the ladies' room had looked like. But she could remember the terror of being alone, huddled up in the corner, too scared to even cry. She had known then and there that her parents weren't coming back. She hadn't been good enough for them to keep.

Being shuffled through foster home after foster home had only reinforced her beliefs that she had never been good enough. No one wanted her, at least no one wanted her for long. Thomas and Julia St. Claire's love and patience with her had helped ease her fears, but not erase them. She was still waiting for the day when Thomas announced that he had changed his mind—that she wasn't good enough to be his daughter any longer.

It was an unreasonable fear. She knew it was irrational, but that didn't make the fear go away. She had been the one to call a halt to the relationships with her two previous lovers. Both had started to hint about the future and she had panicked. It had been better to break it off early, before things went too far, than to be abandoned later when they discovered she wasn't good enough to be a wife.

What she felt for Ellis was different. Her love for him was stronger, more intense. She didn't have the courage to send him on his way. She wanted to put her faith in him and take the risk.

"Sydney," Ellis's voice was a low purr rumbling against the top of her head. "What's wrong?"

She lifted her head and stared down at his handsome face. The risk pulled at her heart but she couldn't say the words. At least not yet. Maybe tomorrow they would come. "Wrong? There's nothing wrong, Ellis."

She could feel the hardening of his body as her breasts brushed his chest. Her breath quickened as his arousal grazed her thigh. Ellis wanted her again. A smile tugged at her lips as she straddled his hips, catching him by surprise. This time when they made love she wanted to be the one in control. She needed to be in control.

Her mouth teased the corner of his as she wiggled her hips and caused him to groan. The sensitive peaks of her breasts brushed his chest as her fingers trembled against his cheeks.

Ellis pulled his mouth away from hers and dragged in a ragged breath. "Tell me what you want, Sydney."

"You." She nipped at his lower lip. "I want to make love to you, Ellis." Her tongue stroked where her teeth had just nipped. "Will you let me?" She could feel his arousal pressing against her opening. All she had to do was slip down a few inches and he would fill her.

Ellis's hands clutched at her hips and positioned her to receive him. A radiant smile broke across his face. "As often as you like."

She wiped that smile off his face as she lowered herself onto him and slowly rotated her hips. This time she would be the one controlling their journey to the brink and deciding when they would go over.

Sometime deep in the night, Ellis reached down and pulled the blanket back up and over them. Sydney didn't so much as flinch. He didn't blame her. He could barely move, either, after the marathon of loving Sydney had taken them on.

He tucked the blanket up under her chin and pulled her into his arms. Her body was warm and pliable as it melted in perfection against his own. A frown pulled at his mouth as he stared up at the ceiling. There had been a different element added to the second time they had made love. Sydney had added the element, and if he wasn't mistaken, it had been desperation.

Why would she feel desperate? He was the one feeling anxious. Sydney hadn't once told him that she loved him. She hadn't once hinted at the future beyond Graystone's test results. His gut was telling him he was losing her, and he didn't know why. She had demons eating at her soul, but until she shared those demons with him his hands were tied. He didn't know what the demons were, so he hadn't a clue as to how to slay them for her.

His arms tightened around her and his frown deepened. It was a long time before he succumbed to the oblivion of sleep.

Trevor laughed as the little train chugged its way around the figure-eight track laid out on the kitchen floor. "You should see it, Thomas, the giraffes are bobbing their heads and the elephants' trunks go up and down."

Thomas grinned. "That's what Georgette said they would do. What about the monkeys in their car? Are they swinging back and forth?"

"Yes!" Trevor lay down next to the track and peered into each car as the train went past his nose. "There are two clowns waving from the..." Trevor looked at his father for help.

Ellis smiled and willingly supplied the word his son was looking for. "Caboose. The last car on a train is always the caboose."

Sydney sat back against the wall and watched as the brightly colored circus train made its way around once more. Every time the lion's car crossed the intersection where the two tracks overlapped, there was a roar. It was a wonderful train filled with jungle animals made all the more special because her father had been the one to buy it for Trevor.

He had picked up the train set this afternoon while he was in town visiting his friends at the police station. Pete and Harvey had accompanied Thomas to the Two-By-Two shop where he had made the selection with Georgette's help.

Trevor reached over and pressed the button near the on/off switch. The sound of the train's whistle filled the room.

"Do you see the tiger, son?" Ellis leaned down and pointed to the black-caged car near the rear of the train.

"Yeah, Thomas, the tiger goes around and around inside his cage." Trevor's voice held nothing but awe.

"Like a top?" Thomas leaned forward on the wooden chair. He looked about as excited as Trevor.

"No, no. He's, he's...what's he doing, Dad?"

"He's pacing."

Ellis ruffled his son's hair and turned to Thomas. "This was some surprise, Thomas. Are you sure Trevor thanked you enough?"

"Three big bear hugs more than covered it." Thomas chuckled. "I wanted to give Trevor something special to remember us by."

Sydney heard the touch of sadness in her father's voice. He was going to miss Trevor, and probably Ellis too, when they returned home. She felt Ellis's stare, but refused to meet his gaze. He was still giving her the space she had requested, but he wasn't easing up on the courtship. In fact, he was growing more persistent with every day.

Cindy and a couple of her other employees had a pool going as to when Ellis would be popping the big question. No one had even thought about if she would accept or not. It was painfully obvious that she was in love with him, and his son. Trevor spent more time with her at the nursery during the day than he did with his own father and Thomas. She not only enjoyed his company, but the thousands of questions that accompanied him. His endless questions made her think and his indisputable love of flowers made her appreciate their wonder all over again. Trevor had not only brought joy back into their house, he had brought it back to the nursery. Employees no longer talked in hushed tones whenever she was around. Laughter could be heard from the employees as they went about their day. She was once again enjoying her work.

She didn't want to lose Ellis, or his love, but she didn't know how to ask him to stay.

The ringing of the phone pulled her off the floor, away from her depressing thoughts. "I'll get it."

Ellis gave her a concerned look before kneeling down and showing Trevor how to make the train go backward.

Sydney grabbed the phone on its third ring. "Hello, St. Claire residence." She glanced at Ellis and silently prayed. "Yes, he's here. Whom shall I say is calling?" She already knew the answer, but asked away. "One moment, please."

Ellis glanced at her over Trevor's head. She knew instantly when he figured out who was on the phone. His hand, holding the instruction booklet, started to tremble and his gaze shot to Trevor.

She held out the phone, and softly said, "It's the lab."

Ellis slowly got to his feet and took the phone. "This is Ellis Carlisle."

She would have stepped away and given him some

privacy, but his hand stopped her. Ellis's trembling fingers clutched at hers as if she were his anchor. She reached out and wrapped her second hand around their already gripping hands.

Ellis faced the wall and mumbled, "I see." Then there was a series of, "Yes, yes," and another, "yes."

Sydney's glance was riveted on Trevor, who had picked up on the vibrations and was staring at his father's back. She couldn't tell anything by Ellis's voice.

Ellis ended the conversation with, "Yes, of course. I'll be in touch. Thank you very much for everything." Ellis leaned his forehead against the wall and held out the phone to her.

She replaced the receiver in its cradle and waited. Trevor waited. Thomas waited. Everyone was waiting for Ellis to say something, and the longer it took him to turn around the tighter her stomach got. It had to be bad news.

"Ellis?" Her hand lightly touched his shoulder.

A heavy sigh shook his body before he turned around. Tears were streaming down his face as he gazed at his son.

She felt her stomach twist into one big endless knot. Dear Lord, there wasn't a match. The breath she once valued as her life support locked in her throat. What in the world were they going to do now?

She started to reach out for Ellis only to falter. A huge grin was splitting his face. His words confirmed her every hope. "It's a match."

Trevor looked confused and unsure. "What match?"

Ellis reached for his son and spun him around in circles. "We found a match, Trev. You're going to get that transplant."

Trevor's little arms locked around his father's neck.

Sydney leaned against the wall as tears ran like rivers down her face. Arthur Graystone matched! Trevor now had something called hope. She wiped at the tears and watched as Ellis and Trevor hugged each other. Trevor really wasn't understanding what was happening. He was only reacting to his father's joy. But that was okay. Everything was okay.

Ellis lowered his son to the floor and swept her into his arms. His mouth grazed the side of her neck as he squeezed the living tar out of her. "He matched, Sydney! Graystone matched!"

She returned his hug with one of her own. "So I heard, Ellis. So I heard."

Ellis continued to tremble within her arms. She didn't mind. She didn't mind one little bit. She glanced over at Trevor, who had climbed up on her father's lap. Her father was hugging the little boy for all he was worth. The loving scene brought more tears to her eyes.

Within minutes there were all gathered around Thomas's chair hugging one another and crying. It took several more minutes before everyone calmed down enough to actually talk.

Thomas broke the silence. "Well, Ellis, what's the next step?" Trevor was still protectively on his lap, being wrapped in his warm embrace. Sydney remembered that embrace and the sense of security it had brought her. Now she leaned back into Ellis and felt the same sense of protection.

Ellis's hand was warm against her hip as he pulled her closer. "Now the really hard part begins."

Sydney glanced up at the moon and smiled. She couldn't help but smile. She had been smiling all evening, ever since they received word that Arthur Graystone was able to be a donor. Ellis had explained about the next procedure and the actual transplant in calm, sensible words that wouldn't frighten Trevor. She had read in between the words and knew the next step wasn't going to be a picnic. But Trevor's best chance at conquering the disease was a transplant, so a transplant he would get.

"Have I ever told you how beautiful you are in the moonlight?" Ellis squeezed her hand and continued to walk the path through the acres of trees.

"No, we haven't actually been under the moonlight a lot." She moved closer to him and pressed her head against his shoulder. His compliment was sweet, but she wasn't going to hold him to it. Tonight, of all nights, he would compliment a toad if one should happen to hop across his path. His rose-colored glasses were definitely on.

Ellis pulled her closer and stopped. "We can change that, Syd?"

"Change what?" She studied his face, all shadowy in the moonlight. A new note had crept into his voice. She couldn't pinpoint what emotion it was.

"Walks in the moonlights." His hand grazed her cheek.

"You want to walk in the moonlight more often?"

"Yes, every night should do it."

She shook her head and softly chuckled. "Every night?" Ellis was more of a dreamer than she had originally thought. "How do you propose that one?"

"Marry me." Strong arms tugged her closer. "If we

were married, we could walk in the moonlight every night."

Marry me! Good Lord, Ellis had just asked her to marry him! She started to shake her head, only he stopped her with a frown.

"I know it's not fair of me to ask you to take on Trevor's illness, but at least now there's a good chance for a cure."

"What does Trevor's illness have to do with my marrying you or not?" She was getting a funny little feeling in the pit of her stomach.

"It should have everything to do with your answer, Sydney." Ellis brought her hand up to his mouth and kissed the center of her palm. "My son is part of me and his illness touches every aspect of our lives. I love you and I know that you love me even if you have never said the words to me. I can see it in your eyes and feel it in your touch." Ellis stared into her eyes. "I would understand your hesitancy in..."

"Wait a minute. Do you think I wouldn't marry you because of Trevor?" That funny little feeling just turned sour.

"It has crossed my mind."

"Well uncross it, Carlisle." She yanked her hand out of his and glared. "How can you say that you love me when you obviously think so little of me?"

"I'm getting the feeling that you are about to turn down my proposal, Sydney. If Trevor isn't the reason, what is?"

She turned away from Ellis and studied the darkened silhouettes of the trees against the night sky. This was it. This was when she either had to take the risk of loving Ellis, or push him away. If she pushed him away, he would think she was doing it because of Trevor and that would be too cruel. A weary sigh escaped her throat as she jammed her hands deep into the pockets of her jeans. "I don't know who I am, Ellis."

"Are you referring to you being adopted?"

No, I'm referring to me being abandoned. "I guess you could say that." She felt Ellis move closer to her, but she still didn't turn around. "I don't know my real last name. I don't know who my natural parents were." A broken little cry melted into her words. "I don't even know which part of the country I'm from."

Ellis reached out and stroked her shoulders. "If the answers to those questions mean so much to you, Syd, I could help you find them."

She was amazed at the simplicity and straightforwardness of his reply. He would help her learn the answers to the questions. Thousands of adopted children seek out their natural parents years after they have grown up. Did she really want to find her natural mother and father?

She shook her head. She already had one mother, and the father she had now was just fine. "No, thank you." The warmth and strength of Ellis's hands were working out the tension that had built in her neck. She relaxed into his hands. "Do you know they dropped me off at some gas station when I was just four and never came back for me?" She tried to keep the tears and the self-pity out of her voice.

"I already knew that, Syd. Thomas told me." Ellis's hands didn't break the rhythm.

"You're a parent, Ellis. What could a four-year-old do that would make you abandon that child in some gas station bathroom along the interstate?"

Ellis's hands froze.

"It had to be something terrible, don't you think?"

He slowly turned her around. "No, Sydney, I don't think you did anything terrible. Little four-year-old girls couldn't possibly do anything that bad to make their parents abandon them. You didn't do anything, Syd." His hands cupped her cheeks. "It was your parents' failure, not yours."

She shook her head as tears blurred her vision. "The first foster home they put me in was run by a nice lady named Muriel. She had a bunch of foster kids and we all loved it there. We were a family." She couldn't prevent the tears from overflowing. "I was happy there and I loved Muriel and all my foster brothers and sisters."

"What happened?"

"I don't know." She shrugged. "I came home from school one day and my bags were already packed and I was taken away and put into another home."

"Why?"

"Muriel tried to explain, but the lady who took me away wouldn't let her. Muriel said it was about some change in the law and that she had too many kids. I guess I was the one she didn't want." She used the sleeve of her jacket to wipe at the tears. "I never even got to say goodbye to the other kids. They were all sent to their rooms."

"Did Muriel get any other kids after you?"

"No."

"Then don't you see, Syd? You were taken not because you weren't wanted or did something wrong. You were taken because you were the last child she acquired."

She shook her head. Ellis still didn't understand. "No, don't you see? I was never good enough for any of them." She had to make him understand. "What will happen if one day after we are married you wake up and realize that I'm not good enough to be your wife? Don't you see? I love you more than life and I could never withstand being abandoned by you. Especially by you. My heart would never recover."

Ellis hauled her into his arms and hugged her as if she was the most precious thing in the world. "Lord, what have they done to you?"

She pressed her face against his chest and shuddered. She had taken the first step to conquering her fear of abandonment. She'd told Ellis about her fear and she'd told him that she loved him. Maybe today was really the day for miracles.

"Sydney?" Ellis stepped back and cupped her chin and forced her to look at him. "Do you love me?"

"Yes." What else could she have said? It was the truth.

"Do you believe that I love you?"

"Yes." She didn't doubt his love for one moment.

Ellis smiled. "I need you to believe one more thing, love."

"What?"

"Believe with all your heart that I would never leave you." Ellis's lips were light as they skimmed her jaw. "I can't change what was done to you in the past, but I can give you a future. A future that contains a loving husband and a son who has just been given the gift of hope."

She studied his face in the darkness. Nothing but truth radiated from his words and from his eyes. Suddenly it seemed so clear and easy. Loving wasn't hard or hurtful.

Loving was a joyful and happy feeling. She softly smiled. "I believe, Ellis."

"Then will you do me the honor of becoming my wife and the mother of my son?"

She threw her arms around his neck and planted a row of kisses up his throat to the corner of his mouth. Ellis was laughing and swinging her around. Her feet left the ground as she tilted back her head and shouted to the heavens, "Yes, yes, yes!"

Epilogue

Sydney felt the baby's shoulders turn and finally work their way free of her body. The rest of the child followed in a great rush. The pressure dissolved with the birth of her child. She had a child!

She strained to see what the doctor was doing as exhaustion took its toll and she collapsed back onto the pillows.

"It's a girl, Syd! We have a daughter!" Ellis was peering over the doctor's shoulder.

I have a daughter! She smiled at her husband, who was wearing green surgical scrubs and appeared ready to burst with pride. *Correction,* we *have a daughter.* The small cries from the bundle being cradled in the doctor's arms pulled at her heart. "Is she okay?"

The doctor glanced up and grinned. "She looks perfect to me. All little toes and fingers are accounted for."

Ellis was handed a pair of scissors and he carefully

cut the cord. A moment later a nurse handed him his daughter wrapped in a pink receiving blanket.

She studied her husband as he tenderly stroked the back of the baby's hand. Tears were clouding his eyes as he cradled the child closer to his heart. It wasn't possible to love a person more than she loved Ellis. Two years of marriage had only built on that love.

She remembered him telling her about being in the delivery room when Trevor was born and how he had bonded with his son. She had thought it was sweet at the time. Now she knew different. It wasn't sweet. It was powerful. She could feel the love Ellis was pouring out to the child in his arms. To their daughter. To Julia Catherine Carlisle.

Ellis walked to the side of the bed and tenderly placed their daughter on her chest. Strong capable fingers brushed aside a damp curl from her face. "She's beautiful, Syd." He placed a kiss on her parched lips. "Just like her mother."

She could only imagine what she must look like. She had gone through over eight hours of labor and she felt like it. "I think the delivery has damaged your eyesight."

Ellis's hands trembled against her cheeks. "I've never seen better in my life." This time when he bent and kissed her it wasn't some light brush. He kissed as if he meant it.

Sydney smiled against his mouth but she couldn't release the precious bundle cradled on her chest.

Ellis broke the kiss and grinned. "Did I tell you today that I love you?"

"At least a hundred times. I swear, every time I had a contraction you told me." She moved the blanket aside a tiny bit and stared at her daughter. "You are right, Ellis. She's beautiful." Her hand reached out and lightly caressed one of the baby's tiny pink fingers. It was soft. "Hello, Julia Catherine Carlisle, I'm your mommy."

Ellis's strong finger skimmed the baby's cheek.

"Excuse me, but I need to take Julia now." The nurse smiled and carefully lifted the child.

"Oh, can't I hold her a moment longer?" She felt tears fill her eyes. She wanted to hold her daughter.

"We'll only be a couple of minutes. She has to be weighed, measured, footprinted and banded." The nurse gave her a comforting smile and a wink. "I'll hurry, okay?"

She nodded and glanced longingly at the pink bundle as the nurse disappeared through the door. "Is everyone still waiting?"

Ellis reached for her hand and held it. "I haven't been out there in a while, but the last time I checked there seemed to be a party going on."

She relaxed into the pillows as the doctor announced he was done putting the finishing touches to her. "You should go out there and tell Trevor he has a baby sister." Trevor had been a nervous wreck, following her around the house and the nursery for weeks. He had been scared he would miss the big event. She would have crossed her legs and waited for Trevor to get home from school before having the baby without him there. She smiled. Trevor would always be there. His transplant had been a success. The prognosis was for a full and complete recovery.

"I will in a minute. I want to make sure you're all right, first."

"I'm fine, just a little tired." She shifted and found a

more comfortable position. "Who's all out there anyway?"

"Trevor, your father and Rita." Ellis tucked the blanket neatly around her arm, making sure he didn't tangle it in the IV line. "Cindy was there delivering pizza and John was swearing he had been at the hospital on business anyway so he thought he'd check in."

"Sounds like a circus out there." She yawned. "Was Arthur there?" Ellis still had a hard time adjusting to having his father come around, but Arthur was persistent. Thomas and Arthur had become Trevor's grandfathers and the little boy loved them both. She thought it was good for both Trevor and Ellis that Arthur didn't fade into the woodwork. After all, they all lived in the same town and no matter how much they had tried to keep Arthur's part in the transplant a secret, it had become public knowledge. Mostly due to Sophie who, after her initial anger at her husband, declared to anyone who would listen that Arthur was a hero.

"Yeah, he's here." Ellis sounded disgusted.

She reached out and took his hand. "Let him be, love. I feel sorry for him."

"Sorry?" He seemed quite taken aback.

"Yes." She smoothed her fingers over the back of his hand. "Think of all he has missed, Ellis." She nodded to the delivery room around them.

He squeezed her hand lightly. "He missed it all, didn't he."

"Yes, he did." She felt her eyes get heavy and wondered when they were going to bring Julia back to her. "You are the one who taught me we can't change the past, only the future."

"Are you trying to tell me to practice what I preach?"

"Maybe." She lost the battle against the heaviness of her eyelids and closed her eyes. "What I am trying to tell you is that I love you, Ellis, and that you've made me the happiest woman in the world. You're very good at keeping your promises." She felt his light kiss as she softly succumbed to the gentle calling of sleep.

* * * * *

Coming September 1998

Three delightful stories about the blessings and surprises of "Labor" Day.

TABLOID BABY by Candace Camp

She was whisked to the hospital in the nick of time....

THE NINE-MONTH KNIGHT by Cait London

A down-on-her-luck secretary is experiencing odd little midnight cravings....

THE PATERNITY TEST by Sherryl Woods

The stick turned blue before her biological clock struck twelve....

These three special women are very pregnant...and very single, although they won't be either for too much longer, because baby—and Daddy—are on their way!

Available at your favorite retail outlet.

Look us up on-line at: http://www.romance.net

PSMATLEV

MEN at WORK

All work and no play?
Not these men!

July 1998
MACKENZIE'S LADY by Dallas Schulze

Undercover agent Mackenzie Donahue's lazy smile and deep blue eyes were his best weapons. But after rescuing—and kissing!— damsel in distress Holly Reynolds, how could he betray her by spying on her brother?

August 1998
MISS LIZ'S PASSION by Sherryl Woods

Todd Lewis could put up a building with ease, but quailed at the sight of a classroom! Still, Liz Gentry, his son's teacher, was no battle-ax, and soon Todd started planning some extracurricular activities of his own....

September 1998
A CLASSIC ENCOUNTER by Emilie Richards

Doctor Chris Matthews was intelligent, sexy and *very* good with his hands—which made him all the more dangerous to single mom Lizette St. Hilaire. So how long could she resist Chris's special brand of TLC?

Available at your favorite retail outlet!

MEN AT WORK™

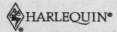 

Look us up on-line at: http://www.romance.net

PMAW2

**Available September 1998
from Silhouette Books...**

THE CATCH OF CONARD COUNTY
by Rachel Lee

Rancher Jeff Cumberland: long, lean, sexy as sin. He's eluded every marriage-minded female in the county. Until a mysterious woman breezes into town and brings her fierce passion to his bed. Will this steamy Conard County courtship take September's hottest bachelor off of the singles market?

Each month, Silhouette Books brings you an irresistible bachelor in these all-new, original stories. Find out how the sexiest, most sought-after men are finally caught...

Available at your favorite retail outlet.

Look us up on-line at: http://www.romance.net   PSWMEB1

Catch more great
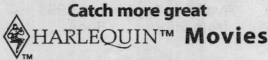 HARLEQUIN™ **Movies**

featured on the movie channel

Premiering August 8th
The Waiting Game
Based on the novel by *New York Times* bestselling author Jayne Ann Krentz

Don't miss next month's movie!
Premiering September 12th
A Change of Place
Starring Rick Springfield and Stephanie Beacham. Based on the novel by bestselling author Tracy Sinclair

If you are not currently a subscriber to The Movie Channel, simply call your local cable or satellite provider for more details. Call today, and don't miss out on the romance!

 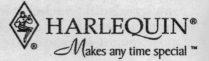

100% pure movies.
100% pure fun.

Harlequin, Joey Device, Makes any time special and Superromance are trademarks of Harlequin Enterprises Limited. The Movie Channel is a service mark of Showtime Networks, Inc., a Viacom Company.

An Alliance Television Production

PHMBPA898

SILHOUETTE·INTIMATE·MOMENTS®

They're back! Suzanne Brockmann's **Tall, Dark & Dangerous** navy SEALs continue to thwart danger—*and* find love—in three exciting new books, only from Silhouette Intimate Moments.

EVERYDAY, AVERAGE JONES...
Intimate Moments #872, August 1998

HARVARD'S EDUCATION...
Intimate Moments #884, October 1998

IT CAME UPON A MIDNIGHT CLEAR
Intimate Moments #896, December 1998

So be sure to remember the men of the Alpha Squad. They're who you call to get you out of a tight spot—or *into* one!

Available at your favorite retail outlet.

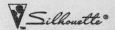

SIMTDD

Look us up on-line at: http://www.romance.net

Noticed anything different lately?

Like all those new flashes on your Silhouette Intimate Moments novels? That's because—just for you— we've created eight new flashes to highlight the appearance of your favorite themes. We've got:

Men in Blue:
Love in the line of duty.

The Loving Arms of the Law:
He's the law of the West, and *she's* the lady he can't resist.

Families Are Forever:
Happily ever after— with kids!

Way Out West:
Because there's nothing like a cowboy.

So look for these new flashes, only on the covers of Silhouette Intimate Moments—available now!

Available at your favorite retail outlet.

Look us up on-line at: http://www.romance.net

SIMTHEME1

**Coming in October from
Silhouette Intimate Moments...**

BRIDES OF THE NIGHT

Silhouette Intimate Moments fulfills your wildest wishes in this compelling new in-line collection featuring two very memorable men...tantalizing, irresistible men who exist only in the darkness but who hunger for the light of true love.

TWILIGHT VOWS
by Maggie Shayne

The unforgettable WINGS IN THE NIGHT miniseries continues with a vampire hero to die for and the lovely mortal woman who will go to any lengths to save their unexpected love.

MARRIED BY DAWN
by Marilyn Tracy

Twelve hours was all the time this rogue vampire had to protect an innocent woman. But was marriage his only choice to keep her safe—if not from the night...then from himself?

*Look for **BRIDES OF THE NIGHT** this October, wherever Silhouette books are sold.*

Look us up on-line at: http://www.romance.net

SIMBON

COMING NEXT MONTH

#877 LONE WOLF'S LADY—Beverly Barton
Way Out West
The last person dark and dangerous Luke McClendon ever wanted to see again was his former lover Deanna Atchley. With just a few careless words she had stolen five precious years of his life—and now she was at his doorstep, looking for salvation. Was this Luke's golden opportunity to seek revenge...or rediscover love?

#878 IF A MAN ANSWERS—Merline Lovelace
Molly Duncan was being hunted for what she'd heard! The love-shy lady had *intended* to call her supremely obnoxious, superbly masculine neighbor Sam Henderson to insist he quiet down, but instead of Sam's deep, sexy "hello," she heard gunshots. Could this spirited woman who'd accidentally dialed *M* for murder, redial *L* for love?

#879 A STRANGER IS WATCHING—Linda Randall Wisdom
Years ago, Jenna Wells had gotten too close to federal marshal Riley Cooper, and it had cost her everything—true love, career, even her identity. Now a dangerous stranger had pieced together her past... and was determined to destroy her future. Impenetrable Riley was once again her protector, but who was keeping watch over this loner's heart?

#880 GIRLS' NIGHT OUT—Elizabeth August
Men in Blue
Detective Adam Riley's investigation uncovered the rocky terrain of Susan Hallston's secret past. In fact, proving her innocence to this cynical cop would be about as effortless as climbing Mount Everest. But unearthing the truth could cause a monumental landslide of emotion...in granite-hearted Adam!

#881 MARY'S CHILD—Terese Ramin
Whose Child?
Gorgeous Hallie Thompson had agreed to be a surrogate mother for her best friend, Joe Martinez, and his wife. But that was before Joe's wife was killed, and before Hallie discovered that she was pregnant...with Joe's child. Now Hallie wanted to adopt the beautiful baby girl —but was she willing to take on a husband, as well?

#882 UNDERCOVER LOVER—Kylie Brant
John Sullivan was the one man Ellie Bennett trusted. He was her dearest friend—and now he was her lover. But what she *didn't* know about him was immense. Like his troubled past, his top-secret profession...and whether he could love her forever....